Gifts for
the Family

—◆—

Gifts for the Family

Over 120 Projects to Make for Those You Love in under 30 minutes

Reader's Digest

The Reader's Digest Association, Inc.
Pleasantville, New York/Montreal

A READER'S DIGEST BOOK

This edition published by The Reader's Digest Association by arrangement with Amber Books Ltd.

Produced by
Amber Books Ltd
Bradley's Close
74–77 White Lion Street
London N1 9PF
www.amberbooks.co.uk

FOR AMBER BOOKS
Project Editor: Charlotte Judet
Design: Brian Rust

FOR READER'S DIGEST
U.S. Project Editor: Mary Connell
Canadian Project Editor: Pamela Johnson
Project Designer: Jennifer R. Tokarski
Senior Designer: George McKeon
Executive Editor, Trade Publishing: Dolores York
Director, Trade Publishing: Christopher T. Reggio
Vice President & Publisher, Trade Publishing: Harold Clarke

Library of Congress Cataloging-in-Publication Data

Gifts for the family: over 120 projects to make for those you love in under 30 minutes
    p.cm.
    Includes Index.
    ISBN 0-7621-0609-3
    1. Handicraft. 2. Gifts. I. Reader's Digest Association

TT157.G4517 2005
745.5--dc22   2005041861

Address any comments about *Gifts for the Family* to:
        The Reader's Digest Association, Inc.
        Adult Trade Publishing
        Reader's Digest Road
        Pleasantville, NY 10570-7000

For more Reader's Digest products and information, visit our website:
www.rd.com (in the United States)
www.readersdigest.ca (in Canada)
www.readersdigest.com.au (in Australia)
www.readersdigest.co.uk (in the United Kingdom)

Printed in Italy

1 3 5 7 9 10 8 6 4 2

Contents

Needlecraft and fabric projects

Why live with plain, dull fabrics when there are so many simple ways of enlivening linens such as table runners, towels, and napkins?

This chapter contains over fifty exciting ideas for gifts that use just a few well-placed stitches to transform everyday fabric items. From leaf-stamped linens to pillows with a more personal touch, these projects are full of simple but inspiring ideas to help you create some very special fabric gifts.

Antique Table Runner

No need to comb the land for an antique table runner for Grandma…the exquisite craftsmanship may be found with a quick rummage in the attic! Her elegant handkerchiefs, put aside as mementos of a bygone era, can be joined together with renewed function and status. The delicate handkerchiefs are positioned on a dresser scarf with fusible webbing. The old embroidery will grace her table with what is, ultimately, timeless beauty.

QUICK & EASY ALTERNATIVES

Option 1

Take a lovely antique handkerchief out of hiding and put it on display! Choose an antique version with a large embroidered or appliquéd area. Remove backing from 5"x7" (13x18cm) frame. Cut white cardboard to same size. Position white cardboard over embroidered area of handkerchief and fold it to back of cardboard. Keep folding until front is smooth and centered. Tape over folds tightly with acid-free tape. Insert handkerchief in frame, then replace backing.

Option 2

A "snippet" of a vintage handkerchief adds a touch of history. Paint small rectangular box blue. Dip wooden end of paintbrush in white paint and dot around box sides. Select damaged antique handkerchief with embroidery intact. Press it flat and lay embroidered corner on lid. Turn lid over while holding handkerchief in place. Trace around lid in pencil. Cut out, adding enough to cover sides and to tuck inside. Spray with adhesive. Smooth onto top and sides of lid.

Option 3

Place the prettiest corner of an antique handkerchief onto a velvet pillow as shown in photo. If damaged or stained, cut handkerchief in half on the diagonal, plus 1" (2.5cm). Place on pillow with fold to the back. Fold in corners. Iron a strip of fusible webbing on fold. Peel off backing and iron onto back of pillow with point of hankie folding over to front. If hankie is in good shape, do not cut it. Instead, fold over to back of pillow and tack in front and back.

Materials You'll Need

- 12"x42" (30x100cm) dresser scarf
- Antique or embroidered handkerchiefs
- Fusible webbing
- Scissors
- Iron & ironing board

1 Purchase 12"x42" (30x100cm) dresser scarf. Arrange the four handkerchiefs along runner, with one arranged on top, in the center of the runner.

2 Cut squares of fusible webbing to fit each handkerchief and iron to the back of each.

3 Peel backing paper off the webbing of the first handkerchief. Place in previously determined position on runner.

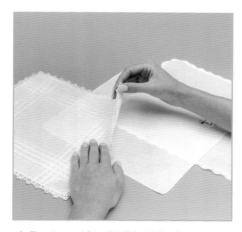

4 Iron handkerchief into position. Repeat Steps 3 and 4 until the runner is decorated with four of the handkerchiefs.

5 Peel backing paper off fusible webbing of the last handkerchief. Position in center of runner and iron in place.

6 Fold under corners of handkerchiefs that extend beyond the edges of the runner. Press under and tack in place, if desired.

Leaf-Stamped Linens

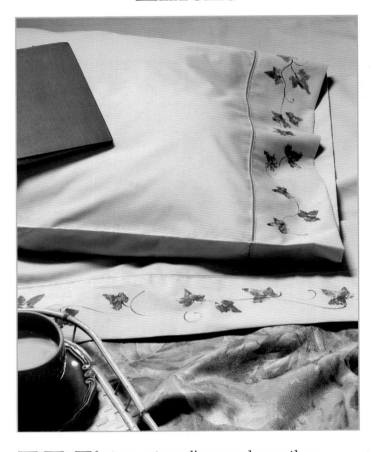

QUICK & EASY ALTERNATIVES

Option 1

Welcome a visiting aunt with these lovely towels in the guest bath. Cut a 4¼"x4 ¼" (10.5x10.5cm) square of organdy or other sheer fabric. Iron a ¼" (6mm) hem all the way around. Use a 3" (7.5cm) foam stamp with a leaf design and dip it in fall-colored fabric paint. Stamp the design in the center of the fabric square. Allow to dry. Attach square to center of folded fingertip towel with hem bonding tape, following manufacturer's directions. Use a matching color marker to form "stitches" around the border of the square.

Option 2

Help your daughter set a striking fall table using autumn leaves to stamp napkins. Lay a napkin on a flat surface with paper towels beneath. Clean off, then dry a fresh, 3" (7.5cm)-long leaf. Using a foam brush, paint the underside of leaf with a mix of green, gold, and burgundy fabric paint. Carefully lay the painted leaf on the fabric on an angle, as shown. Press the leaf with fingers to make sure entire leaf contacts the fabric. Lift leaf straight up to avoid smearing. Touch up with brush, if needed. Add second leaf print to napkin.

Option 3

If she loves to entertain and set a beautiful table for the fall season, she'll love this gift. Dip a foam brush into fabric paint in a mix of autumnal hues. Brush the paint onto a foam stamp with a leaf design, then press near edge of neutral-colored table runner. Lift straight up to avoid smearing. Paint the cut edge of half a walnut shell and press beside leaf stamp, lifting straight up to remove. Continue this pattern all around edge of table runner. Allow paint to dry, then heat-set with iron.

W hat an extraordinary welcome these hand-painted sheets will extend to a dear one planning a long-awaited visit. The distant miles mean time between family reunions, so you'll want to make this relative's stay as memorable as possible. Golden hues of autumn are used to paint garden-fresh ivy leaves, which create a beautiful, stamped impression. Your guest will adore these lovely linens and sleeping on a "bed of ivy."

Materials You'll Need

- Cardboard
- Set of sheets with pillowcases
- Long-bristle paintbrush
- Round paintbrush
- Fabric paint: green, yellow & brown
- Fresh ivy leaves
- Roller
- Tweezers

1 Place a sheet of cardboard inside the pillowcase or beneath the edge of the sheet, so that paint doesn't seep through.

2 Dip long-bristle brush in leaf-green fabric paint and form curvy "ivy vine" lines along border of the sheet or pillowcase.

3 Dip round brush in all three fabric-paint colors and paint a clean, dry ivy leaf.

4 Carefully press leaf, painted side down, onto the sheet or pillowcase fabric.

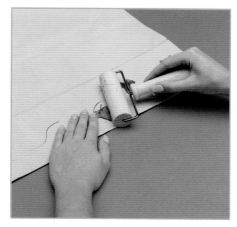

5 Roll over leaf with a roller, applying even pressure. Remove leaf from fabric using tweezers, lifting leaf straight up to avoid smearing.

6 Repeat to form leaves along painted vine. If needed, touch up leaf prints with the small round paintbrush.

Plaid Cross-Stitch Towel

What could be easier? This towel provides you with a natural cross-stitch chart. Just follow the squares in the design of the plaid to stitch perfect cross-stitches and you can easily embellish a homespun towel. This is such a quick way to decorate kitchen towels— several can be stitched up in no time at all, boxed up, and shipped off to a favorite relative just to say "I'm thinking of you."

QUICK & EASY ALTERNATIVES

Option 1

This towel will be a gift appropriate for giving and using during the holiday season. Purchase a fringed, green towel with small checks. Group a square of nine small checks on the towel to use as a pattern. Make a cross-stitch in the square following directions on the opposite page. To form snowflake, make a straight stitch in the center of the cross going down and another going across. Repeat snowflake stitch at evenly spaced intervals across the towel. Knot at back.

Option 2

Send your love with this towel to a cousin in another city. Press an iron-on heart appliqué onto a purchased terry towel, following manufacturer's instructions. Use six strands of red embroidery floss to thread an embroidery needle. Outline about ¼" (6mm) around the heart with a running stitch. Push the needle up from the back of the towel to the top, then back down again, forming ¼" (6mm) top-stitches. Repeat, spacing the stitches ¼" (6mm) apart. When stitches are complete, knot the floss on the back of the towel.

Option 3

This pretty towel will be a sweet gift for a sister. Purchase a lavender plaid towel. Thread embroidery needle with six strands of white floss. Starting at lower left side of towel in first check and from back, bring needle up from left corner and down through lower right corner. Repeat until end of towel is reached on first row. Move needle up to second row, starting from lower right corner, take needle up, then through upper left corner. Repeat across the length of the towel. Tie a knot in back.

Materials You'll Need

- Purchased red, plaid kitchen towel
- Skein of white embroidery floss
- Embroidery needle
- Scissors

1 Open towel on a flat surface. Thread needle with six strands of embroidery floss. Bring needle from back of towel up through bottom left corner of a red square.

2 In the same square, form a half-stitch by inserting the needle in upper right corner of the red square.

3 In the next square, from the back, bring needle up in the lower left corner and down through the top right corner. Repeat pattern across bottom edge of towel.

4 When you're at the end of towel, cross your stitches in the opposite direction by bringing the needle up through the lower right-hand corner.

5 Complete the cross-stitch by bringing the needle back down through the upper left corner. Repeat pattern back across towel.

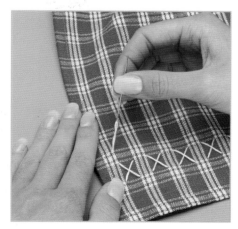

6 Repeat the process across the second row. When that row is completed, knot the end of the embroidery floss on the back to secure the stitches.

Napkin Envelope Pillows

I magine how Grandma's eyes will gleam when she sees this hand-sewn pillow made just for her. Not just an ordinary pillow covering, this feminine, floral beauty boasts the added surprise of a flap accent made of exquisite Battenburg lace. The best surprise of all is that the whole cover is made of fine cloth napkins. This is a great way to use favorite napkins that are no longer part of a complete set.

QUICK & EASY ALTERNATIVES

Option 1

This pillow will suit a budding equestrian or a child's cowboy-motif bedroom. Choose horse-print fabric and a coordinating, checkered fabric napkin. Cut napkin in half and cut two 17" (43cm) squares of horse-print fabric. With right sides together, sew cut napkin edge to top side of one fabric square. Sew second square to the first, keeping right sides together and an opening at top. Turn inside out and iron all seams flat. Insert 16" (40cm) pillow, then fold flap to front.

Option 2

This lovely pillow is made using three 17" (43cm) napkins. To form a pillow flap, measure down 7½" (19cm) from one corner of napkin towards center. Cut diagonally across at that measurement. Sew ivory lace to two short edges of flap. With right sides together, sew raw edge of flap to top of second napkin. Place second and third napkins right sides together and sew on three sides, leaving top open. Turn right-side out and press. Insert 16" (40cm) pillow form.

Option 3

Coordinating fabric napkins create a pretty pillow, with the added charm of buttoned-down flaps. Choose one floral and two plaid napkins. Cut floral napkin into thirds and discard the center strip. With right sides together, sew cut sides of strips to either side of first plaid napkin, then sew second plaid napkin to top and bottom of first. Turn right-side out and press. Insert pillow. Fold in flaps and attach by sewing three buttons on each side.

Materials You'll Need

- Scissors
- Square Battenburg lace doily
- Sewing machine & thread
- Two floral cloth napkins
- Iron
- Iron-on floral appliqué
- 16" (40cm) pillow form

1 Cut lace doily in half diagonally. With right sides together, sew cut edge of doily to top of one of the napkins.

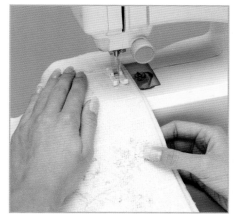

2 Keeping right sides together, sew the second napkin to the first, leaving top side unstitched.

3 Turn the sewn pillow cover right-side out and pull the lace flap free.

4 Press with hot iron, smoothing the sewn seams flat. Fold over lace flap and press the seam flat.

5 Follow instructions given on matching floral appliqué to press appliqué onto the center of the lace flap.

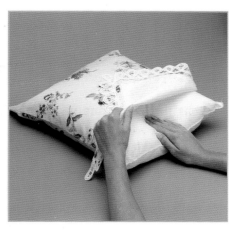

6 Gently ease pillow form into envelope case. Fold flap over and fluff.

Button Napkin Rings

This elegant napkin ring is easy to make, yet looks as if it were purchased at a fancy boutique. It's made of rich velvet ribbon and delicate lace, and enhanced with antique-style buttons. If your daughter, mother, or sister loves to decorate her home with antiques, a set of these napkin rings will be a much-appreciated gift. Wrapped around fine linen napkins, these rings will help her set an exquisite table for her next dinner party.

QUICK & EASY ALTERNATIVES

Option 1

If your husband has a passion for golf, these napkin rings sporting tiny golf clubs and balls are sure to make him smile. These playful table accessories will be a sure-fire hit at a dinner party for his golfing buddies. Measure the circumference and width of a plain napkin ring and cut a length of plaid ribbon to fit. Use a hot-glue gun to glue ribbon around ring, then follow with decorative buttons in the shape of a golf club and golf ball.

Option 2

A boy who loves race cars will get a kick out of these napkin rings for a party or for everyday use. Paint plain, wooden napkin rings with black acrylic paint; let dry. Use masking tape to cover all but a ⅜" (1cm) stripe around the center of each ring, and paint stripes with white acrylic paint using a small brush. (Two coats may be needed.) When dry, use black paint to break the white stripes into long segments. Glue micro cars to the napkin rings with a hot-glue gun.

Option 3

If your mother is a devoted bird-watcher, this handmade gift will really touch her heart. A set of napkin rings featuring pretty birds will make a charming table setting and spark many conversations about her favorite topic. Choose wooden napkin rings in a color to coordinate with the selected artificial birds (may be purchased in craft shops). Use a hot-glue gun to attach a natural 2" (5cm)-long twig to each napkin ring. Glue small birds to "perch" on twigs.

Materials You'll Need

- Plain napkin rings
- Measuring tape
- Scissors
- Velvet ribbon
- Glue gun & glue sticks
- Lace ribbon
- Needle & thread
- Small antique-style buttons

1 Measure circumference and width of first napkin ring with measuring tape.

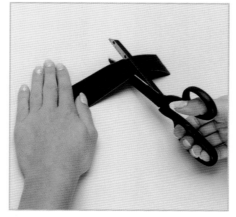

2 With scissors, cut a length of velvet ribbon to fit the exact measurements of napkin ring.

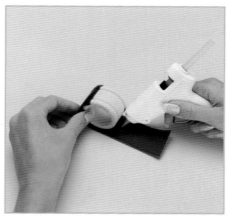

3 Adhere the strip of velvet ribbon to the napkin ring using hot-glue gun.

4 Make a gathering stitch in one end of a 6" (15cm) piece of lace ribbon. Starting at one end, pull thread tightly until the lace is gathered into a rosette shape.

5 Secure the rosette with one or two stitches and center it on the napkin ring Use a hot glue gun to affix the rosette to the ring.

6 Glue a cluster of several tiny antique-style buttons buttons to center of rosette with hot-glue gun. Follow this procedure with other napkin rings for a set.

Cozy Embellished Slippers

Here's a creative birthday or Mother's Day gift idea, an offering of comfort and beauty for Mom or Grandma. These warming, chenille slippers are a nice gift on their own, but the ribbon roses add just the right touch. The roses and leaves are created with luxurious wire-edged ribbon, then attached with a few simple stitches. Watch her eyes light up when she learns you "made" these slippers yourself!

QUICK & EASY ALTERNATIVES

Option 1

A few quick stitches and plain slippers boast a monogram initial and delicate ribbon roses. Consider this gift idea for your sister or daughter! Purchase a pair of ladies' slippers. With needle and thread, attach a monogram letter appliqué to center toe area, using a whip stitch. Or use an iron-on alphabet appliqué. Stitch three ribbon rosebuds, following inner edge of slipper top, with middle rose centered above monogram letter. Repeat for the other slipper.

Option 2

Warm slippers are a practical holiday gift for your son or little brother, but alas, not always exciting to a child. Using a bit of ingenuity, you can bring on the smiles with these whimsical appliqué slippers featuring a favorite furry friend. Select child-size slippers and animal-themed appliqués. Teddy bear appliqués were used here. Center the appliqué over the toe area of slipper. With threaded needle, stitch appliqué to slipper. Or, use an iron-on appliqué. Repeat for second slipper.

Option 3

Gold tassels add a classic, elegant touch to a gentleman's cloth slippers. This easy-sew project is a warm gift of love that any grandfather will appreciate. Select a pair of gray or black men's furry slippers. Tie hanging loops of two gold or black tassels together to form one double-sided tassel. Use needle and thread to stitch the tassels to the upper middle area of the slipper, stitching only at the center point where they're tied together. Repeat the same steps for second slipper.

Materials You'll Need

- Two 22" (56cm)-lengths of wire-edged ribbon
- Two 8" (20cm)-lengths of green satin ribbon
- Needle & thread
- Chenille slippers

1 To make ribbon rose, tie a knot in one end of first 22" (56cm) length of wire-edged ribbon. Use ribbon with a graduated blend of colors, or use a solid rose color.

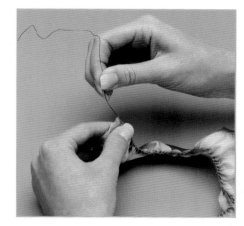

2 Pull wire gently at other end of the ribbon, gathering the ribbon along the wire until you come to the knot.

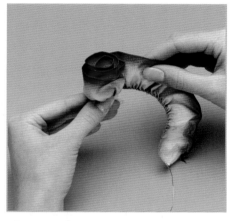

3 Hold knot in one hand and begin wrapping gathered ribbon around it to form the rose.

4 Fold the cut end of the ribbon and secure it and the rose by wrapping exposed wire around the base several times.

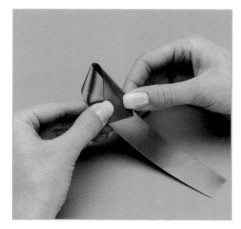

5 To make the leaves, fold one end of a length of green satin ribbon one-third of the way down. Repeat on opposite end, so looped ends meet in center.

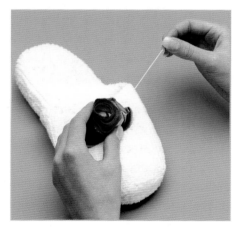

6 Stitch leaves, then base of the rose, to upper center of slipper. Repeat Steps 1 through 6 for the second slipper.

19

Stamped Velvet Bottle Bags

T his intriguing velvet bag—ideal for holding a gift of wine or spirits—is much easier to make than it looks. The unique pattern on the velvet is debossed using a rubber stamp and a household iron. Your choice of stamps customizes the velvet fabric before the bag is sewn. This interesting technique is easy and inexpensive to achieve and duplicates the look of costly cut velvet.

QUICK & EASY ALTERNATIVES

Option 1

Delicate jewelry or accessories will travel safely when tucked into their own velvet envelope. Zigzag-stitch around the edges of a 10"x21" (25x53cm) piece of velvet, then fold and pin a ¼" (6mm)-wide seam on both short sides. Fold bottom up 7½" (19cm), right sides together, and sew sides with a ¼" (6mm) seam allowance. Turn right-side out. Fold sides of flap in and sew with a ¼" (6mm) seam allowance. Scrunch a wire-edged ribbon strip, cut an inverted "V" into each end, then glue to flap. Glue a silk flower and leaf to ribbon.

Option 2

Crushed velvet embellished with iridescent beads makes this opulent container for potpourri a luxurious scented addition to a room. Create the bag in a size of your choice. Sew crushed green velvet into a pouch with right sides together. Turn the pouch right-side out, turn down a cuff at the top, and then zigzag-stitch. Sew or glue bugle beads to the front of the bag. Fill the bag with potpourri, then tie it closed beneath the cuff with a double strand of metallic cord. Tie cord into a bow.

Option 3

For an alternative potpourri container take a round box, wider than it is high. Cut velvet double the height of the box and the same length as its circumference, plus ¾"(2cm). Fold both long sides down ¼" (6mm) and glue. Fold in half, widthwise, right sides together; sew with ¼" (6mm) seam. Turn tube right-side out. Apply glue to outside of box; pull tube over box and press to secure velvet evenly around box. Baste around top of velvet with embroidery floss; tighten. Knot ends. Tie bow. Glue on gems.

Materials You'll Need

- ¼ yd. (23cm) burgundy velvet
- Sewing machine
- Hard rubber stamp
- Pressing cloth
- Iron

- ¾ yd. (70cm) gold cord
- Pins
- Bottle of wine
- Needle & thread

1 Cut two 7"x14" (18x36cm) pieces of velvet. Fold wrong side down and top-stitch a 3" (7.5cm) cuff with a ¼" (6mm) seam allowance on one end of each piece.

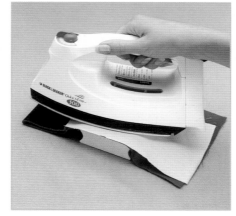

2 Place velvet right-side down over hard rubber stamp. Lay pressing cloth over the velvet. Set iron at hottest setting and place over stamp for 10 seconds.

3 Repeat process for other piece of velvet. Align cuffs and pin the two pieces of fabric right sides together. Sew around three sides with a ½" (1.5cm) seam allowance.

4 Sew across each corner 1¼" (3cm) in from the corner point on each side, creating a small triangle, then cut off corner fabric leaving a ½" (1.5cm) seam allowance.

5 Turn bag right-side out. Tie a knot at each end of the gold cord, fold it in half, then tack the center of the cord on a seam, 3" (7.5cm) down from the top.

6 Slip the gift bottle of wine into the bag, wrap the cord tightly around the neck of the bottle, and tie into a bow.

Heritage Keepsake Pillow

S ome pillows are so cherished that they are passed from generation to generation. This pillow has been fashioned from a family heirloom tea towel and trimmed with antique buttons from a treasured sewing basket. Pillows of all types grace our homes: cushiony ones for lazing on a sofa or firm ones for a reading chair. Most pillows serve as delicate decorations, but nothing compares to a pillow lovingly made of family memories.

QUICK & EASY ALTERNATIVES

Option 1

Indulge a mother's love of flowers with a rose-trimmed pillow to grace her boudoir. To make this pretty accessory, cut two 23" (58cm) squares of pastel floral fabric. Pin the pieces right sides together and sew around all four sides with a ½" (1.5cm) seam allowance, leaving a 6" (15cm) opening. Turn right-side out, insert a pillow form, and hand-stitch opening closed. Wrap pillow like a package with green ribbon. Hot-glue silk leaves and a white silk rose over the ribbon. Scent silk rose with essential oil, if desired.

Option 2

Help a sister brighten a dorm room with a colorful, no-sew harem pillow. Lay a 38" (96cm) square of fabric right-side down. Pinch together 1" (2.55cm) of fabric in the center. Wrap it tightly with a rubber band, then place a 12" (30cm)-round pillow form over it. Pull fabric up around the form, gathering it evenly, and secure it with a rubber band. Trim excess fabric. Wind fiberfill around rubber band, pull fabric tight, and tuck it under fiberfill, forming a rosette. Wrap a rubber band around rosette to secure it.

Option 3

Small enough for baby hands, this cuddly pillow trimmed with a toy will brighten a nursery. Cut two 7" (18cm) squares of fleece fabric, pin the pieces together, and sew around all four sides with a ½" (1.5cm) seam allowance, leaving a small opening. Stuff with fiberfill and close opening. Hand-sew a small baby toy to the front of the pillow, then tie a yellow ribbon bow and tack it to the pillow. As an option, to make toy removable, machine-sew ribbon length to the pillow, then tie on toy.

Materials You'll Need

- 14"x18" (36x46cm) vintage linen tea towel
- Sewing machine
- Vintage button assortment

- Needle & thread
- Pillow form
- Polyester fiberfill
- Silk rose

- Glue gun & glue sticks
- Ribbons
- Plastic ring of keys

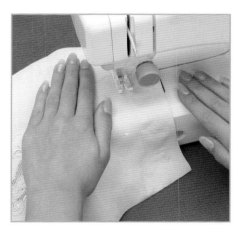

1 Fold long sides of tea towel (wrong sides together) into the center, overlapping about 1" (2.5cm); pin. Machine-sew 1½" (4cm) in on short sides of towel.

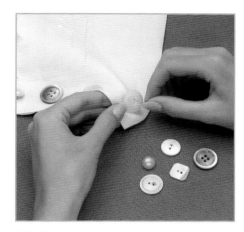

2 Hand-sew the vintage buttons, evenly spacing them out along the pillow edges.

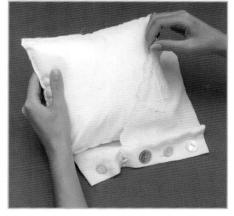

3 Slip pillow form into finished pillow cover. (Pillow form can be purchased, or one can be made using the measurements of the finished pillow cover.)

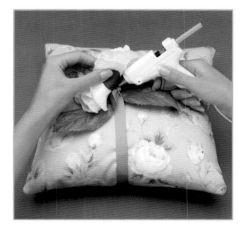

4 To create the floral pillow, remove the stem from a silk rose, then use hot glue to affix the flower head and green leaves to top of the ribbon tie.

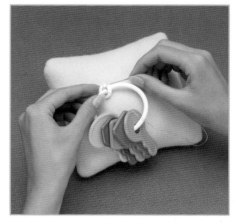

5 For the fleece baby pillow, add the plastic ring of keys by hand-sewing it securely to the front of the pillow with needle and thread.

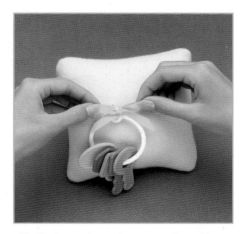

6 Fashion a bow of narrow yellow ribbon, then tack it to the top of the plastic ring. Or, sew ribbon length to pillow and tie keys to the ribbon.

Lace-Edged Hand Towels

C lassically beautiful lace adds elegance to a monogrammed hand towel. Purchase a new towel or find one in an antique shop or at a garage sale. Sew a lovely strip of new or vintage lace to the edge of the towel, creating a perfect gift for your favorite aunt. She'll be delighted to display your handiwork in her guest room or bath.

QUICK & EASY ALTERNATIVES

Option 1

A denim plaid dish towel is beautifully trimmed with crocheted lace for a special gift. Measure the width of the towel. Cut wide crocheted lace long enough to edge towel, plus two additional inches. Pin lace to towel and turn under ½" (1.5cm) on each end. Fold ½" (1.5cm) over front edge of towel. With the sewing machine and matching thread, sew the lace along the bottom edge of the towel. After lace is sewn to towel, press for a finishing touch.

Option 2

Transform a damask napkin into an elegant guest towel by adding a scalloped or pointed lace trim. Pretty damask napkins can be found in linen and bath shops in a variety of colors. Measure the bottom edge of the napkin and cut non-gathered lace that measurement plus 1" (2.5cm). Pin lace onto the damask napkin. Turn lace under ¼" (6mm) on each end and then ¼" (6mm) again to fold around edge. Machine-stitch lace along napkin's bottom edge. Press with a cool iron.

Option 3

Trim a towel for Dad with a black-and-white gingham ribbon. Measure the bottom edge of a terry hand towel. Cut ribbon to that measurement, adding an additional 1" (2.5cm). Pin the wide strip of ribbon onto towel about 2" (5cm) up from the bottom edge. Turn under ¼" (6mm) on each end, and ¼" (6mm) again to fold around edge. Top-stitch along both edges of the ribbon to secure to the towel. Press with an iron. If desired, add a ribbon-trimmed facecloth to the gift.

Materials You'll Need

- Measuring tape
- White linen hand towel
- White lace, 2" (5cm) wide
- Ribbon with pearls

- Scissors
- Pins
- Sewing machine & white thread
- Iron

1 Measure the width of the bottom of the towel. Cut the lace to that measurement, adding 1" (2.5cm). Cut pearled ribbon to this same measurement.

2 Pin the lace to the bottom edge of the towel. Turn under ¼" (6mm) on each end, and ¼" (6mm) to fold around towel edges.

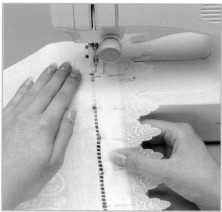

3 Using the sewing machine, stitch the trim onto the towel. Remove pins.

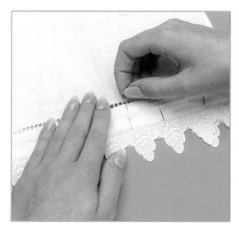

4 Pin the pearled ribbon over the lace. Experiment with various laces and trims to create other interesting guest towels.

5 Machine-stitch the pearl-trimmed ribbon over the lace. Remove the pins.

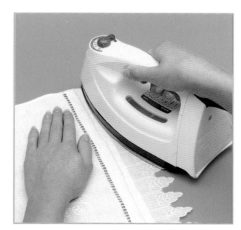

6 With a fairly hot iron, carefully press the trim and the towel for a crisp, finished look. If desired, use a pressing cloth.

Clothes-Closet Freshener

These no-sew sachets make wonderful gifts for male family members. When sachets are handsomely decorated, they also make attractive additions to hall closets for the temporary storage of guests' coats or great accessories for closets in guest rooms to add a welcoming aroma. Richly colored tartan fabric is fashioned into sachets containing pine-scented potpourri and decorated with tiny pinecones.

QUICK & EASY ALTERNATIVES

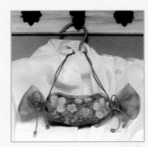

Option 1

An organza napkin filled with potpourri becomes a decorative closet sachet. Place the napkin on a flat surface and glue small silk flowers in the center, then mound potpourri on top of the flowers. Form a rectangle by folding napkin lengthwise, covering the potpourri, and glue seam. Fold each end toward the back seam, then secure ends with a doubled length of gold cord. Tie one end into a bow, then, allowing for a hanger, tie the other end.

Option 2

A child who loves cats will adore having two little kittens scented with a lovely fragrance for her closet. Find tiny wooden cat cut-outs at craft stores, then sand them lightly to remove any rough edges. Coat them thoroughly with essential oil in a light scent, such as lavender or vanilla. Cut little bandannas from colorful fabric scraps and tie them around the necks of the wooden cut-outs. Cut a piece of twine or ribbon to form a hanger, then hot-glue a cut-out to each end.

Option 3

Scent a pretty prom dress stored for its debut with a lovely flower-trimmed floral sachet. A miniature grapevine wreath and artificial flowers are used to create the pretty result. Brush a floral-scented essential oil, like lavender, gardenia, rose, or carnation, onto the grapevine wreath, saturating it well. Glue tiny blue and white silk flowers, green silk leaves, and a few pearl stamens to the wreath. Glue ends of white silk gimp to the wreath, then tie a bow for hanging.

Materials You'll Need

- 12"x6" (30x15cm) tartan wool
- Scissors
- Pins
- Glue gun & glue sticks
- Large spoon or scoop
- Pine-scented potpourri
- 1 yd. (92cm) red cotton cord
- Miniature pinecones

1 Fold fabric in half lengthwise. Match pattern of tartan plaid, then trim raw edges if necessary. Mark bottom fold line with a pin.

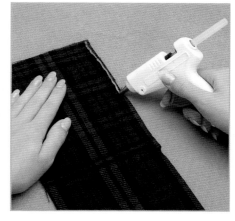

2 Open the fabric and apply hot glue along each side from the top to the bottom fold line. Refold the fabric and press sides together with fingertips to secure.

3 Using a spoon or scoop, fill the the sachet with long-lasting, pine-scented potpourri.

4 Wrap the red cord around the top of the pouch tightly and finish with a secure knot.

5 Use hot glue to attach miniature pinecones to the front of the sachet below the knotted cord.

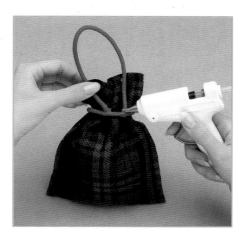

6 Fashion a hanging loop from red cord, then hot-glue it to the back of the pouch.

Appliquéd Scarf Set

A warm and cozy scarf and cap are just the thing for a winter sleigh ride. Made of polar fleece and appliquéd with jaunty hearts, this duo is the perfect gift for family members living in snow country. Easy to make using scraps of fabric, these colorful accessories will keep them warm while listening to the jingle of sleigh bells, ice skating, skiing, or just enjoying the winter wonderland.

QUICK & EASY ALTERNATIVES

Option 1

For nighttime cuddling, this cozy, polar fleece blanket will find a permanent place on a favorite sofa. Purchase a ready-made blanket in midnight blue, then cut a moon shape from purple fabric and two stars from yellow fabric. Appliqué images to blanket with fusible web, following manufacturer's instructions. Machine-stitch a zigzag or satin stitch around appliqués with gold thread, and then whipstitch around entire blanket with matching gold floss. Make simple pillow covers to match.

Option 2

This charming, child-size tote holds toys to take for a visit to Grandma's or the babysitter's house. Select a canvas tote bag just the right size for little hands, then embellish with cartoon-decorated, iron-on letters in bright colors. Iron fusible web to the reverse side of the fabric, cut out letters, and then iron them onto the tote bag. If you can't find letters that you like at the craft store, consider creating your own letters with juvenile-print fabrics and fusible web.

Option 3

Create the perfect nap time pillow from polar fleece, felt, and a pillow form. Cut two 12"x12" (30x30cm) squares of aqua fleece, two 3" (7.5cm) felt circles (one fuchsia and one lilac), two 1½" (4cm) circles of plum felt, and four leaves from green felt. With black floss, hand-sew fuchsia and lilac "flowers" (and their plum-colored centers), leaves, and flower stems onto one 12"x12" (30x30cm) square. Machine-sew the squares right sides together on three sides. Turn right side out, insert pillow form, and hand-stitch opening closed.

Materials You'll Need

- ⅛ yd. (11cm) black-and-white checked flannel
- Iron
- Scissors
- Paper for pattern
- ⅛ yd. (11cm) red fabric
- Fusible web
- Red polar fleece scarf & hat
- Sewing machine
- Yellow rickrack

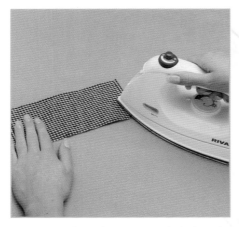

1 Cut a 4" (10cm)-wide strip of black-and-white checked flannel, then press ¼" (6mm)-wide seam on all sides.

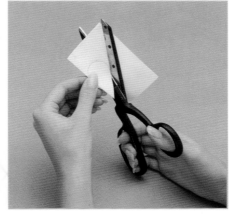

2 Fold paper in half and draw half of a heart at the folded edge. Cut image from folded paper to create a full-sized heart pattern.

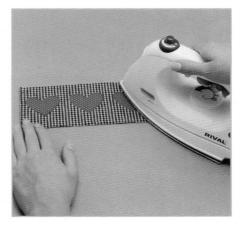

3 Iron fusible web to back of red fabric. Trace heart pattern on fabric and cut out. Peel off fusible web backing and iron hearts onto checked fabric strip.

4 Pin checked fabric strip to polar fleece scarf. Machine-sew all around, staying close to the edge of fabric strip.

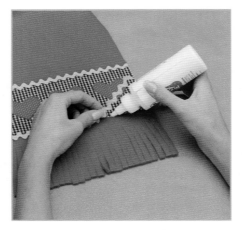

5 Cut rickrack to the width of the scarf, then glue or sew it along the top and bottom edge of the black-and-white fabric strip.

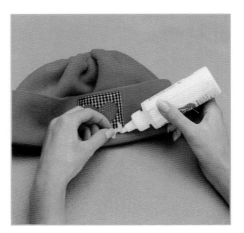

6 Create and appliqué a similar design for the hat with a square of black-and-white checked fabric, one heart, and one strip of rickrack.

No-Sew Wrapped Pillows

Whether it's for your sister or aunt, this elegant pillow will be an appreciated gift. The lovely floral fabric, which features bunches of violets, contrasts nicely with the solid polished cotton of the pillow. This pillow comes together quickly with absolutely no sewing involved. So fast in fact that several can be made in an evening—one for each member of the family.

QUICK & EASY ALTERNATIVES

Option 1

Make this charming pillow for a friend's new home. Select a 32" (81cm)-square silk scarf in colors that coordinate with the decor. Place a 12" (30cm) square pillow form on a diagonal in the center of the scarf. Fold two opposite corners over the pillow, folding one corner under the other. Bring the two remaining corners of the scarf together and tie them into a knot. Fluff out the ends and leave them free, or tuck them under the knot to create a rosette.

Option 2

Present a favorite aunt with a pillow decorated with a faux leopard print. Buy a gold-brocade neckroll pillow, then wrap the center of the pillow with a 36"x4" (91x10cm) strip of leopard-print fabric. Fold the raw edges of the fabric to the backside of the strip before wrapping. Tie the fabric strip tightly, then tuck each end under the knot to form a bow. Hot-glue the ends in place. Glue two black tassels under the fabric bow.

Option 3

Just the right size for cushioning a neck while reading, this pretty white pillow was once a cutwork tea towel. Use a new tea towel or look for a vintage one. Cut the towel into a 14"x14" (36x36cm) square. Fold the raw edge under the cutwork edge, and fuse with lightweight fusible web. Sew a gathering stitch at one end, pull tight, then stuff neckroll with batting. Sew a gathering stitch at opposite end; pull tight. Sew on a yellow satin bow, or attach with hot glue.

Materials You'll Need

- Purchased pillow, 20" (50cm) square
- Measuring tape
- Scissors
- Floral print fabric, ¾ yd. (69cm)
- Iron
- Heavy-duty rubber band
- Craft glue
- Glue gun & glue sticks

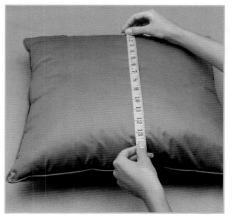

1 Purchase a 20" (50cm) pillow. If using a pillow in a different size, adjust fabric wrap size to fit.

2 Measure the print fabric, then cut it into a 20"x60" (50x150cm) strip using sharp scissors.

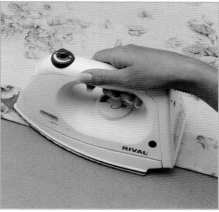

3 Fold over each long end of fabric 2" (5cm) , then press a hem along these folds.

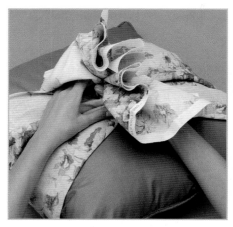

4 Wrap fabric strip snugly around pillow, pulling the ends together in the middle.

5 Pull the ends of the fabric through a rubber band. Make sure to wrap band tightly.

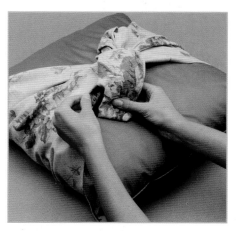

6 Tuck the ends under the wrapped sides or under the banded center. Glue the ends under the knot using a hot-glue gun, if desired.

Dad's Handy Armchair Caddy

This easy-to-make armchair caddy will keep Dad's reading glasses, remote control, and television schedule close at hand. Make this useful holder out of felt and classic plaid fabrics. Finish with an interesting trim, and it's ready to be tucked into a sofa or favorite easy chair right by Dad's side. He'll never lose the remote control again.

QUICK & EASY ALTERNATIVES

Option 1

A fabric-covered wastebasket perfectly appoints a home office. Measure the circumference at the top and bottom of the wastebin, adding ¾" (2cm). Measure the height, adding 2" (5cm). Cut fabric and hot-glue onto side of waste-basket, over-lapping one raw edge with a ¼" (6mm) hem. Glue hem. Tuck corners at the bottom to fit. Glue tucks onto bottom. Cut felt base. Glue onto bottom, covering raw edges. Fold a 1" (2.5cm) strip of fabric with raw edges in. Glue to cover upper raw edge. Hot-glue braid around rim.

Option 2

Plaids in winter hues are beautiful to use all year long. These are easy to make and can be embellished with fancy trims. For one coaster, cut two 5"x5" (13x13cm) squares of fabric. With right sides together, sew a ¼" (6mm) seam all around, leaving a 2" (5cm) opening. Turn right side out, then press. Pin opening closed, then topstitch around coaster as close as possible to edge. Hot-glue trim over topstitching. Several of these can be cut at a time and sewn quickly. Consider giving a set of six or eight coasters with a gift of matching tumblers and stemware.

Option 3

Using ready-made place mats makes this project simple. Purchase place mats in an appropriate color. Add a pocket to the right side by first cutting a 7"x6" (18x15cm) piece of color-coordinated fabric. Turn down, then topstitch a ½" (1.5cm) hem at the top. Press a ½" seam on each side and bottom; top-stitch onto place mat. Use hot glue to add coordinating braid on pocket, and around place mat edge. Tuck a matching napkin into the pocket of each place mat for a unique gift.

Materials You'll Need

- Sewing machine
- 10"x13" (25x33cm) red plaid fabric
- 13"x16" (33x40cm) green plaid fabric
- 13"x24" (33x60cm) black felt
- Pins
- 2⅛ yds. (194cm) green trim
- Glue gun & glue sticks

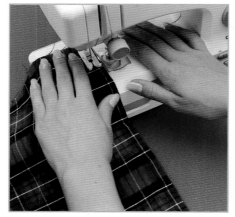

1 Fold the green plaid piece to 5"x13" (13x33cm) and the red piece to 8"x13" (20.5x33cm). Topstitch a ½" (1.5cm) hem along folded edge of the red plaid piece.

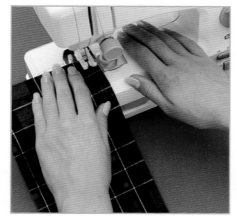

2 Topstitch a ½" (1.5cm) hem along folded edge of the green plaid.

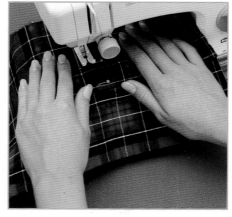

3 Pin both pieces of plaid together at the bottom, then machine-stitch vertically down the center to form pockets.

4 Pin plaid pockets onto one end of the black felt, then machine-stitch to the felt on three sides. Sew up the center a second time to strengthen pockets.

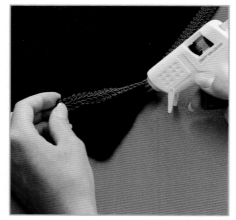

5 With a glue gun, hot-glue the green trim completely around the armchair caddy.

6 Fill the pockets with a remote control, a television guide, and other gifts for Dad.

Muslin Bath Sachets

QUICK & EASY ALTERNATIVES

Option 1

Select fluffy new facecloths to match bathroom decor, or choose feminine or masculine hues to suit the gift recipient. Bundle the facecloths with a fine-milled, rich and creamy soap, and a tube of facial scrub. Tie with a coordinating organza bow and strip of rosebud trim for a beautiful and feminine gift. Or, for a masculine package, tie with a deeper-hued ribbon, and finish with a simple braid trim. Complete the presentation with a sprig of dried or artificial flowers.

Option 2

Beautiful fragrant soap look wonderful packaged in a delicate and feminine froth of organza. Make this little pillowcase from a 7"x9" (18x23cm) piece of organza. Machine-sew lace trim border along 7" (18cm) edge. Fold to 3¼"x9" (8x23cm), right sides together, then sew along bottom and long side; turn right side out. Slip soap into pillowcase. Secure with a coordinating metallic organza ribbon tied in a bow. Finish this lovely gift by tucking in a sprig or two of dried lavender under the gold ribbon bow.

Option 3

Affix a flower petal to the tag of these tea bags for the bathtub. One-sided, fusible interfacing is used as the fabric for the bags. To make, cut an 8"x10" (20.5x25cm) strip of fabric, fold lengthwise, then fuse a ¼" (6mm) seam with a hot iron. Flatten fabric with fused seam inside. Fold at the center, bringing open ends up. Fill each side with herbs. Fold open ends over, lay a 12" (30cm) piece of white twine on the fold, staple closed, then staple a small identifying tag to bottom of twine.

G ifts of fragrance are welcomed by everyone in the family. These muslin bath bags filled with herbs are wonderful additions to the ritual of bath time. Create a sachet using a mixture of restorative lavender or a therapeutic blend of eucalyptus and cedar for sore muscles. Easy-to-sew muslin squares tied with cotton twine keep herbs intact but allow their aromatic oils to be released in a steamy tub or shower.

Materials You'll Need

- Thin muslin, 18"x36" (45x91cm)
- Ruler
- Scissors
- Sewing machine
- Herbs
- White cotton twine
- Dried or artificial flower buds
- Glue gun & glue sticks

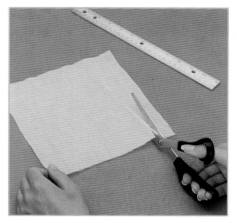

1 Measure and cut eight 8"x8" (20.5x20.5cm) squares. To speed the process, fold the fabric and cut through several layers. Separate squares.

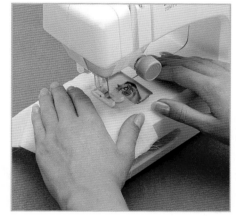

2 Fold lengthwise and sew a ¼" (6mm) seam along side and bottom. Make sure seams are secure to prevent herbs from dislodging.

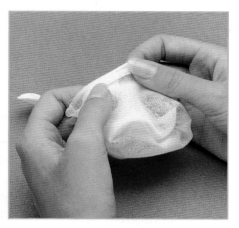

3 Turn raw-edged seam inside. (Open end does not require sewing.) Iron bags flat to permit easy filling.

4 Fill approximately one-half of open end of bag with herbs used for the bath. Choose a blend specifically designed for therapeutic use.

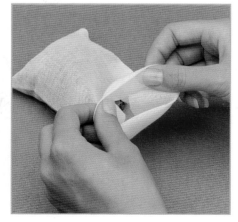

5 Turn raw edge of bag down 2" (5cm) inside, touching dried herbs. Do not iron; a soft fold is prettier. Tie a secure knot with white cotton twine, Tie a loose bow.

6 Use a glue gun to affix small dried or artificial flower bud onto knotted twine. Place in a gold wire basket for presentation.

Padded Fabric Hangers

F abric-covered padded hangers are perfect closet accessories for hanging delicate silk and knit garments. Choose a luxurious vintage floral material for each in the set, or coordinate fabrics around a central theme. Add tiny crocheted doilies or antique handkerchiefs, and trim with bows of silk, taffeta, or grosgrain ribbon. These lovely hangers make wonderful gifts for grandmas, aunts, and cousins.

QUICK & EASY ALTERNATIVES

Option 1

Make these beverage coasters using a single fabric pattern, or coordinating fabrics. Add a single layer of felt to make them more absorbent. Cut 5"x5" (13x13cm) squares of fabric; two squares make one coaster. With right sides together, sew ¼" (6mm) seam on three sides to close. Turn right side out. Insert felt squares. Fold the raw edge inside, making a small hem. Press. Topstitch ⅛" (3mm) in on all four sides with contrasting colored thread.

Option 2

Accent bathroom towels by adding colorful fabric borders. Cut fabric strip widths as needed based on size of towels. Hem each strip of fabric ¼" (6mm) in on each long side. Measure up from edge of towel about 2" (5cm). Lightly mark edge with pencil. Pin fabric to towel. Machine-sew all four edges evenly. Topstitch to secure thread at each end. Trim loose thread. Add pretty color-coordinated textured braid, lace or rickrack trims for special added interest.

Option 3

Brighten a corner with a glowing spot of light. Cover a plain lamp shade with color-coordinated fabric. Make a lampshade cover pattern. Cut fabric to fit. Cut two strips for the trim. Spread craft glue over lamp shade (or use a spray adhesive in a area that's well-ventilated). Use your fingertips to press fabric onto the shade and trim to fit as needed. Hem the edges, and glue the fabric strips at top and bottom of shade. Glue contrasting gimp trim over the fabric strips to embellish. This shade makes a wonderful gift for a new homeowner.

Materials You'll Need

- Scissors
- Ruler
- 14"x18" (35x45cm) batting
- Wooden hanger
- Thread

- Vintage fabric, 45"x18" (115x45cm)
- Needle
- Wire-edged ribbon
- Glue gun & glue sticks

1 Cut batting into a 14"x18" (35x45cm) piece. Cut two 8"x11" 20.5x27.5cm) pieces from the vintage fabric.

2 Wrap batting around hanger, and then loosely wrap with thread. Continue wrapping until batting covers hanger completely. Trim excess.

3 With right sides together, hand-stitch one end of fabric closed, gathering as you go. Repeat this step with the other piece of fabric.

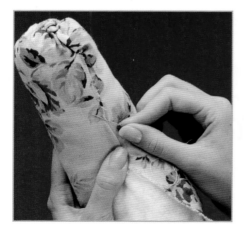

4 Turn right side out, and slip one piece of fabric onto one end of hanger over the batting. Stitch this piece closed to the middle of hanger

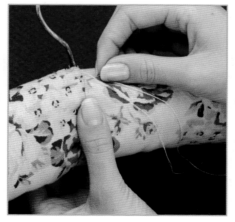

5 Repeat Step 4 with the second piece of fabric then hand-stitch these two pieces together at center part of the wooden hanger.

6 Wrap ribbon around the seam to hide the stitches. Tie another piece of ribbon into a bow and hot-glue to top of hanger.

Whimsical Welcome Mat

This delightful doormat is as fresh as a springtime garden. Your Grandma or Aunt will love the butterflies fluttering above a white picket fence where springtime flowers "grow" in abundance. Fabric paints and stencils were used to impart this cheerful scene—a perfect welcome to a country cottage or a gardener's hideaway.

QUICK & EASY ALTERNATIVES

Option 1

Graceful green ivy weaves its way along a flag-stone path on this stenciled welcome mat for a family member's porch. Use masking tape to tape stencil with a pathway design to a light-colored mat. Follow the instructions on the opposite page for stenciling techniques. Stencil edges of stones with brown and rust fabric paint mixed together, darker on edges and lighter towards center. Tape ivy design stencil to mat. Paint leaves green and stems brown. Seal with clear acrylic spray.

Option 2

Create a rich, woven look of twigs on this mat to frame the word "WELCOME." It makes a delightful gift for a summer cottage. Tape twig stencil to a light-colored mat or rug. Follow the stenciling technique on the opposite page to stencil twigs with brown fabric paint. Stencil leaves green. Dip the end of the stencil brush in red paint and dot on berries. Tape stencil with "WELCOME" design on the mat and paint green. Spray mat with a coat of clear acrylic sealer.

Option 3

Give a Noah's ark rug to a favorite nephew to brighten up his room. Tape the stencil with a Noah's ark design centered on a blue mat. Follow the instructions on the opposite page for stenciling techniques. Stencil the ark brown, roof red, Noah's robe red, hair and beard gray, and face light brown. Tape the animal stencils, as pictured, and paint zebras black and white, elephants gray, lions gold, alligators green, and giraffes yellow with brown spots.

Materials You'll Need

- Masking tape
- Stencils: fence, flowers, & butterfly
- Beige, tassel-trimmed mat or rug
- Stencil brushes
- Fabric paints: white, green, light &
- dark pink, light & dark yellow, & light & dark purple
- Plastic foam plates
- Clear acrylic spray sealer

1 Use masking tape to secure stencil to mat. Start with the fence design, lining the bottom of the stencil with the bottom edge of the mat.

2 Dip stencil brush in white fabric paint and dab brush on a paper towel so that it's almost dry. Paint the fence onto the mat in a circular motion, holding brush upright.

3 Stencil the slender green stems and leaves over the top of the fence, using green fabric paint.

4 Stencil the flowers next. Continue applying the paint in a circular motion.

5 Finish the mat by adding the butterflies, each in a different color, to the top corners.

6 To provide longevity to the rug and protect it from wear, spray on a coat of clear acrylic sealant.

Fabric-Covered Canvas Headboard

A favorite friend or relation will love the simple beauty of the abstract bouquet of flowers on this headboard. This gift looks as if it would cost a few hundred dollars to purchase, but actually is inexpensive and easy to make. A large artist's canvas was covered with designer fabric—stretched across the frame and stapled. The result is a beautiful designer headboard.

QUICK & EASY ALTERNATIVES

Option 1

Give a unique gift of art by making this four-paneled canvas presentation from scenes on fabric. Determine which four images you'll want to frame. Using one of the four 12"x12" (30x30cm) artist canvases, lay the fabric down and center the canvas over an image. Add 1½" (3cm) on all sides. Mark measurement with a pencil, then cut out the square. Repeat for remaining three panels. Follow directions on the opposite page for applying fabric to each canvas.

Option 2

A piece of vintage fabric finds renewed life as a decorative wall hanging. Present this gift with a ribbon edged in a matching color. Follow directions on the opposite page for applying fabric to a 5"x5" (13x13cm) artist canvas. After the fabric is applied to canvas, use hot glue to affix 1½" (3cm)-wide wire-edged ribbon around the canvas edges, starting and ending at bottom center. Tie another piece of ribbon into a bow and hot-glue it to the top of the canvas.

Option 3

A dainty embroidered tea towel rises to new heights as a wall hanging. Center embroidered area of tea towel on a 5"x5" (13x13cm) stretched canvas. Allow for enough fabric to cover the fronts and sides of the canvas, so it can wrap around the back and be stapled securely. Follow directions on the opposite page for applying fabric to canvas. Cut a 24" (60cm) piece of ribbon and staple it around sides of canvas. Use another 8" (20.5cm) piece to make a hanger by stapling to each side. Glue a bow to top of hanger.

Materials You'll Need

- 56"x45" (140x115cm) upholstery fabric
- 36"x36" (90x90cm) stretched artist's canvas
- Yardstick
- Pencil
- Scissors
- Staple gun & staples
- Craft glue
- Satin ribbon: 4½ yds. (410cm)

1 Lay fabric face down. Center the stretched canvas on the fabric. Use the yardstick and pencil to measure and mark 2½" (6cm) out from all sides of canvas.

2 Use the edge of the yardstick to draw lines connecting all the measurement marks.

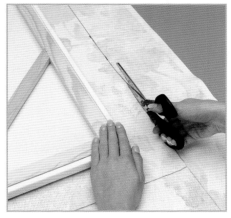

3 After all the lines are drawn, use scissors to cut along the pencil-marked lines.

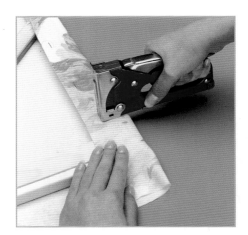

4 Fold the fabric up and over the frame. Staple to secure. Stop 1" (2.5cm) from each corner.

5 Secure the corners by pinching fabric together and folding tightly to one side. Staple to secure.

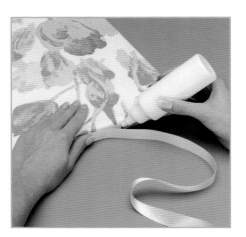

6 Spread craft glue evenly around one edge of frame. Lay the ribbon on the glue to secure. Repeat process around the frame.

Poem Pillow

There's a lot to love about this exquisite little pillow, which can be made for a friend near and dear to your heart. The beautiful Battenburg lace of the doily delicately complements the pretty hand stitching and sweet ribbon roses. A satin ribbon suspends the pillow from a knob to display its warm message, specially selected and poetically expressed. One look and she will know…this gift was handcrafted by someone who really cares.

QUICK & EASY ALTERNATIVES

Option 1

Hanging from a doorknob, this message pillow will make a teacher's day, everyday. Copy your message onto heat-transfer paper, available at craft stores. Cut two 4"x6" (10x15cm) pieces of natural-colored fabric, using pinking shears. Transfer design to center of front. Cut two pieces of batting to 3"x5" (7.5x13cm). Pin the two pieces of fabric wrong sides together, with batting in between. Sew a running stitch ½" (1.5cm) inside edge of pillow using embroidery floss. Sew heart buttons in corners. Make hanger of twine.

Option 2

What a beautiful little gift to delight a gardener. Copy or write "Earth laughs in flowers" message on heat-transfer paper, available at craft stores. Fold a vintage floral-print handkerchief in half diagonally. With iron, transfer message to handkerchief. Cut two pieces of batting 1" (2.5cm) smaller for center area. Place batting in folded handkerchief. Pin to secure. Hand-sew a running stitch around inside edge of pillow with embroidery floss. Tie a bow with satin ribbon and sew to top corner of pillow's inside edge.

Option 3

A great gift to offer inspiration. Write a dream-themed message on heat-transfer paper and iron to a piece of star-print fabric. Trace a moon shape onto fabric using a stencil. Lay two pieces of fabric wrong sides together and cut out with scalloped edges. Cut a piece of batting 1" (2.5cm) smaller all around than fabric. Place batting between the two pieces of fabric and pin. Sew a running stitch 1" (2.5cm) in from edge using embroidery floss. Glue scalloped edges of moon together using fabric glue. Sew on star button.

Materials You'll Need

- Typed or handwritten message on heat-transfer paper
- Battenburg doily & scissors
- Narrow satin ribbon
- Very thin quilt batting
- Potpourri
- Polyester stuffing
- Pins
- Embroidery floss
- Needle
- Thread or fabric glue
- Ribbon roses

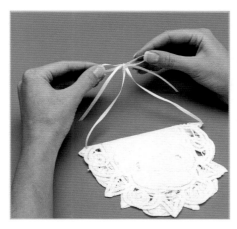

1 Type or write message on heat-transfer material (available at craft stores). Fold doily in half. Cut ribbon to 18" (45.5cm) and place in the fold of the doily. Tie into a bow.

2 Preheat iron (do not use steam). Place transfer ink-side down on center of fabric and iron transfer onto front of doily. Do not slide iron. Remove iron and paper transfer.

3 Cut a piece of thin quilt batting the same size as center of doily. Fold in half, then tuck some potpourri and polyester filling inside for stuffing.

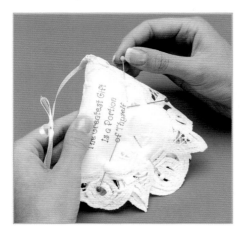

4 Fold doily, to encase the stuffing and secure edges with pins.

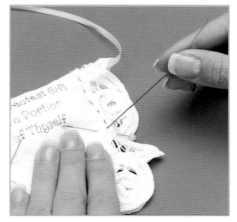

5 Thread needle with embroidery floss that coordinates with the ribbon roses. Sew a running stitch around the inner edge of the doily. Remove pins.

6 Sew or use fabric glue to attach a few ribbon roses to front of pillow. Attach one rose to the bow of the ribbon hanger.

Paper and card projects

When it comes to art and craft projects, the simplest materials are often the best. With a little imagination, a few simple scraps of paper can serve as the base for all manner of gifts—but it can be difficult to know where to start.

The projects in this chapter will provide all the guidance and inspiration you need to help you turn your ideas into beautiful gifts that you'll be proud to give away. But watch out—you may decide they are just too special to let go!

Découpaged Photo Memories Box

Old family photographs are priceless treasures handed down from generation to generation. They're often used to trace genealogy and to illustrate wonderful stories chronicling family history. Every home should have a place to store these family heirlooms, and this box—which is découpaged with old family photographs—is the perfect container.

QUICK & EASY ALTERNATIVES

Option 1

Present an aunt who loves cats with a frame box in which she can showcase a photo of her own pet. Select a small, black frame box, then cut images of cats from magazines or gift wrap. Brush backs of images with a coat of découpage medium, place them on the box in a pleasing design, and smooth them with your fingers. Let dry, then cover the entire box with a coat of découpage medium. For a glossy effect, apply several coats of medium, letting the box dry between applications.

Option 2

Create this découpaged album to present to parents on their anniversary. Choose a selection of photographs, then color-copy them for the album cover and spine. Cut out the photo images, then brush the backs with découpage medium. Affix images to the album cover; let dry. Cut a square of ecru paper with fancy-edged scissors; glue to slightly larger gold square. Write a title for album on ecru paper, then glue assembled square to album. Brush the entire album with découpage medium.

Option 3

When a vacation or once-in-a-lifetime school trip results in too many postcards, this frame provides a solution for displaying them. Purchase a ready-made frame with wide molding, then color-copy a selection of postcards. Arrange them on the frame, trim to fit, then brush a coat of découpage medium on the back of each and place them on the frame until it is covered. Let the frame dry thoroughly. Add a glossy finish with additional coats of medium, allowing the frame to dry between coats.

Materials You'll Need

- Photocopies of old photographs
- Scissors
- Wooden box
- Cutting board
- Découpage medium
- Sponge brush

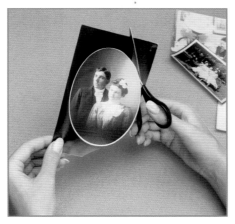

1 Photocopy old photographs in color or black-and-white, depending on the original. Trim photocopied images.

2 After all of the images are cut out, arrange them on the box in a pleasing pattern.

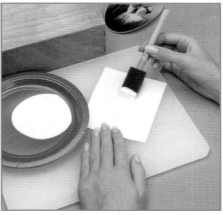

3 Brush a coat of découpage medium on the back of each image using a sponge brush.

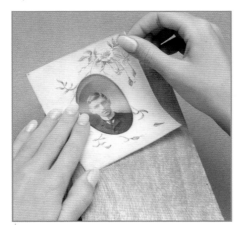

4 Position the damp photocopied image on the box and smooth it down with your fingertips.

5 Trim away excess paper from edge of box. Continue placing photos on remainder of box until entire surface is covered. Let the box dry completely.

6 When box is thoroughly dry, apply a final coat of medium over the entire surface.

Vacation Placemats

Option 1

A child can use this placemat to practice table setting techniques. Cut two clear, self-adhesive sheets 13"x18" (33x45cm). Cut a piece of decorative paper 12"x17" (30x43cm). Use dishes and utensils as patterns to draw and cut shapes out of contrasting paper. Attach shapes to paper using a glue stick. Lay one clear sheet face down, add glued papers, face down, then the second clear sheet, face up. Trim to form a ¼" (6mm) clear border around design.

Option 2

Pictures, maps, and photos of a prized catch can be used here to delight a special fisherman. Cut two clear, self-adhesive sheets 13"x18" (33x45cm). Cut colored background paper 12"x17" (30x43cm). Assemble design items, then attach to paper with glue stick. Peel off backing and lay one clear sheet face down. Top with the design, face down, then the second clear sheet, face up. Press out any bubbles, then trim the edges for a ¼" (6mm) border all around.

Option 3

Group together photos, drawings, and ad headlines, all pertaining to her favorite antiques. Cut two sheets of clear, self-adhesive film 13"x18" (33x45cm). Cut a 12"x17" (30x43cm) sheet of colored paper. Cut out images and headlines, then adhere them to paper with glue stick. Peel backing and lay first film sheet face down. Place design face down on top, then second film sheet, face up. Press away bubbles and trim film to form ¼" (6mm) border.

Placemats are a useful gift, appropriate for almost anyone, and are easy to create with the help of clear, adhesive sheets. In fact, almost any flat item can be placed between two sheets, with theme possibilities limited only by the imagination. Here, vacation souvenirs, including a map, postcards, photos, and ticket stubs, create one placemat—imagine a complete set, each a memorial to a fun family trip from days past.

48

Materials You'll Need

- Scissors
- Clear, self-adhesive plastic (repositionable), two sheets
- Ruler
- Map
- Highlighter marker
- Vacation memorabilia
- Glue stick

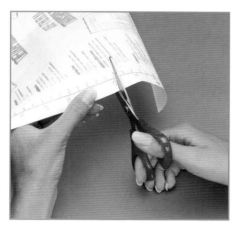

1 With sharp scissors, cut both sheets of clear plastic film to 13"x18" (33x45cm) in size.

2 Cut street map showing vacation route to 12"x17" (30x43cm). Highlight route taken on trip, if desired.

3 Assemble postcards, brochures, photos, and other memorabilia. Trim each piece to desired size for placemat.

4 Lay memorabilia on map, arranging at various angles and overlapping. When satisfied with result, adhere pieces to map with glue stick.

5 Peel backing from one plastic sheet and lay face down. Lay map face down on top, smoothing with fingers to eliminate any bubbles or wrinkles.

6 Peel backing and lay down second sheet of plastic, face up. Smooth out wrinkles, then trim edges of placemat to create a ¼" (6mm) border around map.

Tabletop Collage

Glass-topped, round tables have long been a popular way to display a lovely tablecloth. Now, consider creating a decorative collage to display beneath clear glass on an occasional table. Attractive items of special appeal to a family member can be arranged on just about any tabletop, beneath a shiny pane of glass. This table displays vintage postcards against a white cloth, a thoughtful gift for an antique lover.

QUICK & EASY ALTERNATIVES

Option 1

All little girls like cut-out dolls. Make color copies of her favorites to make this tabletop collage. Or, use antique-style cut-out dolls found in books or antique stores to coordinate with vintage furniture. From the color copies of the paper dolls, cut out figures, clothing, and accessories. Arrange them on top of a nightstand until you're pleased with their appearance. Cover the design with a purchased piece of glass precut to fit the nightstand.

Option 2

She can use this tray while enjoying her patio garden. Select a tray with a removable glass center. Cut a piece of heavy, white paper the same size as glass area of tray. Make color copies of antique-style seed packets, then cut out. Arrange copies on the paper, overlapping them until satisfied with the results. Apply découpage medium to each copy with a small sponge brush and press them onto the paper. When dry, place on tray, with glass on top.

Option 3

Here's a way to display his keepsakes from a memorable vacation, and turn a plain bedroom table into a conversation piece. Your son, the travel buff, will love this! Collect vacation memorabilia such as tickets, brochures, postcards, luggage stubs, pictures, and a copy of your son's passport. Arrange items at different angles on top of a small side table until pleased with collage. Cover table with a piece of glass cut to fit top.

Materials You'll Need

- Color photocopy machine
- Antique postcards
- Scissors or craft knife
- Round table with removable glass top
- Tablecloth

1 Make copies of postcards on a color copy machine. Also copy any card backs containing interesting written messages.

2 With scissors or craft knife, carefully cut copies of postcards from background paper.

3 Drape a white tablecloth over the table. Or, choose a colorful tablecloth to coordinate with the recipient's decor.

4 Arrange postcards on tabletop, beginning with outside edge and working toward center. Place them horizontally and vertically, interspersing message cards.

5 Continue arranging cards, overlapping a few, until desired effect is achieved.

6 Place glass top on table when design is complete, covering and securing postcards.

Decorative File Folders

A nimal prints are springing up everywhere, with exotic patterns decorating clothing, accessories—even furniture. Wrapping paper is also part of the trend, providing an ideal way to splash everyday items with a little "jungle fever," creating unique, stylish gifts. Here, paper-decorated manila file folders become trend-setting office or dorm room organizers, perfect for your wild-at-heart sister.

QUICK & EASY ALTERNATIVES

Option 1

The family animal print lover will "go wild" for this desk accessory set. It's an easy, inexpensive gift for a style-conscious student. Cut a piece of animal-print wrapping paper to fit pencil. Spray pencil with adhesive, then roll in paper, beginning at one edge and ending at the other. Repeat to wrap more pencils in different prints. Tie pencils together with twine and present in the pencil holder. For pencil holder, repeat this same procedure to decorate a soup or other can with paper.

Option 2

This gift will help keep her organized at school or work, and further her fashion-forward image at the same time. Select animal-print wrapping paper to complement the color of an accordion file folder. Lay folder down on wrong side of paper and trace with a pencil. Open fold over flap and trace flap twice, then cut out all shapes. Spray front of folder with adhesive, then smooth on paper with fingers. Trim any excess paper. Repeat to affix paper to both sides of fold over flap.

Option 3

Here's a useful gift for your daughter when she lands her first job. Select a desk pad with a calendar or purchase a separate calendar. Measure the border strips on either side of the desk pad. Cut pieces of animal-print paper to fit these measurements, plus some for wrapping under. Spray the back of paper with adhesive, then press onto pad, wrapping the excess to back. If desired, wrap a matching pencilholder for a great desk set.

Materials You'll Need

- Wrapping paper, a variety of animal prints
- Pencil
- Colored manila file folders
- Ruler
- Scissors
- Surface covering
- Adhesive spray
- Durable surface
- Craft knife

1 Place wrapping paper print-side up, then use pencil to trace file folder. Use different paper for each file, if desired.

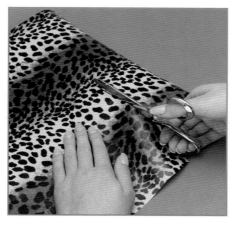

2 Extend bottom line an additional 1" (2.5cm) on each, redrawing lines with ruler. Cut out shapes with scissors.

3 Place cut-out paper on a covered work surface and spray the back side with adhesive.

4 Press cut-out paper onto front side of folder, smoothing with fingers to prevent wrinkles. An extra inch (2.5cm) will remain at bottom.

5 Fold extra paper over to other side of folder, spray lightly with adhesive, and press with fingers to adhere.

6 Place folder on a durable surface. Clean up any excess paper at edges, cutting along the edges of the folder with a craft knife. Repeat for other folders.

Decorated Clocks

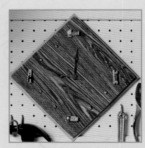

Delight Grandma with a clock she will cherish. Just right for her sewing room, this special timepiece is sure to become a conversation starter. Easy-to-cut foam board is used as the base of the clock, which is then covered with an old-fashioned gingham fabric. Buttons and spools of thread cleverly represent the numbers. All you add are the whimsical decorations and the clockworks.

QUICK & EASY ALTERNATIVES

Option 1

A teenaged girl will enjoy this bright blue feather boa-decorated clock. Trace a plate onto a piece of foam board. Use a utility knife to cut traced circle. Using a daisy rubber stamp, stamp flowers onto clock at 12, 3, 6, and 9 marks. Color the stamped flowers using colored markers. Use hot glue to attach colorful rhinestones in flower centers and for the rest of numbers. Attach blue boa around outside edge of clock using hot glue. Follow manufacturer's directions for attaching clockworks.

Option 2

Young boys are fascinated with tractors. This clock will be their dream. Use a utility knife to cut foam board into a square. Cut black card stock ¼" (6mm) larger than foam board and hot-glue it to the back of board. Use a black ink stamp pad and checkerboard stamp to decorate the edges of the clock. Stamp tractor designs for 12, 3, 6, and 9, then color in with markers. Affix button for other "numbers" on the clock face. Stamp middle design, color, then punch holes for clock parts.

Option 3

Dad can hang this clock above his workbench. Use a utility knife to cut core board into a square. Cover with wood grain contact paper. Mount gray card stock that is cut ¼" (6mm) larger than the foam board, behind the board, using hot glue. Turn foam board into a diamond shape. Glue tool buttons on clock face at 12, 3, 6, and 9. Punch screws into foam board to simulate the other numbers. Anchor the backs of the screws with hot glue. Punch a hole in the center using a screwdriver. Add the clockworks.

Materials You'll Need

- Utility knife
- Cutting board
- Foam board
- Burgundy card stock
- Glue stick

- Fabric scissors
- Plaid fabric
- Craft glue
- Halved wooden spools
- Scraps of plaid fabric

- Glue gun & glue sticks
- Buttons
- Screwdriver
- Clock parts kit

1 Use the utility knife and cutting board to carefully cut the foam board into an 8"x8" (20.5x20.5cm) square.

2 Cut the burgundy card stock ¼" (6mm) larger than the foam board square. Use a glue stick to attach to back of board.

3 Cut plaid fabric the same size as the foam board. Fringe the edges. Affix the fabric to the foam board clock face using craft glue.

4 Cover four wooden spool halves with craft glue and scraps of various plaid fabrics. Use hot glue to affix each spool to clock face at 12, 3, 6, and 9 marks.

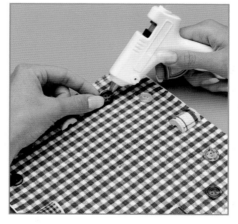

5 Use a hot-glue gun to affix the buttons to the clock face for the other numbers.

6 Punch a hole in center of the clock using the end of the scissors or a screwdriver. Follow manufacturer's directions to attach the clock parts.

Family Bulletin Board

Active families sometimes find it difficult to keep everyone on schedule with so many events, invitations, and telephone messages to keep organized. One solution to desktop clutter is a bulletin board, with pushpins to hold written reminders and notes. Here, a handsome bulletin board was created, complete with painted, personalized stripes to organize items for each individual. A great gift for the whole family.

QUICK & EASY ALTERNATIVES

Option 1

This is a charming wall accessory for a little boy who loves trains. Paint, ticking fabric, and a bandanna are all you need to transform a board. Measure cork area and cut fabric to fit, then adhere fabric to bulletin board with spray adhesive. Brush blue acrylic paint on frame of bulletin board. Allow to dry. Tie the bandanna in knot and hang on corner of board. Include train pushpins to complete.

Option 2

Brighten a girl's room with this hanging bulletin board featuring specially made pushpins. Cover the wooden frame of a bulletin board with white acrylic paint. Let dry, and cut a length of yellow-checked fabric ribbon for a hanger. Hot-glue each ribbon end behind top corners of board. Cut a new piece of ribbon, form a bow, and glue to center of hanging ribbon. Glue white- and yellow-flower buttons on top of plain, flat pushpins to create your own original, designer pushpins.

Option 3

This decorative bulletin board displays kids' school schedules and family messages. Apply white acrylic paint to frame of bulletin board. Allow to dry. With square-shaped stencil and black paint, create checkered pattern on frame. Use a variety of vegetable stamps and stamp pads in green, orange, red, and purple to decorate cork area. Include vegetable-themed push pins.

Materials You'll Need

- Ruler
- Masking tape
- Wood frame, cork bulletin board
- Acrylic paint: gold, white, & green
- Paintbrushes

- Stencil brush
- Alphabet stencils
- Wood stain
- Gloss varnish
- Scissors

- Beige flat trim
- Glue gun & glue sticks
- Pushpins
- Three types of notepaper

1 With ruler and masking tape, divide bulletin board into three equal sections. Then divide off a 3" (7.5cm) lengthwise panel at top.

2 Alternating three colors, paint sections, using masking tape to prevent paint from one area running onto another area.

3 Using stencil brush, stencil "DAD," "MOM," and "KIDS" (or other names) in center of each small top section of board.

4 With small paintbrush, apply wood stain to wood frame of bulletin board. Let dry.

5 Cover stained wood frame with a gloss varnish, using clean, small paintbrush.

6 Hot-glue flat trim across board, beneath name sections. With themed pushpins, apply matching-themed notepaper (appropriate to each family member) on their section of bulletin board.

Leaf-Collecting Album

Create a gift for the naturalist in the family—a handsome binder embellished with an assortment of dried leaves surrounding a beautiful nature photograph. The binder can be used to hold a collection of leaves and plants and also to record important data. Whether the recipient is an experienced collector or just starting a new hobby, this is an ideal gift for the young botanist.

QUICK & EASY ALTERNATIVES

Option 1

Create an album for a feather collector. Cover the album with brown corrugated paper cut to fit. Tear purple corrugated paper into a square, slightly smaller than the cover front. With a large needle threaded with natural raffia, sew the raffia around the edge of the corrugated paper and finish with a bow. Tear a strip of orange mulberry paper and glue to the corrugated paper along with two natural feathers. Glue to cover. Fill the binder with paper.

Option 2

This album, decorated with pressed flowers, is a wonderful gift for a wildflower collector. Cut a piece of natural handmade paper embedded with leaves and petals (available at craft and paper stores) large enough to cover binder. Cover the album with the handmade paper and affix pressed flowers and ferns on cover using a sponge brush and découpage medium. Tie a bow and glue to the bouquet. Fill the binder with paper for collecting the specimens.

Option 3

Make a discovery game out of your evening walk with the family and store the treasures in this album. Cut and glue light brown card stock to a binder. Using pinking shears, cut green gingham fabric for the front cover and attach it with craft glue. Smooth out wrinkles with your fingertips. Hot-glue twigs around edge of fabric as a frame. Glue corrugated leaf cut-outs to album front. Tie a twine bow and glue it along with a leaf button to the leaves.

Materials You'll Need

- Small photo album with a removable plastic cover
- Ruler
- Scissors
- White handmade paper
- Craft glue
- Small nature photo or color copy
- Various dried leaves
- Light brown construction paper

1 Measure small album with a ruler. Cut white handmade paper ½" (1.5cm) less than the size of the album all the way around.

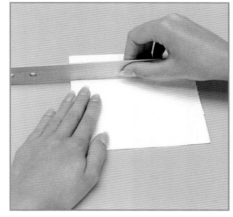

2 Place paper on album and mark placement of the spine. Score paper at each side of spine by folding sides up against ruler edge and creasing.

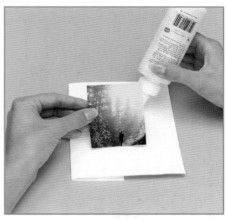

3 With craft glue, affix a nature-themed photocopy to the center of the paper.

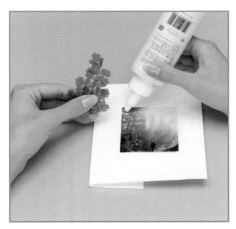

4 Affix leaves surrounding the photograph on the cover front using craft glue.

5 Cut brown construction paper to fit album. Glue white decorated paper to the brown paper.

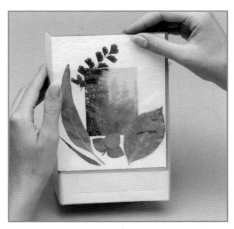

6 Gently peel plastic cover away from top third of photo album. Tuck cover paper in and readhere plastic to the album.

Home Office Desk Set

Offices have become essential rooms in today's homes as many workers are choosing lifestyles that combine both a career and home. A woman's home office reflects aspects of both her career and her personal style. This elegant, feminine desk set, put together with ready-made components covered in chic fabrics and trims, fits both categories beautifully.

QUICK & EASY ALTERNATIVES

Option 1

Handy little notepads by the phone are important tools for keeping track of busy lives. Place one in a beautiful cover and it could serve as a pretty desk accessory, too. Cut two 3½" (9cm) cardboard squares and one 3½"x½" (9x1.5cm) cardboard strip. Hinge the pieces together with tape, inserting the small strip in the center. Cover both sides with decorative paper. Fold to 3½"x½"x3½" (9x1.5x9cm) and glue notepad to the inside back cover. Embellish the cover with contrasting paper and a bow.

Option 2

One of the most common wrist injuries, tendonitis, results from typing at a computer keyboard. Resting wrists on a padded armrest placed in front of a computer keyboard is known to alleviate this ailment. To make one, cut a piece of 7"x16" (18x40cm) fabric, place right sides together, then machine-sew all sides to create a tube. Leave a small opening. Turn right side out, fill the tube with small white beans, and hand-stitch opening closed. Sew a double line of stitching on each long side.

Option 3

Monograms are elegant and tasteful ways to personalize objects of any type. CD-ROM disks, which permit telecommuters their work-at-home luxury, often have little to identify them on their labels. Purchase a plain CD holder, then stencil the recipient's monogram on the cover. For a decorative effect, stencil a border of symbols. This gift is also ideal for a teen who needs to store audio CDs. Look for CD holders in bright colors for a teenager.

Materials You'll Need

- Four-piece desk set: accordion file, pencil cup, paper clip holder & desk blotter
- Fabric
- Iron
- Aerosol spray adhesive
- Glue gun & glue sticks
- Wide ribbon
- Narrow ribbon

1 Cut a piece of fabric large enough to cover the exterior front and another to cover the back of the accordion file. Add 2" (5cm) to each measurement for hems.

2 Fold under a 1" (2.5cm)-wide strip on each edge, then press the strips to form a hem.

3 In a well-ventilated area, spray adhesive on the file front and wait five minutes.

4 Affix fabric to file front with gentle pressure, smoothing the fabric down with your fingertips. Repeat Steps 3 and 4 to cover back of file.

5 Trim top edge of file front with a strip of wide ribbon. Use hot glue to affix ribbon edges securely.

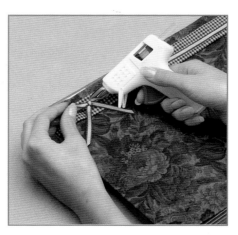

6 Embellish wide ribbon edge with a narrow decorative ribbon and a bow. To complete desk set, follow basic instructions to cover the remaining items.

Grandmother's Stamped Family Album

Beloved family photos become cherished possessions when placed in a beautifully decorated album. Boxed for years in attics, they tell no story, but collected into an album, they become part of a prized historical document. Surprise Grandmother with this personalized album waiting to begin its passage through the generations.

QUICK & EASY ALTERNATIVES

Option 1

The paw print on the cover of this album hints that a collection of photos of a beloved pet are inside. Your dog will help make this album by obligingly placing his paw onto an ink pad, then pressing it onto card stock. A purchased purple velvet album is embellished with four layers of colorful paper and topped with the paw print. Softly frayed edges of handmade paper mimic the furry print, and a ribbon bow completes the gift for a dog lover.

Option 2

So tiny, this album can be tucked into a purse or briefcase. It is perfect for someone to take on a business trip or to the office for a quick peek at beloved faces any time of the day. Select number of photos, then cut colored card stock to match. Crop and trim photos to fit, allowing for a ⅛" (3mm) black mat around each. Cut mats. Glue photos onto mat, then onto card stock. Laminate each card. Punch small holes in cards. Link cards with small brass rings.

Option 3

Capture the first day of a couple's life together on the front of a beautiful album. Start their collection of family photos with this gift. Purchase a rich, velvet-covered photo album and replace the binding tie with gold cord. Adorn the upper left corner with a gold and white organza bow, centered with a spray of white silk roses and leaves. Hot-glue ribbon and roses securely. Finish by hot-gluing a mat with a photo of the bride and groom onto the cover.

Materials You'll Need

- Handmade paper, off-white
- Scissors
- Lavender, purple & white card stock
- Craft knife & cutting surface
- Lavender wire-edged ribbon, 1½" (4cm) wide
- Glue gun & glue sticks
- Initial stamp & purple ink pad
- Glue stick
- Album
- Sponge

1 Cut purple card stock to size of album cover. Cut lavender card stock ⅛" (3mm) smaller, and handmade paper ⅛" (3mm) smaller than lavender piece. Glue these together and then glue to album cover.

2 Measure a 2" (5cm)-wide strip on lavender card stock and draw a light pencil line. Carefully tear along this line. Do the same with a piece of purple card stock, measuring 2¼" (5.5cm) wide.

3 Place lavender strip over purple strip, so that purple card is exposed ¼" (6m). Cut a ¾" (2cm) vertical slit on left side, ¼" (6mm) from bottom. Cut a second slit, on right side, 1" (2.5cm) from bottom. Repeat at 1" (2.5cm) intervals.

4 Starting at lower left, thread wire-edged ribbon through slits from back. Hot-glue ribbon on the back. Tie a bow and trim tails. Hot-glue bow at top of stitched paper strip.

5 Cut squares of white, lavender, and purple card stock, graduating sizes by ⅛" (3mm), and glue together. Stamp initial onto white card. With a sponge, lightly rub stamp pad ink onto edges of white card.

6 Glue ribbon-stitched paper strip to the left side of the album cover. Hot-glue initialed card onto front in lower right hand corner. Fill album with photos.

Felt-Covered Books

P resent a wished-for book in its own handsome felt wrapping to a favorite relative. The book covering will perform double duty as a very special gift wrap and then as a protective covering for the cherished book. In lovely muted colors with simple closures, these felt covers will be used again and again. Find just the right buttons and trim to suit the person receiving the gift.

QUICK & EASY ALTERNATIVES

Option 1

Understated enough for a man, this felt cover could easily hide the latest book on investments or improving a golf score. To make, cut a strip of felt ¼" (6mm) wider than height of book and long enough to wrap around the book, plus two 2½" (6.5cm) pockets at each end. Secure top and bottom edges of pockets with hot glue. Sew button to the center edge of the front cover. Wrap twine around the button, then glue ends to inside edge of back cover. Glue small piece of felt over ends of the twine.

Option 2

A ribbon-embellished pillow in bright burgundy felt is especially nice for reading in bed. Make this one with two 12"x12" (30x30cm) felt pieces, 1 yd. (90cm) wide ribbon, 1 yd. (90cm) narrow ribbon, and pillow stuffing. Cut felt, then pin two wide ribbon strips vertically and two narrow ribbon strips diagonally onto pillow front. Cover with pillow back and sew around four sides, leaving a 2" (5cm) opening. Turn right side out, stuff the pillow, then hand-stitch the opening closed.

Option 3

These cases are so easy that you can make one for everyone on the gift list who wears glasses. Cut a 6½"x8" (16.5x20cm) piece of felt. Cut one of the short edges with pinking shears. Place a pair of glasses in center of felt (pinked edge at top), then fold up lower third to cover glasses. Hot-glue along both sides of this fold (very close to edges) to form a pocket. Fold upper third of felt over pocket to form a flap. Sew a button onto the inside pocket under flap. Cut a button hole slit on outside flap; fold over and button.

Materials You'll Need

- Beige and green felt
- Pencil
- Scissors
- Glue gun & glue sticks
- Pins

- Pinking shears
- Brown satin ribbon, ½"x4" (1.5x10cm)
- Gold sealing wax & stamp
- Hook-and-loop self-adhesive tape

1 Lay book on felt and draw around edge with pencil. Add ¼" (6mm) to top and bottom, and 5" (13cm) to width. Cut out.

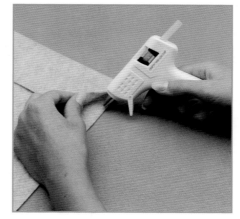

2 Fold in one end of felt 2" (5cm) and hot-glue along top and bottom edge, ⅛" (3mm) in, to slip over back cover of book.

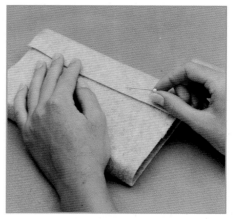

3 Slip book inside, placing back cover into pocket, and then wrap edge around to form a flap.

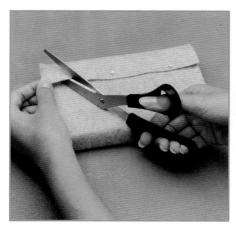

4 Cut a 1½" (4cm) diagonal corner at each side of flap. Try other decorative cuts, such as pinked or scalloped edges.

5 Cut ends of a 4" (10cm) piece of ribbon at an angle. Fold, then glue onto center of flap. Cut a 2" (5cm) green felt circle with pinking shears. Hot-glue onto ribbon. Melt a wax seal onto moss green felt, and stamp.

6 Cut a 1" (2.5cm) piece of hook-and-loop self-adhesive tape. Affix to back of flap under seal and to front of book cover.

Shadow Box Memory Frame

A beautifully arranged shadow box collection of shared memories is a sentimental way to present a personal gift to someone. This framed tribute to the sea displays shells discovered along a romantic shoreline by honeymooners. It will always remind your special someone of those special moments shared by the two of you. Included might be a favorite poem or a romantic beach photo.

QUICK & EASY ALTERNATIVES

Option 1

Touch your mother with a framed tribute to her mother. Gather scraps of damaged quilts and a copy of Grandma's photo. Fold the largest quilt scrap and place it inside a disassembled shadow box frame. Lay photo on top of one quilt piece, then fold and place second quilt piece to the right over the first. As an accent, thread a needle and stitch through top quilt, leaving needle and thread on top of quilt. Assemble the frame.

Option 2

This tribute to intertwined lives is a loving gift from one sister to another. Cut printed paper to fit inside shadow box frame. Remove cardboard liner from box and lay flat, then spray front with adhesive. Smooth paper on and trim any excess. Arrange collage of photos and pin to cardboard with pearl-head corsage pins. Tie a bow around stem of one of five porcelain roses, and hot-glue at top between photos. Glue on other roses. Reassemble shadow box.

Option 3

A veteran will be touched by this tribute to his service. Cut a piece of fabric from soldier's military shirt or use a piece of fabric resembling a uniform. Remove cardboard liner from shadow box, lay flat, and spray with adhesive. Smooth on fabric. Spray backs of flags, insignias, patches, and printed message and attach to fabric. Use pins on the backs of medals and uniform decorations to secure to assemblage and lay dog tags at bottom. Reassemble frame.

Materials You'll Need

- 11"x14" (28x35cm) shadow box, wood frame
- Scissors
- Pastel paper

- Poem printout or copy
- Spray adhesive
- Sponge
- Small shell, watercolor or print

- Sand dollar
- Starfish: 1 small, 1 medium & 1 large

1 Disassemble shadow box and remove cardboard backing. Cut pastel paper to 11"x14" (28x35cm). Print poem, place face down and cover with spray adhesive.

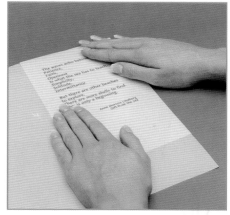

2 Smooth poem onto one side of pastel paper. Spray back of pastel paper with adhesive and smooth down on cardboard.

3 Gather items and plan arrangement of collage. Cut a square of sponge to fit behind watercolor or print of shell.

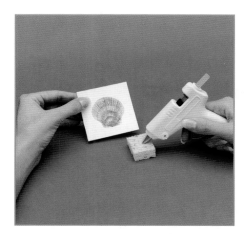

4 Hot-glue sponge to back of shell print as a spacer, then dab glue on other side of sponge and affix to pastel paper.

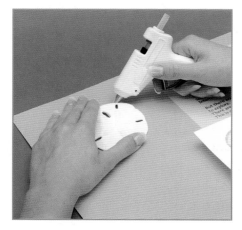

5 Hot-glue sand dollar or other large shell in desired place on pastel paper.

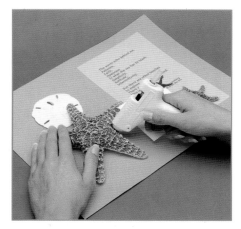

6 Hot-glue three starfish (or other large and smaller shells) onto paper to complete collage. Reassemble shadow box.

Quilled Paper Cards

Decorate a greeting card with a quilled paper design, and get ready for some admiring exclamations. Quilling, or tightly curling small strips of paper, is a unique decorating method for a design that looks complicated but is really quite simple. A charming, quilled ladybug enhances this featured card—an artistic way to convey a special "thank you" or other message to a friend.

QUICK & EASY ALTERNATIVES

Option 1

Quilled paper makes a lovely border for framing decorative items on greeting cards. The bird sticker on this card looks adorable in its quilled frame. This card uses beige card stock and four 4"x¼" (10cmx6mm) strips of paper in two colors to match bird. Use a toothpick to tightly curl up 1" (2.5cm) of ends of each strip. Apply thin lines of white glue to form a border in center of card; press quilled paper strips onto glue, alternating colors. Place sticker in center.

Option 2

Show your handiwork with these pretty gift tags. Cut two rectangles of card stock; angle the corners. Cut 2"x¼" (5cmx6mm) strips of paper: six pink, two peach, and two white. Quill all strips by tightly winding each one on a toothpick. Glue a pyramid of pink quills to center of one tag, and form a vertical line of other quills on a second tag. Glue scraps of green ribbon to make stems and leaves. Punch holes at top of tags and thread a narrow ribbon through to hang.

Option 3

Quill a pretty card for that special note. You'll need 1¼ x ¼" (4.5cmx6mm) strips of paper: nine blue, eleven yellow, and five green. Quill seven blue and six yellow strips with a toothpick. Glue a line of yellow and blue coils near left edge of the note card. Loop and glue ends of five yellow strips and glue to card to form flower petals. Glue two blue coils to flower center. Add a straight green stem glued to the bottom edge of flower. Add green coils to stem.

Materials You'll Need

- Scissors
- Ruler
- Red & black paper
- Craft glue
- Blank white card
- Toothpick
- Eight tiny, black pom-poms

1 Cut a strip of red paper (card stock or drawing paper works well) to 7"x¼" (18cmx6mm) wide.

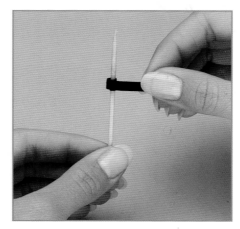

2 Form a circle out of a red paper strip, overlapping ends about ¼" (6mm) and securing with glue.

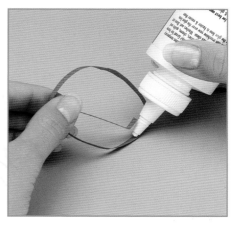

3 Cut a ¼"(6mm)-wide strip of red paper to fit inside diameter of circle, folding a small tab on each end. Apply glue to tabs and affix strip to inside circle.

4 Cut six 1"x¼" (2.5cmx6mm) black strips of paper and one 4"x¼" (10cmx6mm) strip of black paper.

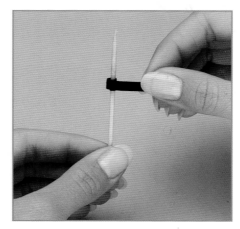

5 Tightly wind one end of each small black strip around a toothpick to curl, leaving ¼" (6mm) uncurled. Fold longer strip in half and curl each end with toothpick.

6 Glue red circle and black strips to front of white card, using smaller strips for legs and folded strip for antennae. Glue pom-poms to form ladybug dots.

Stamped Herb Note Card

This handmade card is so lovely it's likely to end up in a frame, hung on the wall, or placed on the desk of a grateful recipient. If you have a special thank you, or some other important message, to bestow on a nature-loving friend, create this card using natural handmade papers in rich tones and the surprise of real twigs bordering a stamped botanical design. Someone who appreciates nature will be truly impressed.

QUICK & EASY ALTERNATIVES

Option 1

These beautiful floral "postage" stamps are created with simple rubber stamps and colorful ink. Brush the front of a blank, white note card with sage green acrylic paint. While it's drying, stamp four multicolored flowers onto white paper. Cut a square around each stamp with scalloped scissors until you have four shapes resembling postage stamps. Use a glue stick to affix stamps to the card front in a square.

Option 2

Hanging on the front door handle, this pretty tag tells visitors where they're apt to find an avid gardener. Decorate the center of a plain, white door tag using a botanical stamp and colored stamp pad. Cut a rectangle of a complementary shade of mulberry paper larger than the door tag to form an approximately ⅛" (3mm) border all around. Tear the edges of the mulberry paper and use spray adhesive to attach to the back of the door hanger. With marking pen, write "I'm in the Garden" beneath the stamp.

Option 3

Whoever said there's beauty in simplicity captured the charm of this lovely note card, which celebrates fresh color and clean lines. Cover a plain, white 4"x5" (10x13cm) card with pastel blue acrylic paint and set aside to dry. Use a green stamp pad to stamp a fern in the center of a 4"x2⅝" (10x6.5cm) rectangle of cream-colored paper. When dry, turn paper over and trace round curve of a quarter (coin) at corners. Cut corners and glue paper to card.

Materials You'll Need

- Basil rubber stamp
- Multi-colored stamp pad
- 2¾"x3" (7x7.5cm) green paper
- 5"x6" (13x15cm) card

- Pen or pencil
- Green & blue natural papers
- Craft knife
- Cutting board

- Ruler
- Spray adhesive
- White glue
- Twigs
- Marking pen

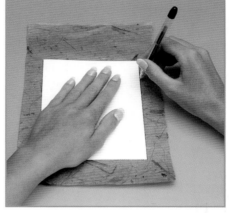

1 Apply inked botanical stamp to the center of a small piece of green paper. Set aside to dry.

2 Place note card on sheet of green paper and trace its shape with a pen or pencil.

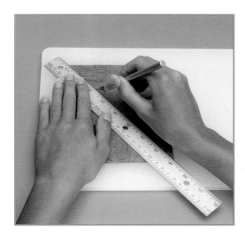

3 Repeat previous step with sheet of blue paper, tracing card onto paper.

4 Cut out traced shapes from natural paper, then cut them in half diagonally with craft knife to form triangles. Trim to fit on card front, allowing for center design.

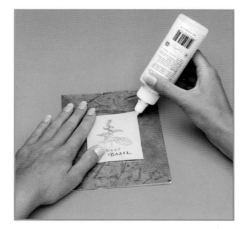

5 Glue triangles to card with spray adhesive, then glue stamped paper in the center area with white glue.

6 Use white glue to attach twig border around stamped paper. If desired, write a small caption or message below stamp with colored marking pen.

Personalized Tags with Stamped Edges

Decorate a pot of pretty violets with a delicate, handmade gift tag. Use your imagination and experiment with the variety of supplies available to create personalized cards and tags. The final results will be an expression of your individuality, and your gifts will be all the more special with the addition of your gift tag creations.

QUICK & EASY ALTERNATIVES

Option 1

For instant personalized gift tags, keep white card stock, rubber stamps, colored markers, and decorative-edged scissors on hand. Rubber stamps add a floral motif, which is then hand-colored with markers and brightened by the addition of gingham ribbon. To make this tag, cut an oval shape from card stock. Rubber-stamp the design on the oval and then color in the details. Sponge card edges with a bit of stamp pad ink. Punch a hole near the edge of the tag and add a ribbon tie.

Option 2

Create this card and gift wrap for a child's present. Cut a piece of colored card stock, then cut a piece of white paper ⅛" (3mm) smaller. Dip the end of a pencil eraser in acrylic paint and "dot" the paper. Use a variety of cheerful primary colors. Finish the card by gluing dotted paper onto the card stock. Punch a hole in the upper left-hand corner of the card and add a ribbon tie. A sheet of butcher paper can be painted to match. Wrap a box with the matching paper and add the tag.

Option 3

"Finger-painted" roses adorn this folk-art gift tag. Cut out a tag from white card stock or purchase blank tags from a stationery store. Dip the tip of your pinky finger in mauve paint; dab finger on paper towel to wipe off excess paint. Then imprint the trio of roses onto the tag. When the paint is dry, place a white acrylic dot on each of the mauve "roses" using the end of a small paintbrush. Add mauve dots around the edge of the card and green dotted leaves to the roses. Punch hole in card and add a ribbon tie.

Materials You'll Need

- Scallop-edged scissors
- White & purple card stock
- Rubber stamp
- Black & purple stamp pads
- Colored markers
- Sponge
- ⅛"(3mm)-wide wooden dowel
- Organza ribbon

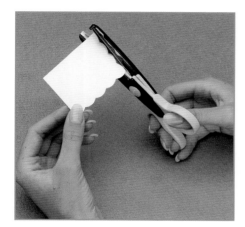

1 Cut the white card stock to the desired size using a pair of scallop-edged scissors.

2 Stamp the tag with a flower image, using a black stamp pad. Practice on scrap paper before stamping final image.

3 Hand-color the details of the floral image using a variety of colored markers.

4 Add the greeting to the card. Then lightly sponge the edges of the white card with purple stamp pad ink.

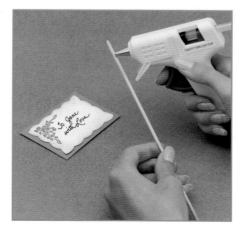

5 Cut small piece of purple card stock ¼" larger than white card. Glue white card to top of purple card, then use hot glue to affix card to dowel.

6 Insert dowel into the plant. Wrap the organza ribbon around the dowel just below the tag and tie into a bow.

Keepsake Wedding Portrait

Preserve the announcement of the wedding nuptials along with a photo of the bride and groom in an elegant gold frame. Further enhance the presentation by including the new family name. Color-coordinate the background color to achieve a formal display. This beautiful and thoughtful gift will become an instant family heirloom.

QUICK & EASY ALTERNATIVES

Option 1

Golden charms at the corners of a plexiglass frame create glamour for a small portrait of the bride and groom. The size is perfect for a desktop or nightstand. Purchase charms in a variety of styles, shapes, and finishes at a craft store. Frames are also available in many sizes. Use epoxy glue to affix charms to the frame. Let dry thoroughly, then insert the wedding photo. This frame is so easy to make that several could be made in one evening—one for each member of the wedding party.

Option 2

Love blooms on this Victorian-inspired glass plate decorated with roses, paper doilies, and a portrait of the bride. Use a plain glass luncheon plate for this gift. Brush découpage medium onto the front side of the trimmed paper rose prints, then smooth prints onto the back side of the plate with your fingertips. Repeat this process with the wedding photo, and then the paper doilies. Clean up any découpage medium with a wet cloth. When the plate is completely dry, brush a coat of red paint onto the back.

Option 3

This creation uses a ready-made frame and mat. Purchase burgundy velvet fabric to cover the mat, adding enough to permit "ruffling" the fabric. Trace mat on back of velvet. Cut fabric, leaving a 1" (2.5cm) border all around and in center. Spread craft glue on mat and lay velvet wrong-side down on glue. Scrunch and wrinkle the velvet, pressing into the glue. Miter outside corners and clip into the inside, opening corners, and glue to the back of the mat. Hot-glue a piece of wire-edged ribbon to velvet. Add flat, heart-shaped charms to ribbon. Place mat in frame.

Materials You'll Need

- 11"x14" (28x35cm) piece of foam core
- 11"x14" (28x35cm) sheet crinkly metallic gold paper

- Spray adhesive
- Cream card stock
- Alphabet rubber stamps & stamp pad

- 5¼"x7¼" (13.5x18.5cm) metallic gold paper
- 5"x7" (13x18cm) photo

- Wedding invitation
- Shiny metallic gold paper strip & ribbon
- Frame & glass

1 Spray foam core with spray adhesive. Position the crinkly metallic gold paper evenly on top; smooth gently and firmly with fingers to secure.

2 Stamp family name onto cream card stock. Trim letters, then glue onto metallic gold paper strip. When completed, name card will have a ⅛" (3mm) gold border. Glue name card to cream card stock.

3 Glue photo onto shiny metallic gold paper. When completed, photo will have a ⅛" (3mm) border on all sides. Glue mounted photo onto cream card stock and then onto crinkly gold paper.

4 Glue a bow to the wedding invitation, and then glue the invitation to the left of the wedding photo.

5 Center the stamped family name at the bottom of the arrangement before gluing.

6 When glue is dry, position the finished piece in the frame. Add a cardboard backing and secure with tape.

Nature-Stamped Gift Boxes

Bold color, intricate leaf shapes, and pure white paper offer dramatic contrast on nature-stamped gift wrap. A cream silk ribbon and a real leaf further enrich the handsome result. Match paint color to natural leaf hues, color-coordinate ribbon, or let the cream silk ribbon shimmer on its own. Either way, the beauty of Mother Nature's splendid leaves will add their uniqueness to the packages.

QUICK & EASY ALTERNATIVES

Option 1

A gift box looks intriguing wrapped in organza. Cut a square of organza to cover the box, allowing for a 5" (13cm) ruffle on top, then fold into fourths. Round off one corner, then unfold into a circle. Cut two 3" (7.5cm) organza squares to create a three-sided pocket. Pin pocket to center front of organza circle, placing a leaf in between with a dot of glue. Sew pocket in place with a gold zigzag stitch. Wrap the box in the organza, tying ruffled top with a rubber band. Finish with a green organza bow.

Option 2

The natural shapes of green fern fronds add native beauty to a simple white box tied with gold ribbon. Purchase pressed fern fronds at a craft store or dry your own (pressing them between pages of a book). Brush découpage medium onto a fern frond, then position on the box, smoothing frond onto the box with your fingertips. Repeat the pattern around all sides, covering the box as desired. When completely dry, wrap the box with gold metallic ribbon and tie into a bow.

Option 3

Transform a terra-cotta pot into a decorative gift container using pretty ribbon and a wonderful leaf-painted design. Coat a plain terra-cotta pot with white acrylic paint. Brush plum-colored acrylic paint onto the textured side of a leaf, then press leaf onto white pot. Lay a piece of paper over the leaf and smooth with fingers. Carefully lift paper and leaf away from pot. Repeat process to cover pot. When paint is dry, brush on matte varnish. Hot-glue ribbon around pot rim, adding a bow.

Materials You'll Need

- White paper
- Scissors
- Green acrylic paint
- Sponge brush
- Leaf
- Scrap paper
- Transparent tape

1 Start with a large piece of white paper. With sharp scissors, cut paper large enough to fit box.

2 Using a sponge brush, coat the textured side of the leaf with green acrylic paint.

3 Carefully place paint-coated side of the leaf onto the white paper.

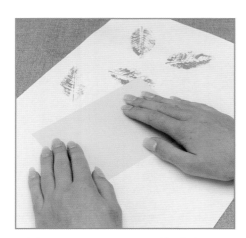

4 Lay scrap paper on top of leaf, then press with fingers, being careful not to move leaf.

5 Lift leaf and repeat steps until entire paper is imprinted with leaves in a random pattern.

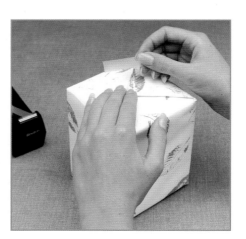

6 Neatly wrap the box, using transparent tape to secure the edges. For variety, experiment with different paint colors, ribbons, and types of paper.

Punched-Edge Thank You Card

A very special gift warrants an equally special "thank you." Send a handmade card to honor the thoughtfulness of the gift-giver, and your gratitude will make a lasting impression. Use paper punches and inexpensive card stock in a variety of colors to produce creative cards that can be adorned with ribbons, sponged edges, and buttons. Add your special "thanks" to the front of the card with a pen or charming rubber stamp.

QUICK & EASY ALTERNATIVES

Option 1

A formal "thank you" inscribed on a card made from beautiful textured papers creates an understated yet elegant result. Cut and fold pink card stock. Trim mauve paper to fit with a pair of fancy-edged scissors, then glue to the folded card. Repeat process with white card stock. Sponge around the edges of the white section with pink stamp pad ink. Write "Thank You" in center of card using a calligraphy pen. Practice on a piece of scrap paper first.

Option 2

Send your Valentine a ribbon-trimmed card with a row of cut-out hearts. A heart paper punch makes the job easy! Cut and fold red card stock. Use pinking shears to trim one edge of white card stock to fit the front of the red card. Punch heart shapes at evenly spaced intervals along the pinked edge. Then, glue the white card onto the red card. Tie a red organza bow and glue to the top of the finished card. Add a heartfelt Valentine greeting to the inside.

Option 3

Bright yellow lights glow on a green tree with a matching wooden star on the top. Cut and fold white card stock. Cut a tree shape with pinking shears, then glue to card front. Punch holes in the white card surrounding the tree. Then cut a piece of green card the same size as white card, and glue onto inside. Punch several holes in yellow paper, then glue the dots to the tree. Paint a wooden star yellow and hot-glue to treetop. Vary the design by punching and gluing multi-colored dots to the tree.

Materials You'll Need

- White & pink card stock
- Scissors
- Hole punch
- Pink stamp pad
- Sponge

- Fine-tip marking pen
- Ribbon
- Glue stick
- Envelope (for template)

1 Use scissors to cut three scallops on a piece of white card stock. The center scallop can be larger than scallops to either side of it, if desired.

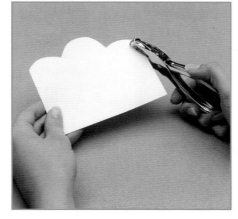

2 Punch small holes along edge of scallops, spacing at even intervals to resemble eyelet lace.

3 Lightly sponge edges of the white part of the card using pink stamp pad.

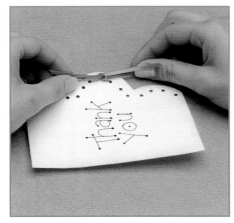

4 Use marking pen to inscribe greeting on front of card, then thread a narrow ribbon through holes on center scallop. Tie the ribbon into a bow.

5 Fold a piece of pink card stock in half to create card. Then line up white scalloped piece on three sides and glue in place.

6 Using a pre-made envelope as a template, create an envelope from white card stock. Cut scallops along back flap, and sponge with a pink stamp pad.

Marbleized Place Cards

QUICK & EASY ALTERNATIVES

Option 1

Place cards embellished with paper fans add a dramatic component to a table setting. Cut an ivory place card to the desired size, then fold it in half. Cut a gold rectangle ⅛" (3mm) smaller than place card and a navy blue rectangle ⅛" (3mm) smaller than gold rectangle. Cut out small ivory rectangle to write the guest's name. Layer and glue rectangles to front of place card. Fold marbleized paper into adecorative fan and glue it to the place card.

Option 2

Marbleized paper imparts one-of-a-kind beauty. A rustic table setting can be enhanced with a place card made with green marbleized paper and a dried leaf. Assemble this card from tan corrugated paper, beige handmade paper, green marbleized paper, and ivory-colored paper inscribed with the guest's name. Create this charming place card by layering cut papers and gluing them together with a glue stick. Select shapely dried leaves to glue to fronts of place cards.

Option 3

Marbleized paper in shades of pink and lavender evoke femininity, making a perfect addition to place cards for showers, luncheons, and all-girl get-togethers. Create this place card with ivory card stock, pink- and lavender-marbleized paper, gold thread, and a gold charm. Cut, fold, and glue papers together, then inscribe the guest's name with a calligraphy pen. Glue three loops of gold thread to the corner and top with the charm.

Marbleized paper is enjoying a revival and is being used to enhance books, stationery, gift wrap, and even table decor like these place cards. In rich jewel hues, marbleized paper adds sophistication; in watery pastel pinks, it lends an old-fashioned quality. Change to soft greens, and the effect is natural and organic. These complex colorations are simple to achieve with modern materials and techniques.

Materials You'll Need

- Shallow plastic tray
- Liquid starch
- Acrylic paints
- Cups
- Water
- Comb
- White paper
- Tweezers
- Cookie sheet
- Scissors
- Ivory card stock
- Gold paper
- Glue stick
- Calligraphy pen

1 Pour a ½" (1.5cm)-deep layer of liquid starch into a shallow tray. Place acrylic paints into cups, then thin them with a small amount of water so that they pour easily. Pour the paint in stripes onto the starch.

2 Gently swirl a comb through the mixture to get a feathery effect. Do not overmix, or the paint will have a muddy appearance.

3 Carefully dip paper onto the surface of the mixture until all of the paper is covered with paint. Do not agitate the paper or immerse it in the mixture. Use tweezers to handle the paper.

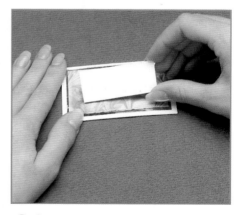

4 Lift paper from the surface of the mixture, allowing excess paint to drip straight down into the tray. Place paper on a cookie sheet to dry.

5 When paper is completely dry, cut it into rectangles. Repeat process for additional paper. Cut ivory card stock to desired size; fold in half.

6 Cut gold paper ⅛" (3mm) larger than marbleized paper rectangle; glue both to folded card. Glue smaller ivory rectangle to center and write guest's name.

81

Stationery Greeting Cards

A handmade greeting card shows you care. Start with colored or off-white stationery—the perfect paper for these cards because it comes with its own matching envelope. Use prints or illustrations cut from magazines. Add ribbons, buttons, and other trinkets to create your own unique style. Collect vintage papers, reproduction stickers, and photocopies from antique books to have on hand when making your greeting cards.

QUICK & EASY ALTERNATIVES

Option 1

Cut a sheet of green stationery in half. Fold a slightly smaller piece of handmade paper in thirds. Glue this to the green piece. Glue a piece of gold mesh ribbon to the center of the flap. Start gluing the green ribbon under the flap. Wrap it around the card and glue to top of flap leaving a tail. Cut in inverted "V". Hot-glue a loop of pearls on top of the ribbon and drip sealing wax on this. Stamp wax with an initial seal to personalize.

Option 2

Make a cone from a 4" (10cm) round paper doily. Place rose petals on a small white circle of tulle. Gather up and tie with thread or ribbon and glue into the doily. Glue doily to a piece of pink corrugated paper that has been cut with fancy-edged scissors. Glue the pink corrugated piece to the ivory card stock and then onto a piece of the folded pink stationery. Tie a wire-edged ribbon into a bow and then glue to the doily cone.

Option 3

Create fancy edges on simple card stock using a corner punch (available at craft stores in various designs). Glue these corner-punched pieces together. Fold the green paper in half and cut pieces of pink and ivory papers slightly smaller than the green stationery; glue these pieces together. Glue the layered, corner-punched pieces to this and top with a floral sticker, a ribbon bow, and a heart charm.

Materials You'll Need

- Scissors
- Photocopy of image
- Glue stick
- Card stock, various colors
- Stationery & hole punch
- Narrow ribbon
- Large-eyed needle
- Glue gun & glue sticks
- Button

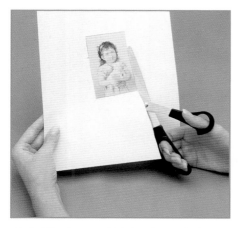

1 Cut the image which has been photo-copied from a magazine or book. Color copies can be made at print shops.

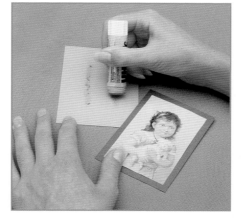

2 Cut three pieces of card stock in graduated sizes. Glue the image to the smallest piece and then glue this to the next larger piece.

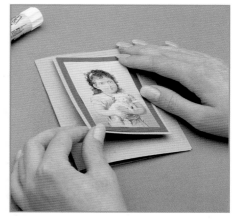

3 Glue these layered pieces to the center of a piece of stationery that has been folded in half.

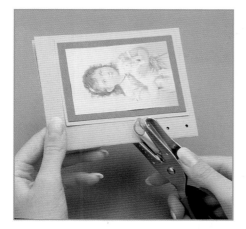

4 Use a hole punch to punch around the top and left side of the card about every ½" (1.5cm). This measurement may vary depending on the weave desired.

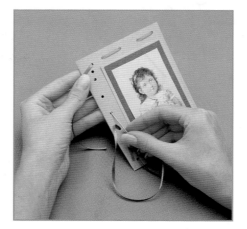

5 Thread the narrow ribbon through a large-eyed needle and stitch the ribbon through the punched holes.

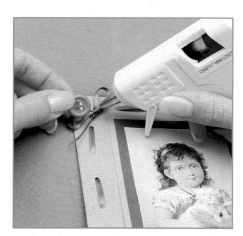

6 Tie ribbon into a bow and glue to the upper left corner of the card. Glue a button over the bow.

Houseplant and flower projects

Nothing brightens up a room like a beautiful basket of flowers or a leafy plant. With a few simple ideas—and a little creativity—it is easy to turn a floral arrangement or plant into unique and unforgettable gift.

Whether you want to transform a plain vase or make a handsome wreath or floral centerpiece to impress your friends, this chapter is full of ideas to help you to show off your plants and flowers to their very best effect.

Faux-Finished Flowerpots

Y our Mom will never guess this was once a garden-variety terra-cotta pot. To her delighted eyes, it looks like an expensive, marble planter! The secret is in the painting technique, layering several hues with subtle streaks and feathery "veins." A glossy varnish polishes the finish, echoing the sheen of nature's gorgeous marble stone. It's "faux," yes, but since it was created by her favorite artist, she will love it all the more!

QUICK & EASY ALTERNATIVES

Option 1

For a "rustic" lover, this technique mimics the effects of time on a copper surface. Brush metallic, copper acrylic paint on a terra-cotta pot, then let dry. Mix teal green paint with an equal amount of clear glaze. Repeat with light green paint. Cut two small pieces off a sponge. Dampen sponge piece; dip in teal paint-and-glaze mixture and dab excess on a paper towel. Sponge-paint pot. Repeat with light green paint, making sure copper color is visible. Spray with sealer.

Option 2

Brush a terra-cotta pot with gold acrylic paint. Fill a splashing tool (available in craft stores) with rubbing alcohol and a spray bottle with water. Mix copper and black paint separately with equal parts of clear glaze. Dab copper mixture on pot using a sponge, followed by black. While paint is wet, spray pot with water. Use splashing tool to apply alcohol over paint. Use soft-bristle brush to smooth edges.

Option 3

With a taste for antiques, the brand-new look just doesn't appeal. Let a little paint wizardry lend a time-worn feel for a gift she'll love! With a sponge brush, apply blue acrylic paint to a terra-cotta pot. Let dry. Add a little water to white paint to form a thin "wash." Paint the wash on top of the blue paint on pot. Before it dries, rag off some of the wash with a soft, dry cloth. Allow to dry. Dip another piece of cloth into brown antiquing gel and rub lightly onto pot.

Materials You'll Need

- Terra-cotta pot
- Acrylic paint: white, light gray, light blue & charcoal
- Sponge brushes
- Plates & spoons
- Clear glaze
- Soft cloth
- Soft-bristle brush
- Fine artist's brush
- High-gloss spray varnish

1 Using a sponge brush, coat terra-cotta pot with white acrylic paint. Allow to dry.

2 Mix light gray paint with an equal amount of clear glaze. On a separate plate, do the same with light blue paint and glaze.

3 Paint clear glaze onto the dry pot, covering the white base coat. Apply gray and blue paint-and-glaze mixtures in diagonal strokes. Allow some white to show through.

4 Use a soft cloth to lightly wipe off some of the gray and blue color and to blend the colors.

5 Use a soft, dry-bristle brush to soften any distinct edges left in the pattern.

6 Mix charcoal paint with an equal amount of glaze. Paint light "veins" diagonally across the pot with the fine brush. Let dry, then spray with varnish.

Découpaged Vase

A shower of falling leaves is an ideal escort for a bouquet of fresh-picked flowers. Exquisite skeleton leaves transform a simple glass vase into a breathtaking work of art, a gift for a family member who loves fine things. In soft shades of mauve, green, and ecru, these delicate, transparent beauties reveal their intricate structure and provide pleasing texture. Those prized cut flowers deserve a lush, leafy display!

QUICK & EASY ALTERNATIVES

Option 1

Doilies form a pretty fringe! Cut the corners off two 8" (20.5cm) square doilies. Use a sponge brush to apply découpage medium to exterior of a tall glass vase. Press one doily corner into place, aligning wide edge with bottom edge of vase. Repeat with other pieces, slightly overlapping if necessary. Affix widest edges of doilies flush with top edge of vase, forming a zigzag design to center of vase. Add another coat of découpage medium. When dry, wrap wire-edged ribbon around top of vase, gluing on back to secure.

Option 2

Cut wrapping paper to the height of a tall glass vase and 1" (2.5cm) wider than the width. Brush découpage medium onto vase and back of paper, then smooth paper onto glass. Cut out a small square from leftover paper and affix photo corners with hot glue. Glue the piece onto natural-colored card stock. When dry, cut the card stock to form border around design. Cut small image from paper and glue to the corner of tag. Cut rectangle of black card stock and use mounting tape to attach partly on, partly off vase.

Option 3

Painted checkerboards and farm-friendly cut-outs create a cheerful, country flower vase for the kitchen. Use a ½" (1.5cm) flat brush and black acrylic paint to decorate a glass jar with a checkerboard pattern. Leave top and bottom section of jar unpainted. Let dry completely. Cut rooster and chicken pictures from a magazine. Use découpage medium and a sponge brush to affix pictures onto vase, angling in opposite directions and overlapping slightly.

Materials You'll Need

- Tall glass vase
- Glass cleaner & cloth
- Découpage medium
- Sponge brush
- Matte spray varnish
- Two sizes of skeleton leaves in mauve, green & ecru (available in craft stores)

1 Clean tall glass vase with glass cleaner and cloth, rubbing away any visible marks.

2 Coat entire outside area of vase with découpage medium, using a sponge brush.

3 Press a few large skeleton leaves into place on vase, smoothing with fingertips.

4 Add small skeleton leaves, filling in some open spaces between larger leaves. Alternate colors.

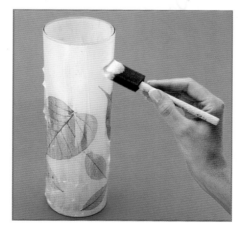

5 When finished with design, brush over entire surface again with découpage medium, covering leaves.

6 When vase is completely dry, place on covered work surface and spray with matte varnish.

Tiered Dried Flower Basket

She displays flowers to celebrate every occasion, an endearing expression of her joyous nature. Present your passionate sister with a gift that will speak to her heart. Rows of dried flowers assembled in soft pastel stripes create this one-of-a-kind floral arrangement. The bouquet will fit right in at her home, shaped in a long narrow basket, the colors of larkspur and safflower arranged alongside delightfully cheery poppy pods.

QUICK & EASY ALTERNATIVES

Option 1

This gift caters to her love of flowers! Cut floral foam to fit snugly into a low square container and secure with hot glue. Lightly score foam with a craft knife to divide the area into six equal sections. Select dried flowers in coordinating colors to use in the arrangement. Clip the stems and arrange flowers (such as yarrow, white and pink Australian daisies, coneflower, coxcomb, and hydrangea) into its own small section of foam.

Option 2

Silk flowers combine to create a three-part bouquet. Select three pots in different sizes and shapes. Using a craft knife, cut a block of dried floral foam to fit the bottom of each pot. Clip the stems of silk hydrangeas and arrange the flowers in one of the pots. Add silk greenery to the arrangement. Repeat to fill other pots—one with silk peonies, and the third with silk hydrangeas.

Option 3

Take Grandmother's well-loved, well-used teapot out of retirement. This gift is a wonderful way for her to continue to enjoy the company of a dear old "friend." Fill the teapot to the top with foam popcorn. Select an assortment of silk flowers that coordinate with the color of the teapot (such as red zinnias, gold ranunculus, red poppies, and golden waffles). Loosely arrange the flowers in the container, clipping stems as necessary.

Materials You'll Need

- Floral foam
- Rectangular basket
- Clippers

- Dried botanicals: sweet Annie, dark purple larkspur, poppy pods, pimentina grass, safflower & moss

1 Cut a piece of floral foam to fit snugly into a rectangular basket. Place foam in basket.

2 Clip a bunch of preserved sweet Annie to the desired height for the the back row of the arrangement. Insert stems into the back of the foam in a row.

3 Clip a bunch of dried, dark purple larkspur a bit shorter than the sweet Annie. Insert into the foam to form a second row.

4 Clip a bunch of dried poppy pods slightly shorter again, to fit in front of the larkspur. Insert into the foam.

5 Clip a bunch of dried pimentina grass shorter than the poppy pods, and insert into the foam.

6 Clip a bunch of dried safflower for the front row of the arrangement. Fill any gaps in the arrangement with dried moss.

Decorated Herb Pots

QUICK & EASY ALTERNATIVES

Option 1

A small plaster urn becomes a home for an indoor herb. Paint the urn with three different shades of green acrylic paint. Rub with a soft rag between each paint layer to give it a distressed look. Then, spray an uneven coat of transparent wood-toned paint over the painted urn. Let dry. Add drainage material and potting soil to urn, then transplant an oregano plant from its pot into the urn. Wrap raffia around the urn base, tie into a bow, and tuck in two dried roses. Add an "oregano" plant marker.

Option 2

She'll be fascinated with the interesting array of papers you used to cover this container. Tear a collection of natural-fiber papers into strips. Spray adhesive onto the back of each piece. Smooth each paper onto the outside of a florist's papier-mâché plant container, overlapping as you go. Plant a small collection of herbs such as oregano, basil, thyme, and chives into the pot, loosening root balls and adding drainage material and potting soil as needed.

Option 3

Since lavender is known for its soothing properties, this aromatic herb gift is just the thing for someone who needs some relaxation. On a gray clay planter, use a lavender floral stencil and green and lavender acrylic paint to stencil the design four times onto the sides of the dish. Then, stencil the word "Lavender" in between the floral stencils on the dish. Place the lavender plants into the dish, adding additional drainage material and potting soil as needed.

E namelware cups make perfect little containers for planting herbs. She'll love these, placed on a sunny window in her kitchen. These humble little potted plants will yield big rewards when basil leaves are pinched to toss with pasta and garlic, or thyme is added to a hearty soup. Potted herbs make wonderful gifts and take only a few minutes to label and plant.

Materials You'll Need

- Alphabet rubber stamps
- Pigment-colored ink pad
- Three enamel mugs
- Embossing powder
- Embossing gun
- Three herbs in 2" (5cm) pots
- Drainage material and potting soil
- Water

1 Using the alphabet rubber stamps and pigment-colored ink pad, stamp the name of each herb onto the front of the enamel mugs.

2 While the ink is wet, sprinkle embossing powder over the stamped herb name.

3 Hold the embossing gun about 6" from the mug and heat the stamped area until it is raised.

4 Place a small amount of drainage material and potting soil in each of the mugs. Add a little water to each mug.

5 Carefully remove the planted herbs from their pots, loosening the root ball gently.

6 Transplant an herb to each mug, then fill in around the herb with additional potting soil.

Lavender and Rosebud Wreath

Remember your daughter's anniversary with a gift symbolic of all the love associated with her and her husband's wedding day. A grapevine wreath is loosely wrapped with a wide romantic ribbon. Tiny bouquets shaped from fragrant lavender, sprigs of boxwood, and the delicate, unopened blooms of a rose embellish a path along the heart-shaped wreath—creating a fitting tribute to their love.

QUICK & EASY ALTERNATIVES

Option 1

Enhanced with sprays of rose-buds and lavender, a trio of moss-covered spheres create a lovely centerpiece or decorative shelf accent. Spray some sheet moss with water to soften. Allow moss to dry, then hot-glue onto three 3" (7.5cm) foam balls with cool-melt glue sticks. When balls are moss-covered, wrap each ball with ribbon and tie at top. Gather small bundles of lavender, rosebuds, and a combination of the two. Glue bundle under the ribbon.

Option 2

The color and delicacy of tiny dried rosebuds are enhanced with sprigs of dried lavender. To achieve the whitewashed effect, water down a small amount of off-white acrylic paint. Use a sponge brush to paint wooden candlestick; let dry. Form a little bouquet of dried lavender, rosebuds, and boxwood leaves following the design pictured. Attach the bouquet to the candlestick with a few dabs of hot glue. Wrap a wire-edged ribbon around base of the candlestick and tie into a bow. Present gift with a pretty taper candle.

Option 3

Delicate "corsages" dress a picture frame you can present to your sister who stood by as your maid of honor. Attach two sprigs of boxwood on an upper corner of a picture frame with a glue gun; form an angle with the sprigs. Repeat on opposite lower corner. Glue long sprigs of dried lavender and rosebuds that have been clipped short over boxwood on each corner. Glue small pieces of ribbon to peek from underneath the boxwood.

Materials You'll Need

- Heart-shaped grapevine wreath
- Wide sheer ribbon
- Small bunch of dried lavender
- Scissors
- Green floral tape
- Glue gun & glue sticks
- Dried boxwood
- Dried rosebuds

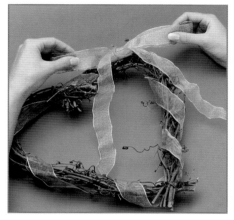

1 Loosely wrap heart-shaped wreath with wide, sheer ribbon. Tie ends into bow.

2 Trim stems of dried lavender with scissors. Create five small bunches of trimmed lavender. Wrap bottoms of each bunch with green floral tape.

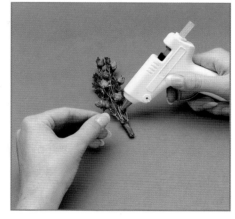

3 Use glue gun to attach several rosebuds to each bunch of lavender sprigs.

4 Using scissors, cut five stems of boxwood to fit under bouquets of lavender and rosebuds.

5 Apply the boxwood stems around the right-hand side of the wreath using hot glue.

6 Attach the small bouquets of lavender and rosebuds onto wreath over the boxwood.

Potted Lavender Sheaf

Dried lavender provides a lovely scented addition to any room of the house. In the bath, its delicate fragrance will be enhanced by moisture. On a bedside table, its lulling, relaxing qualities will be appreciated. In the kitchen, snips of the buds can be used to flavor cuisine. Clustered in a tall blue topiary pot and tied with a pretty ribbon, this striking arrangement will add lively color and scent wherever it is placed.

QUICK & EASY ALTERNATIVES

Option 1

Decorate a berry basket with a stenciled lavender pattern and small bows, then fill basket with lavender cookies. To make cookies: Cream 1 cup (225g) unsalted butter and ⅔ cup (115g) (minus 1 tablespoon) sugar. Add one egg; beat well. Stir in 1 tablespoon lavender flowers and 1¼ cups (190g) (minus 1 tablespoon) self-rising flour. Drop by teaspoon onto a parchment-lined cookie sheet; bake at 350°F (180°C) for about 18 minutes. Cool cookies on waxed paper.

Option 2

Lavender fragrance and color embellish a charming gift wrapped in green tissue paper, lavender stems, and a matching ribbon. Wrap box top and bottom in tissue paper then glue one end of lavender ribbon to underside of lid and bring to the top. Weave ribbon through lavender stems, gluing stems in the process. Finish by gluing ribbon tail to underside of lid. Tie a knotted ribbon bow and hot-glue it to the ribbon on the top of the package. Trim stems evenly.

Option 3

Lavender, rosemary, thyme, and rosebuds bunched in a doily create a delicate tussie-mussie. Place stems of fresh herbs and flowers in the opening of a tussie-mussie holder (or through a hole in a small doily) and glue stems to holder. Tie a multi-looped bow from pastel organza ribbon, then tie an additional length of wider organza ribbon around the bow's center. Trim ribbon tails and glue assembled bows to the tussie-mussie beneath the bouquet. Consider wrapping stems with matching wide ribbon.

Materials You'll Need

- Large sheaf of dried lavender stems
- Florist's wire
- Scissors
- Painted terra-cotta pot
- Florist's foam
- Spanish moss
- Wire-edged ribbon

1 Create an attractive arrangement of dried lavender stems by placing tallest stems in the center and shortest stems on the outside of the sheaf.

2 Wind florist's wire around the sheaf, securing it tightly. Fasten wire by twisting one end into preceding strand.

3 Trim end of sheaf evenly with scissors. If stems are extremely thick, use garden clippers to create a neat edge.

4 Fill a terra-cotta pot halfway with dry florist's foam, then push stems of lavender sheaf into foam to hold it upright.

5 Fill the pot with Spanish moss, placing it around the sheaf over the florist's foam.

6 Complete lavender sheaf arrangement by tying a wire-edged ribbon bow around the stems, covering the florist's wire.

Easy Teacup Gardens

T he intriguing symmetry of topiary-trimmed plants has fascinated gardeners for decades. Create these topiary teacups as gifts for a favorite cousin or aunt. Easily crafted in color-coordinated teacups adorned with matching bows, these topiaries require no watering! Antique teacups and pitchers add beauty of their own, but any cup and saucer combination can be used with charming results.

QUICK & EASY ALTERNATIVES

Option 1

This velvet-covered pincushion can be adapted to any cup. Purchase a plastic foam ball slightly smaller than the inside diameter of cup. Place a piece of quilt batting, large enough to cover ball, onto the wrong side of the velvet (approximately 6"x6" [15x15cm]). Pull fabric tightly around ball with a rubber band. Trim excess fabric. Insert ball into cup, then wrap its circumference at the cup rim with color-coordinated cording, sewing it where it overlaps. Affix a bow with hot-glue onto the cord above the cup handle.

Option 2

Use candle wax (available at craft stores) to make this simple teacup candle. If candle wax is not available, use paraffin (available in grocery stores). Melt candle wax in a double boiler or microwave oven. For a shaded candle.add 2-3 drops of food coloring The wax can also be scented with essential oil to give the gift fragrance. Carefully pour the melted wax into teacup, then when the wax is partially set, insert a birthday candle in the center for a wick. Wrap teacup candle in cellophane and tie a bow at the top for an elegant gift.

Option 3

Give the gift of fragrance in a lovely teacup filled with potpourri. Cut a piece of tulle approximately 10"x10" (25x25cm). Mound the potpourri into the center of the tulle, draw the fabric sides up, and secure tulle with a rubber band. Place the tulle-wrapped potpourri into the cup, with rubber band at the bottom. Select a potpourri that coordinates nicely with the teacup and has a fragrance that the recipient will enjoy. Present the gift with a bottle of essential oil for freshening.

Materials You'll Need

- Plastic foam ball
- Twig
- Glue gun & glue sticks
- Dry floral foam
- Teacup & saucer
- Sheet moss
- Wire-edged ribbon

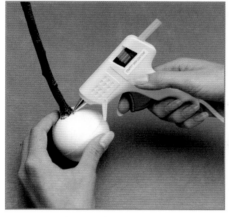

1 Insert a twig into the plastic foam ball. Secure the twig using a hot-glue gun.

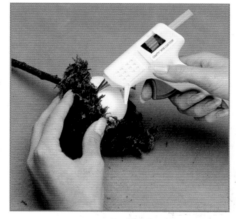

2 Hot-glue sheet moss to cover the plastic foam ball. Fill in any exposed areas with more moss.

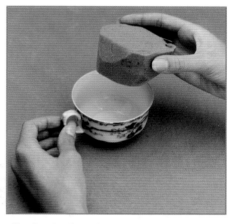

3 Cut dry floral foam so that it fits snugly into cup. Foam may be hot-glued to cup.

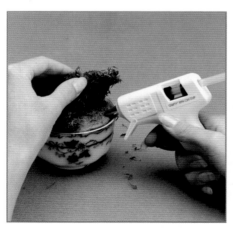

4 Cover the top of the foam with sheet moss, hot-gluing as necessary.

5 Insert the trunk of the topiary through the sheet moss and into the floral foam.

6 Straighten the trunk of the topiary, then wrap a ribbon around it. Tie the ribbon into a bow.

Fresh Grass Summer Centerpiece

T his wicker basket filled with grass and perky daisies is ready to bring cheery country color to a picnic table set for a gathering of good friends. Nestle nursery pots of bright white daisies into a layer of tall sod grass and add a blue-handled trowel and vibrant red bandanna to punctuate the arrangement. Present this basket of flowers to the hostess of an outdoor summer barbeque.

QUICK & EASY ALTERNATIVES

Option 1

Silk daisies and artificial strawberries are reminiscent of lazy summer days. Combine them with red-and-white gingham bows on a blue plate to create a patriotic centerpiece. Wire three ribbon bows onto a candle ring. Affix silk daisies around the ring with florist's wire, then fill in the open spaces with artificial strawberries. When ring is complete, place a dripless pillar candle in the center. As an option, substitute with fresh flowers and berries.

Option 2

Four frames surround a flowering plant for a Memorial Day table. This interesting planter is made from family photos and bits of family history. Put family photos in two of the frames and cards with written details about the individuals pictured in the other two frames. Cut four strips of corrugated cardboard to height of frames; fold each one lengthwise to create a hinge. Hot-glue hinges to frames to form an open-ended box. Place potted plant inside box.

Option 3

A wooden toolbox filled with colorful flowers and decorated with the precious photos of his kids is a wonderful gift for a dad. Line the inside of the toolbox with florist's foil, then fill with a selection of potted flowers or garden vegetables. Color-copy children's photos, then glue to card stock. Have kids write special messages on the backs of the photos. Place each photo into a florist's card pick; insert picks into soil.

Materials You'll Need

- Green florist's foil
- Scissors
- Basket
- Sod grass
- Water (if necessary)
- Potted daisies
- Red bandanna
- Blue-handled gardening trowel

1 Cut a piece of green florist's foil large enough to cover the bottom and sides of basket. Use adequate foil to ensure that the basket liner will be watertight.

2 Press florist's foil into the basket and up the sides as a liner. Use two layers of foil if the arrangement will be on display for a long period of time.

3 Place sod firmly into the basket, filling the corners first and leaving small spaces for the potted daisies. Water sod if necessary, but do not oversaturate it.

4 Insert potted daisies into the open spaces in the sod. Fill in any gaps with more sod to make sure arrangement is snug.

5 Fold bandanna into a rectangle with two corners pointing outward. Tie bandanna around the basket handle, knotting it firmly.

6 Insert blue-handled gardening trowel into the sod or between the sod and the side of the basket.

Seasonal Scented Centerpiece

E mitting scents of pumpkin spice and cinnamon, this autumnal potpourri filled with dried botanicals smells just like Thanksgiving. Simply add colorful pods, nutshells, and dried corn to purchased potpourri, and this fall blend will continue adding its bouquet and beauty for days. Display the mixture in a decorative bowl where its fragrance and color can be admired for the holidays.

QUICK & EASY ALTERNATIVES

Option 1

This delightful little cranberry heart is made from dried cranberries, but any dried fruit—or even fresh red cranberries—could be substituted. Start by bending a piece of wire into a heart shape. Thread the dried or fresh fruit onto the wire until it is completely covered. Bend both ends of the wire and hook them together. Use a hot-glue gun to add a ribbon or color-coordinated fabric, a piece of fresh or dried greenery, cinnamon sticks, and a dried apple slice.

Option 2

Use a collection of small, glass gardening pots for this dainty project. Make the poles with gold-sprayed florist's picks. Wrap the picks with three shades of narrow ribbon, then tie a bow at the top. Use hot glue to affix a rosebud on the top of the pick. Fill the pots with rose-petal potpourri. Place the "pole" directly in the center. Tie a color-coordinated ribbon around the pot, then secure the ribbon with hot glue to prevent slipping. These lovely, ribbon-bedecked poles are perfect for celebrating springtime festivities.

Option 3

For a Valentine luncheon or tea with the ladies, this wide glass bowl with its rosebud rim is a beautiful centerpiece. Use hot glue to affix the dried rosebuds to the rim of the bowl. Place a tall, wide ivory pillar candle directly in the center of the bowl. Fill the bowl with a favorite blend of potpourri. Lavender or an all-rose scented potpourri would be perfect. Easily adaptable for seasonal use, glue tiny pinecones to the bowl and add a pine-scented potpourri blend.

Materials You'll Need

- Wide decorative bowl
- Autumnal potpourri
- Miniature pumpkins
- Miniature ears of dried corn
- Dried oranges & lemons
- Wire
- Cranberries
- Ribbon, greenery & dried apple slice
- Clear glass bowl
- Rosebuds
- Glue gun & glue sticks
- Glass pot
- Maypole
- Ribbon

1 Fill a bowl with a fall-scented potpourri blend containing pods, dried botanicals, nutshells, and an interesting assortment of dried herbs.

2 Add miniature ears of dried corn, miniature pumpkins, and dried oranges and lemons.

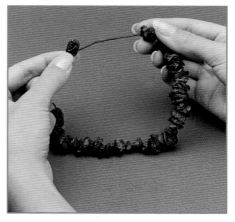

3 For the berry wreath, thread cranberries onto a heart-shaped wire. Bend wire ends to create hooks; hook ends together.

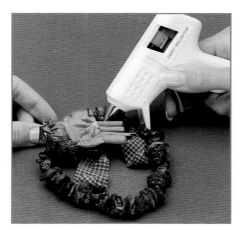

4 Use hot glue to add ribbon or fabric, dried or fresh greenery, and a dried apple slice.

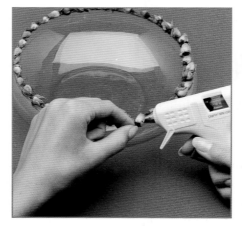

5 For Valentine option, hot-glue dried rosebuds around top edge of wide, shallow, clear glass bowl. Add potpourri and candle.

6 For May Day centerpiece, fill glass pot with potpourri. Add a gold-sprayed florist's pick wrapped in narrow ribbon. Tie ribbon around rim of pot and into a bow.

Hearts and Sunflower Wreath

A sunflower-decorated wreath evokes a bright summer day in the country. The wreath is embellished with wire-edged ribbon and small moss-covered hearts tied on with raffia. Easy to make, this wreath can be fabricated in just minutes, ready to grace a door or wall. Extend rustic charm to a friend, reminding her of lazy days in the country.

QUICK & EASY ALTERNATIVES

Option 1

Show the loving couple how much you care with a beautiful, heart-shaped, moss-covered wreath. Cover the plastic foam wreath with sheet moss using a hot-glue gun. Fill in spaces with moss until the wreath appears lush and cushiony. Tie a multi-looped, wire-edged ribbon bow. Trim the tails into inverted "V" shapes. Ripple bow and tails attractively, then hot-glue to the top of the wreath. Tuck in color-coordinated silk blooms around the bow, and tack them into place with hot glue.

Option 2

A confection of pink and white announces a girl's fifth birthday. Paint a wooden numeral (sold as address numbers at hardware stores) white with pink edges. Hot-glue the matching papier-mâché boxed "gifts" and clusters of balloons tied with curled ribbon to the wreath. Then hot-glue the number securely onto the wreath. Tie a wide, pink satin ribbon into a bow and glue under the number. Arrange decorations in blue for a birthday boy.

Option 3

Welcome home beloved friends or family members with a wreath embellished with their own photos. Beautiful, plaid ribbon tied in a multi-looped bow is intertwined with silk leaves and a pink silk rose. Tiny silver frames enclose the photographs. Tie, then hot-glue the ribbon to the wreath. Add the framed photos with hot glue, spacing them attractively. Then glue the silk rose onto the ribbon knot. Hang the wreath on the door to greet arriving guests.

Materials You'll Need

- Pencil
- Cardboard
- Heart pattern
- Sheet moss
- Glue gun & glue sticks
- Grapevine wreath
- Strips of raffia
- Blue-and-white striped ribbon
- Artificial sunflowers, blue corn flowers & white dogwood

1 Trace heart pattern onto heavy cardboard, then cut out shape. Make three hearts.

2 Cover front and back of cardboard hearts with sheet moss. Use hot glue to affix securely.

3 Slip the raffia strips through a strand of grapevine at the top of the wreath. Tie a loop and a bow, then hot-glue bows onto hearts. Hang hearts at different heights.

4 Tie a large ribbon bow with long tails. Hot-glue bow to wreath above looped hearts.

5 Arrange flowers on wreath attractively, then hot-glue them into place.

6 Arrange ribbon tails around flowers on the front of the wreath, folding and hot-gluing to secure onto grapevine. Trim ribbon tails.

Holiday Floral Centerpiece

An opulent arrangement of lush flowers replicates a fashionable turn-of-the-century Victorian design in which a French epergne— an ornate tiered holder for displaying flowers and fruit—is used for the centerpiece. This magnificent floral collection relies on a mixture of silver table-service pieces strategically combined to duplicate a costly epergne. Create this display for a grand party, formal buffet, or fancy brunch.

QUICK & EASY ALTERNATIVES

Option 1

Patriotic stars and stripes decorate a terra-cotta pot exploding with white daisy mums for this Fourth of July centerpiece. Purchase a decorated pot or create your own design with stencils or rubber stamps. Line the pot with florist's foil, then fill with saturated florist's foam. Shape top of foam into a mound, then cover with sheet moss. Insert mums into the wet foam to create a loose mound of flowers. Insert gold glitter sticks, wired silver star garland, and tinsel floral picks.

Option 2

Create a centerpiece with live plants to match the exterior of a terracotta planter that's been decorated with glazed tiles. Buy a planter with a floral mosaic tile design, then fill with a selection of ivy and blooming plants. Plant by loosening soil from two 4" (10cm) pots of ivy and place one at each end of the planter. Fill in the center with live, blooming plants. Add potting soil, if necessary. Wrap the planter with a large wire-edged ribbon bow.

Option 3

Gold glitter stars shoot from a basket brimming with delicate, dried hydrangea blossoms dusted with gold. Separate dried hydrangeas into two bunches. Hot-glue florist's foam into a basket, then insert half the stems of dried hydrangea blossoms. Allowing the flower color to show through, dust the remaining hydrangea blossoms with gold spray, then add to arrangement. Insert the sticks of gold glitter stars into the foam. Glue gold bow to the handle.

Materials You'll Need

- Silver plate
- Silver compote dish
- Silver mint julep cup
- Florist's foam
- Water
- Fresh ivy, smilax, green grapes, pink roses, white tulips & pink sweet peas

1 Stack silver compote on top of plate, add mint julep cup (or other deep silver container) on top. Fill plate and compote basin to rims with water.

2 Soak florist's foam in water until completely saturated. Cut foam to fit inside mint julep cup; place foam in cup. Cut stems of ivy and smilax, then arrange on plate to establish trailing lines.

3 Arrange grapes in an attractive manner on plate, compote, and on top of mint julep cup.

4 Cut rose stems short, removing leaves. Place larger roses on the plate, smaller roses in the compote, and rosebuds in the grape bunch on top of the mint julep cup.

5 Cut stems of fresh sweet peas and insert them attractively into all three levels. Leave sweet pea stems longer for a more natural look.

6 Cut fresh tulip stems to various lengths and place them throughout arrangement as accents.

Waxed Flower Bridal Shower Arrangement

An amazing array of just-picked flowers, dipped in wax, ring the base of a stately, tall purple candle. This Victorian-inspired technique enables wonderful floral arrangements to remain fresh-looking for as long as a week. Wax-dipping mutes colors and gives the blossoms a beautiful sculptural quality. And, because they don't need water, you can use them to decorate in new and unexpected ways.

QUICK & EASY ALTERNATIVES

Option 1

Spring's sunny daffodil blooms and their distinctive sword-shaped leaves decorate the sides and base of two white pillar candles. To wax the flowers and leaves for this arrangement, follow step-by-step instructions. However, instead of allowing waxed leaves to harden on paper, press them against the sides of the candles to harden. With leaves in place, hold candle by its wick and dip the base into the hot wax. Let harden, then place the candle on a glass plate and lay the daffodil blossoms alongside.

Option 2

A beautiful rosebud has been dipped in wax to enhance a place card setting for a "just the girls" get-together. Select fresh, firm rosebuds for a long-lasting effect. To wax the flowers and leaves for this display, follow step-by-step instructions. If wax doesn't completely seep into spaces between petals, use a spoon to fill in the gaps. Handle the flowers carefully to prevent cracking. Place cards on table with a rosebud beside each one.

Option 3

A collection of waxed daisy chrysanthemums, green leaves, and a wire-edged ribbon create a beautiful wreath for an anniversary party. Select a grapevine wreath as the base, then wax the daisy mums following the step-by-step instructions. Gather daisies with their leaves in clusters of three, wrap their stems with green florist's tape, and then hot-glue them to the wreath. Glue a gold, looped ribbon bow to the top of the wreath.

Materials You'll Need

- Two blocks of paraffin wax
- Double boiler
- Candy thermometer
- Fresh flowers, such as roses, daisies, paperwhites, tulips,
- hyacinths, stephanotis, & hydrangeas.
- Cookie sheet
- Candle
- Colored plate

1 Heat two blocks of paraffin wax in a double boiler to 150°F (70°C). If wax is too hot, flowers will wither; if too cool, wax will not adhere.

2 Hold the flower by its stem and carefully dip the flower head completely into hot wax.

3 Lift flower straight up, allowing wax to drip back into pan. Lay flower on cookie sheet. Let harden for five minutes.

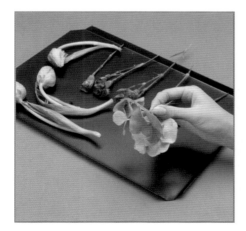

4 Once wax has hardened, dip stem into hot wax twice, letting wax cool slightly between each dipping. Lay waxed flowers on cookie sheet and leave until hard.

5 Drip a few drops of the wax onto the plate and then place the candle into the melted wax to secure.

6 Arrange waxed flowers around candle base. Flowers will last for about a week.

Surprise Party Bouquet

D ecorate a table for a surprise birthday party with a gift-wrapped package holding a tall taper. Combine floral wrapping paper with an array of silk flowers in complementary hues, then add a vibrant wire-edged ribbon to tie these colorful elements together. Planning a surprise party requires secrecy and detailed organization, but the results are gratifying when the guest of honor is truly surprised.

QUICK & EASY ALTERNATIVES

Option 1

Surprise Mom on Mother's Day by planning a special family brunch in her honor. Make the occasion exciting and colorful with individually potted silk flowers at each place setting. Coat the small flowerpots with glue, then smooth fabric over the curves of the pots. Fill pots with florist's foam, insert one flower into each pot, and arrange Spanish moss around its base. Wrap the flowerpots with narrow ribbons and tie them into bows. Try using a variety of fabrics and silk flowers.

Option 2

A bright centerpiece designed for a housewarming party is decorated with silk geraniums, four recipe cards, and a wooden spoon. Write recipes on cards, glue them to a round box, and glue narrow rick-rack around the cards. Glue large rickrack around the rim of the box. Fill box with florist's foam and glue Spanish moss to its surface. Insert geraniums into box, filling it completely. Tie a gingham bow to the spoon and glue onto box.

Option 3

A trip abroad is exciting in its own right, but when the anticipated trip is celebrated with a party, it becomes even more special. Glue travel pictures cut from magazines or brochures onto the base of a round papier-mâché box, overlapping to cover surface completely. Fill box with florist's foam, then insert and arrange artificial flowers. Attach a message to a pipe cleaner and insert it in the center of the decorated box.

Materials You'll Need

- Floral wrapping paper
- Square white gift box
- Scissors & tape
- Wire-edged ribbon
- Wire cutters
- Glue gun & glue sticks
- Florist's foam
- Dried & artificial flowers
- Slender candle

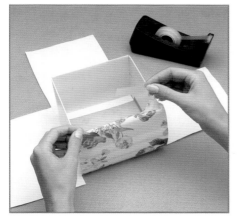

1 Lay floral wrapping paper on a flat surface, place box base in the center, and cut paper to fit, allowing for paper flaps to insert inside the box.

2 Fold flaps inside the box and tape in place. Cut two strips of wire-edged ribbon; hot-glue them around each side of the box.

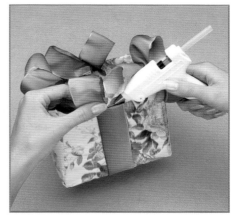

3 Fold ribbon ends into the box and glue in place. Make eight ribbon loops. Glue them to the inside of the wrapped ribbon ends, making them resemble bows.

4 Cut a dry block of florist's foam to fit box snugly, then glue it into the box.

5 Insert a selection of dried and artificial flowers into the foam. Combining dried and artificial flowers results in a more natural-looking arrangement.

6 Insert candle into the center of the arrangement. Choose dripless tapers or place a bobeche around the candle for safety.

Pretty Floral Centerpiece

S pecial occasion gatherings call for pretty decorative items, whether you're bringing a hostess gift or hosting the group in your own home. Using silk flowers and your artistic talents, there are many creative ways to present a beautiful table centerpiece for any occasion. The basket of blooms shown here combines leafy hydrangeas, baby's breath, and artificial apples to enhance a springtime dinner party.

QUICK & EASY ALTERNATIVES

Option 1

Present this lovely centerpiece gift when attending a friend's open house party. Select a pretty wallpaper border to enhance the flowers. Cut wallpaper to fit papier-mâché box. Glue paper to box using craft glue. Let dry. Cut florist's foam to fit snugly in box and insert. Place silk greenery into foam first, then add flowers. Form a ribbon bow, wire it to a wooden floral pick and insert it into the arrangement.

Option 2

Each tiny, pastel-painted pot holds a matching silk peony for a charming effect. Paint each pot a different acrylic shade, using ivory for the rims. Let dry. Cut a piece of florist's foam to fit each pot snugly, then insert. Clip a few leaves from each flower. Insert leaves into florist's foam, so they extend over pot edges. Clip stems of flowers and insert into foam center of each pot. Write a message on each rim with a green felt-tip pen.

Option 3

Choose a ceramic container and silk roses to make a lovely centerpiece for a romantic dinner. Gather nine silk roses in red, dark pink, and medium pink shades. Cut the green leaves from the blooms and trim stems, leaving pieces long enough to insert in the florist's foam. Cut the florist's foam to fit snugly into the chosen container. Firmly insert the foam, then arrange the greenery in the container. Insert the blooms into the foam, among the greenery.

Materials You'll Need

- Knife
- Florist's foam
- Woven basket
- Glue gun & glue sticks
- Wooden floral picks
- Three artificial green apples
- Wire cutters
- White & green silk hydrangea with leaves
- Silk baby's breath stems

1 Use a knife to cut florist's foam to fit snugly inside basket. Press foam into basket, hot-gluing, if desired.

2 Stick a floral pick into the bottom of each of the three artificial apples.

3 With wire cutters, trim leaves from hydrangeas. Trim stems, leaving enough to insert into the florist's foam.

4 Insert leaves into foam so some extend over the rim of basket. Insert some leaves into center foam area.

5 Insert flower stems into the foam between the leaves. Use hot-glue gun to secure, if desired.

6 Stick florist's picks with attached apples into arrangement, spacing attractively between flowers and leaves. Add a few stems of baby's breath for accent.

Herb Planter for the City Dweller

Fragrant herbs on a windowsill bring a sunny garden into the city—or any home without room for a garden. Plant them in matching pots, and tie with blue-and-white checked ribbon. Rosemary, sage, and thyme are perfect for a city dweller because these savory plants will enhance even the simplest cuisine. Herbs as prettily planted as these will be a welcomed gift.

QUICK & EASY ALTERNATIVES

Option 1

A fragrant, pale green bay-leaf topiary reminds one of pots found in a formal garden. Beautiful to look at, this one needs no watering! Use hot glue to cover a small plastic foam ball with dried bay leaves, leaving a tiny area on the bottom of the ball uncovered. Paint a small clay pot. Hot-glue a little square of plastic foam into the pot. Insert a short stick into the center, then hot-glue in place. Press the leaf- covered ball onto the stick, and hot-glue. Wrap the stick with wired-edged ribbon, and tie into a bow.

Option 2

Give the French scent of Provence with this pillar candle completely wrapped with dried lavender. To make this fragrant gift, first cut lavender stems ½" (1.5cm) shorter than candle height. Adjust stems according to size of candle. Paint the bottom two-thirds of the candle base with craft glue, and then affix lavender stems to candle base. Once glue is dry, snip off any uneven stems, and tie with a simple raffia bow. Present gift on an antique plate.

Option 3

Packed full of herbs and edible flowers, this country basket is a gift that will continue to delight for months to come. Line a basket with florist's foil. Tuck a selection of herbs and edible flowers in nursery pots into the basket. Write a greeting onto a tag, then wire tag and a ribbon bow onto a wooden pick. Press the pick into the potting soil of a decorative clay pot.

Materials You'll Need

- Terra-cotta pots with drainage holes & matching tray
- White acrylic paint

- Foam brush
- Culinary herbs in 2" (5cm) pots
- Blue-and-white checked ribbon

1 Coat flowerpots and tray with white acrylic paint. Let dry. Water herbs deeply by allowing their pots to stand overnight in about ¼" (6mm) water. Drain completely.

2 Gently loosen plant from the nursery pot by squeezing the sides of container. Carefully pull plant out, keeping root ball intact.

3 Place the rootball into the painted flowerpot. Tamp the soil down into the pot, being careful not to pack it too tightly.

4 Wrap the checked ribbon around pot. You may wish to add a dot of glue to the back of the pot to secure the ribbon while tying.

5 Tie the ribbon into a neat bow and trim the tails. Cut the ends of the ribbon into an inverted "V."

6 Place the potted herbs in the tray. Wrap cellophane around the three pots and the tray and decorate with a large bow.

Bags, containers and storage projects

I t is often said that the best gifts come in small packages; the exquisite boxes, gift bags, and containers in this chapter will certainly delight the lucky recipient—no matter what you choose to put inside them.

As well as showing you how to make these charming gift boxes and bags, this chapter contains some great ideas for ways to smarten up your home storage. From monogrammed coat hooks to a baby's keepsake box, the projects in this chapter are sure to charm and delight.

Pasta-Decorated Gift Box

Option 1

Known for its fetching shape, farfalle (bow tie-shaped pasta) is always a popular choice among chefs. Here, gleaming with red paint, this pasta's decorative potential is revealed on a perfect little Christmas box. With a hot-glue gun, attach the uncooked pasta in a row around the lid sides of a small, square gift box. Cover entire box with red spray paint, then allow to dry. Cut a length of plaid Christmas ribbon and form a double bow. Glue on lid top.

Option 2

Hot-glue one end of each fettuccini strip along edge of square box lid, placing side by side to cover lid. Break off excess pasta at other end. Cut a length of ¾" (2cm)-wide gold ribbon and weave it over and under pasta, two strands at a time. Let 1" (2.5cm) of ribbon extend at each end. Repeat until whole lid is woven; glue down other end of pasta strips. Glue ribbon ends to lid edge, then trim. Edge lid with more gold ribbon, then add a strip of ¼" (6mm) black ribbon just inside gold ribbon.

Option 3

Three types of pasta create a textured design on this reusable gift box. Spread white glue all over lid of round, papier-mâché box. Cover lid with spaghetti, placing end of each piece in center, fanning out to edge. Snap off excess. Glue six pieces of penne pasta in center of lid, forming a "star," then top with a large pasta shell. Spray entire box with a coat of gold paint. When dry, sponge blue acrylic paint lightly over box and lid.

Not only is pasta a tasty treat, it offers a wide variety of eye-pleasing shapes to tempt creative hands. This box is embellished with six types of pasta, then spray-painted silver to create a one-of-a-kind gift container for a gourmet cook. It makes a wonderful presentation for a kitchen gift, and the box can be reused for countertop storage. How nicely it will blend with today's sleek, stainless steel appliances!

Materials You'll Need

- Glue gun & glue sticks
- Hexagonal, faceted, papier-mâché box
- Spaghetti
- Penne pasta
- Fusilli pasta
- Mini rotelli pasta
- Pennette pasta
- Orechietti pasta
- Surface covering
- Silver spray paint

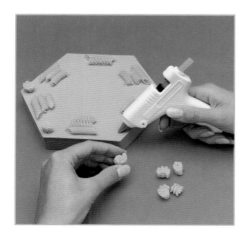

1 Using a hot-glue gun, outline all the faceted edges of the hexagonal box with a spaghetti strip on either side.

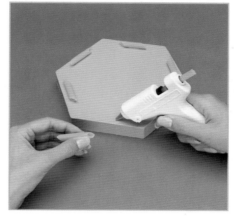

2 Glue a piece of penne pasta near the top edge of each side of the box lid (six in all).

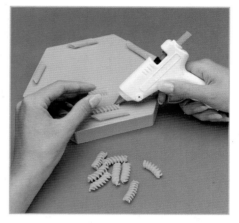

3 Glue two pieces of fusilli pasta beside penne on lid top, forming a row of three on each side.

4 Add a piece of mini rotelli at each corner point on box lid, filling in spaces between other pasta pieces.

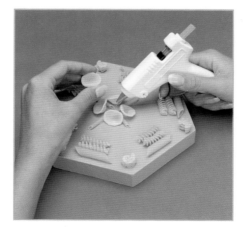

5 Place ends of six pieces of pennette pasta to meet in center of box lid. Glue down, then add a piece of orechietti pasta between each pennette.

6 Cover work area and spray entire gift box with metallic silver paint, covering all sides of pasta embellishments.

Monogrammed Hooks

J azz up the decor and improve organization with monogrammed hooks for the family. Bright brass letters on checkered wooden "tiles" leave no doubt as to the owner of all that is hanging on the brass hook beneath. It's perfect for coats and hats by an entry door and works wonderfully to keep the "who's whose" in bathroom towels straight. They'll be "hooked on" this handsome gift, and all the orderliness that accompanies it.

QUICK & EASY ALTERNATIVES

Option 1

Delight the four-legged members of your family with this personalized accessory holder. Paint a decorative board with brown acrylic paint. Use black paint to stencil paw prints along bottom of board. On a piece of foam board, trace a dog bone cookie cutter to make a bone for each dog. Cut out with craft knife and color with markers. Stamp or stencil dogs' names onto bones and glue to painted board. Screw large cup hooks into board over paw prints.

Option 2

Family members will be delighted with this new and pretty home for their keys. Spray-paint an unfinished wooden plaque with sky blue acrylic paint. Allow to dry. Apply thin coat of white paint over face of board. When dry, stencil house and trees in country colors. Make small "stitches" around house, path, trees, and sun with fine black marker. Use red marker to add apples to the trees. Screw large cup hooks along bottom of the plaque.

Option 3

When garden gloves are left among the flowers, they're often lost for the season. Create this bed of tulips to keep garden accessories handy. Paint a wooden board white. When dry, paint design using plaid stencil and pale yellow paint. Paint leaves and stems green on three wooden tulips. Paint tulips blue, pink, and yellow. Glue to board with wood glue. Screw hooks under each flower.

Materials You'll Need

- Acrylic paint: red and white
- Paintbrush
- 24"(61cm)-long wooden board

- 4" (10cm) square boards
- Checker stencil
- Stencil brush
- Wood glue

- Screwdriver
- Brass screws
- 4" (10cm) brass letters
- Brass hooks

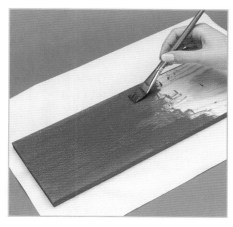

1 Use red acrylic paint to paint face and sides of 24" (61cm) board. Set aside to dry.

2 Paint each 4" (10cm) square with white acrylic paint and allow to dry. Two coats may be needed.

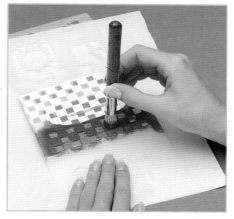

3 When white paint has dried, stencil checks onto squares using red paint, stencil, and stencil brush.

4 Use wood glue to attach checkered squares to red painted board. Allow time for glue to set.

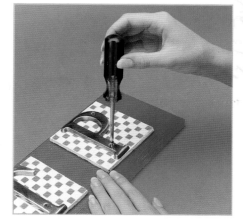

5 With screwdriver and brass screws, attach a brass letter to each red-checkered square.

6 Position a brass hook underneath each red-checkered square and screw into place.

Painted Wooden Boxes

He has no need for a jewelry box, but your husband is apt to warmly welcome a place to organize a watch and pocket items. A simple, two-step staining process lets you create a seemingly intricate inlaid pattern on an unfinished wooden container for his receipts, tickets, wallet, keys, or other belongings. He will love this handsome box...because now that he is newly organized, he'll spend less time hunting for misplaced items!

QUICK & EASY ALTERNATIVES

Option 1

This handsome box doesn't take up a lot of room on Dad's dresser, and will keep cuff links and loose change neat and organized. Select an unfinished wooden box, 3" (7.5cm) round, with a lid. Cut 1"(2.5cm)-wide masking tape into four pieces and stick across lid in a "tic-tac-toe" grid formation. Press edges of tape firmly in place. Use a sponge brush to apply dark gel wood stain to exposed sections of lid. Let dry, then remove tape. Spray entire box with stain in a lighter color than gel.

Option 2

Select an unfinished wooden tissue box. Affix 1"(2.5cm)-wide, paint-quality masking tape on the box, creating diamond patterns down each side and around the tissue opening. With a craft knife, trim the tape as needed. Press the tape edges firmly down with fingertips, then use a sponge brush to apply gel stain to the exposed wood. Allow to dry, then remove tape. Spray entire box with a wood stain in a lighter color than gel.

Option 3

Make a faux inlaid box for an interesting gift. Select an unfinished square wood box with lid and matching square knob. Affix strips of 1"(2.5cm)-wide masking tape to box in different-sized square patterns. Use craft knife to trim excess after overlapping tape ends. Use a sponge brush to apply dark gel stain to exposed wood. Let dry, remove tape, then spray box, lid, and knob with lighter color wood stain. Let dry, then attach knob to lid with wood glue.

Materials You'll Need

- Unfinished wooden box with lid
- Paint-quality masking tape
- Scissors
- Straight-edge ruler
- Craft knife
- Gel wood stain
- Sponge brush
- Unfinished wood
- knob
- Spray wood stain
- Wood glue

1 Select an unfinished wooden box with a hinged lid. Place strips of tape horizontally along the top and bottom edges of sides of box. Trim excess with scissors.

2 Cut strips of tape to fit vertical sides of box. Place evenly spaced strips all around box sides, overlapping the horizontal tape.

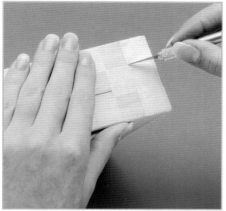

3 Using a craft knife, cut and remove pieces of vertical tape that overlap horizontal tape, leaving squares of tape in the center area of the box sides.

4 Brush the entire box, including knob, with a dark-colored gel stain. Let dry completely.

5 Remove tape from box. Cover work surface and spray entire box and knob with a lighter colored stain. Let dry.

6 Attach the wooden knob to the center of the box using wood glue.

Fabric-Découpaged Market Basket

Fabric cut-outs of brightly colored fruit become bold graphics when applied with découpage medium to a white bushel basket. An apple green rim and a big raffia bow add contemporary country touches. Fill the basket with fruit, wine, and cheese, then tuck in a fresh baguette for a beautiful and bountiful gift.

QUICK & EASY ALTERNATIVES

Option 1

Create a bushel basket of gifts for the gardener. Paint basket deep green, then sponge on white acrylic paint along the rim and base of the basket; let dry. Cut out illustrations of blooms from garden catalogs or magazines. Brush découpage medium on the back of each image, then affix them along the sides of the basket, smoothing them down while still damp. When dry, apply a second coat of medium. Tie twine bows to handles. Fill basket with garden gifts.

Option 2

This pretty basket is embellished with fabric cut-outs to create a charming kit for the seamstress. Brush a coat of acrylic paint on the exterior of the basket; let dry. Cut several fabric squares with pinking shears, then brush a coat of découpage medium on the back of each square and apply along sides of basket. Glue buttons and small spools of thread to the fabric squares. Tie a yellow ribbon bow, glue it to the rim, then sew a pincushion to the bow.

Option 3

This lovely basket takes its cue from the color scheme of the recipient's bathroom. Select a white basket, then cut out floral images from gift wrap that matches your friend's bathroom decor. Brush découpage medium on the back of each image; affix them to sides of basket. Smooth images with fingers while still damp. Let dry. Seal images with a second coat of medium. Glue a bow and spray of silk flowers to basket rim. Fill basket with soaps and oils.

Materials You'll Need

- Bushel basket
- White & green acrylic paints
- Flat sponge brush
- Fruit-patterned fabric
- Scissors
- Découpage medium
- Cutting board
- Raffia
- Glue gun & glue sticks

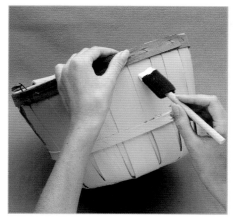

1 Brush a coat of green acrylic paint on the rim of the bushel basket, then paint the base of the basket white. The interior can also be painted to match, if desired.

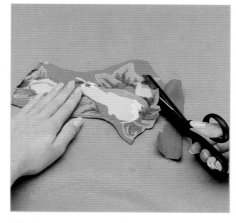

2 Cut out shapes of brightly colored fruit from the fabric. Trim as neatly as possible.

3 Brush a coat of découpage medium on the back of each fabric cut-out.

4 Apply damp fabric cut-out to side of basket, smoothing it to ensure a secure bond. Repeat process with remaining fabric cut-outs until the desired effect is achieved.

5 Tie several strands of raffia into a large bow. If the basket has handles, make one bow for each handle, if desired.

6 Use hot glue to affix raffia bow to basket rim or handle. Fill basket with bread, cheese, wine, and fruit.

Painted ABC Planter

D o you need a "Grade A" gift for your child's favorite teacher? You can't go wrong with a fun planter created to brighten his or her classroom. Here's a project that you and your child can work on together and one that your young student will be proud to present. Designed to look like a chalkboard, this whimsical planter is sure to brighten a teacher's day.

QUICK & EASY ALTERNATIVES

Option 1

This decorated terra-cotta pot is a perfect gift for someone who loves the beach or has a cottage by the water. Begin by painting a flowerpot with lavender or other pastel-colored acrylic paint. Buy seashells at a craft store or collect them on a trip to the beach. Paint the shells in various pastel colors, then affix them around the rim of the flowerpot with epoxy glue. Finish this gift by wrapping a matching pastel ribbon around the pot; tie it into a bow in front.

Option 2

Before pre-sifted flour, sifters were essential tools in the kitchen. Vintage flour sifters with fun designs make charming planters. Find sifters at tag sales or flea markets. Cut a plastic bag to fit inside flour sifter; punch holes in bag for drainage. Fill bag with soil, add plant, and tie a bow to sifter's handle. Add a special touch to planter, such as artificial strawberries, to match the design of the sifter. This is an ideal gift for a person who loves to buy kitchen collectibles.

Option 3

Indulge a friend's love of color and whimsy with this lively, painted flowerpot. You simply need five bright acrylic paints, some sponge brushes, and ¾"(2cm)-wide painter's tape. Paint a flowerpot yellow. Affix vertical strips of tape to the pot, allowing ¾" (2cm) between each strip. Paint each space between the tape strips a different color all the way around the pot. When dry, carefully remove the tape. Glue a rainbow-hued ribbon around the rim of the flowerpot and tie it into a bow.

Materials You'll Need

- Sponge brush
- Flowerpot
- Black & white acrylic paints
- Masking tape
- Alphabet stencil

- Stencil brush
- Ribbon
- Craft glue
- Blackboard charm

1 Using a sponge brush, cover a flowerpot in black acrylic paint. Allow pot to dry completely.

2 Apply tape to the alphabet stencil, blocking letters that will not be used.

3 Tape stencil securely to the flowerpot about halfway between the top and bottom.

4 Stencil "ABC" on the pot using white paint and a stencil brush. Repeat the "ABC" design around the pot, using a mix of lowercase and uppercase letters in straight, diagonal, and curved patterns.

5 Cut a ribbon long enough to fit around rim of pot and tie into a bow. Wrap the ribbon around rim, gluing in several places, then tie into bow in front.

6 Hot-glue a blackboard or other school-related charm underneath the bow.

127

Colorful Snack Bowl

Homemade edibles are always a popular gift for teachers, friends, and family members. The bonus of a lovely hand-painted glass container makes it even more special. Put your artistic talents to work on a plain glass bowl, and then fill it with gaily wrapped gifts of nuts, popcorn balls, or homemade candy. This is a wonderful way to surprise a hostess—and her guests—at her next dinner party!

QUICK & EASY ALTERNATIVES

Option 1

Everyone loves freshly baked cookies, and here's a beautiful way to present them to a hostess—on an elegantly decorated plate that she can use again and again. To make this gift, start with a glass plate embossed with a floral pattern. Prepare the plate's surface with glass conditioner, applying it with a sponge brush. Use pastel dimensional paints with fine-tip applicators, following the floral designs of the plate. Outline the flowers in pink and lavender and the leaves and stems in green.

Option 2

How pretty a plain, glass flowerpot becomes when you add an assortment of colorful, glittering jewels. Give this as a hostess gift filled with cellophane-wrapped snacks and add a bow for a really eye-catching effect. Buy a small glass flowerpot and an assortment of flat-back jewels in a variety of colors. Use epoxy glue to affix a circle of large jewels around the rim, and a smattering of smaller ones to the base of the pot. Wrap candy, trail mix, nuts, or other snacks in cellophane and wrap with a ribbon tied into a bow.

Option 3

This hand-painted glass soap dish with matching decorative soap is an impressive gift for a teacher, friend, bride-to-be or anyone who appreciates fine things. The color theme carried through in paint, soap, and ribbon adds beauty to an already lovely embossed glass dish. Prepare the dish by applying a glass conditioner using a sponge brush. Use bronze metallic dimensional paint with a fine-tip applicator to follow the design on the dish.

Materials You'll Need

- Glass bowl, embossed plate & soap dish
- Glass conditioner
- Glass paint in various colors
- Flat-tipped brushes
- Dimensional paint with fine-tip applicators: lavender, pink, green & copper

1 Prepare glass bowl by brushing on glass conditioner. With a flat-tipped brush, use a downward stroke to apply paint squares in an evenly spaced checkerboard pattern.

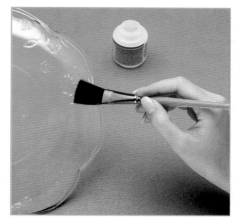

2 For the cookie plate with the embossed flower design, brush on glass conditioner with a large, flat-tipped paintbrush.

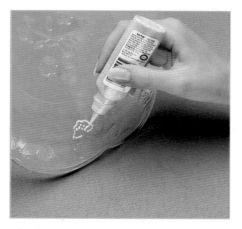

3 Outline a flower with the lavender dimensional paint, carefully following the plate's embossed pattern. Slowly squeeze paint out of the fine-tip applicator.

4 Apply pink paint to a nearby flower using the same method. Continue to paint pink and lavender flowers all around the plate.

5 Use green dimensional paint to outline the leaves and stems of the flowers.

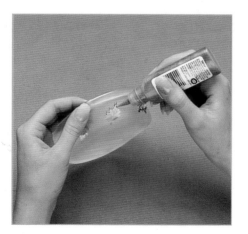

6 For the soap dish, use a dish with an etched or embossed design. Prepare with glass conditioner, then use copper dimensional paint to outline the design.

Paper-Covered Party Favor Boxes

Charming little pastel hat boxes filled to the brim with dainty candies are party favor gifts everyone will want to take home. This selection is decorated with quilt-printed paper, pure white embossed paper trimmed with a ribbon-threaded white lace band, and pastel plaid paper decorated with white paper doilies and ribbon. Crafted in any size, the beautiful collection adds up to a memorable present for each party guest.

QUICK & EASY ALTERNATIVES

Option 1

Even a simple treasure will be prized when lifted from this gift box. Start with a rigid papier-mâché container. Coat the top and bottom with craft glue, then cover with color-coordinated paper. Fold ends, turning excess paper inside, and secure with hot glue. Insert a party favor and close the box. Wrap narrow side of paper-covered box with ribbon; secure with hot glue on bottom. Wrap remaining wide side with ribbon. Tie a shoelace bow, catching center of narrow side in knot.

Option 2

Choose sheets of pastel baby shower wrapping paper for these clever little containers. Cut an 8½"x11" (22x28cm) piece of wrapping paper and an 8½"x11" (22x28cm) piece of thin fabric. Spray adhesive on back of paper, then lay it carefully on the fabric. Press the layers together until dry. Cut the layered paper into two 8½"x5" (22x13cm) pieces, fold long side of paper ¾" (2cm) down over fabric, then fold into "diaper" triangle. Pin in front.

Option 3

Bright tissue paper creates the radiance in these little party favor candy cups. Start with plain paper nut or candy cups. Un-pleat the cup sides, keeping the rim intact. Cut squares of tissue paper, then cover the outside and inside of the cup. Wrap green florist's tape around a pipe cleaner for a handle, then punch two holes across from each other under cup rim. Insert "handle," and twist ends.

Materials You'll Need

- Pencil or pen
- Round papier-mâché boxes with lids
- Wrapping paper
- Scissors
- Ruler
- Craft glue
- Paper doilies
- Ribbon & lace trim

1 On the back side of the wrapping paper, trace around the bottom of a box, then cut four circles. Cut one circle ¼" (6mm) larger in diameter than the others.

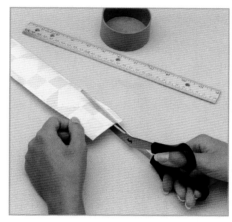

2 Cut a strip of paper twice as wide as the side of the lid and the same length as the circumference plus ½" (1.5cm). Fold ¼" (6mm) under at one end.

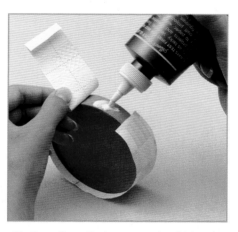

3 Smooth craft glue onto side of lid. Starting with the unfolded end of paper, wrap paper around edge and gently press it against the glue.

4 Use scissors to make perpendicular slits in the paper in ¼" (6mm) increments around the lid edge, then fold and glue slits onto lid top. Repeat with inside edge.

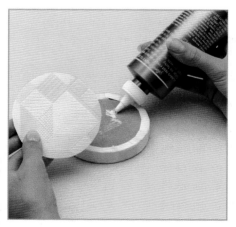

5 Glue large circle to the top of the box lid. Press firmly to smooth, and affix all edges of circle. Glue small circle inside lid. Repeat Steps 2-5 for bottom of box.

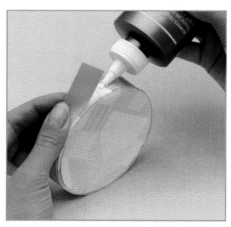

6 Use craft glue to add trim to box lid or box bottom. Vary trims to coordinate with the paper color and party theme.

Fragrant Touches for Gift Boxes

A selection of fragrant botanicals brings natural beauty to a collection of unique gift boxes. Use natural touches such as slender fresh eucalyptus leaves, dried bay leaves, and cinnamon sticks. Some of these fragrant ingredients are as close as your grocery store or your own backyard. The finished results will be gift wraps of fragrance and distinction.

QUICK & EASY ALTERNATIVES

Option 1

This fragrant, feminine gift wrap is easier to make than it looks! Cut a tulle circle 2" (5cm) wider than the lid of a papier-mâché box. Coat box lid with craft glue and top with potpourri. Wrap tulle over the potpourri, gluing tulle around the edge of the lid. Glue satin ribbon around rim, covering tulle. When the glue is dry, trim tulle. Overlap pansy stickers around base of box. Wrap the ribbon around the box and tie into a bow on the top. Hot-glue three or four dried rosebuds to the the bow.

Option 2

An absolutely perfect combination of raffia, green leaves, a tiny wreath, and an aged wooden box creates a one-of-a-kind gift wrap. To make this unusual creation, use craft glue to affix fresh leaves to a piece of cardboard or paper cut to fit slightly smaller than the box top. Let dry completely, then tie to the box top with raffia, catching the small wreath in the bow. Use several strands of raffia for the most attractive result. Fill the box with favorite family recipes and present to a beginner cook.

Option 3

Sprigs of herbs, such as rosemary, lavender, and thyme, enhance gift wraps of all types. They dry beautifully and remain fragrant for months. Brown papier-mâché boxes make perfect containers for natural embellishments. Use craft glue to cover the base with narrow corrugated paper, then cover the top with handmade paper. Fold paper, and glue folds neatly inside lid. Tie with green-and-tan checkered paper ribbon. Tuck a fresh herb sprig under the bow. Use this handsome box to give packaged herbs and spices.

Materials You'll Need

- Corrugated paper
- Dried or fresh bay leaves
- Glue gun & glue sticks
- Dried or fresh lavender
- Raffia
- Eucalyptus leaves
- Small papier-mâché box
- Green corrugated paper
- Cinnamon sticks
- Wire-edged ribbon, ¾" (2cm) wide
- Artificial blueberry spray

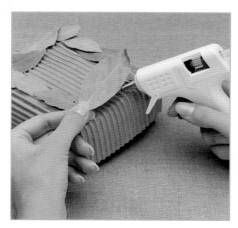

1 For corrugated box, use hot glue to add bay leaves in an overlapping pattern around the outside edge of box top.

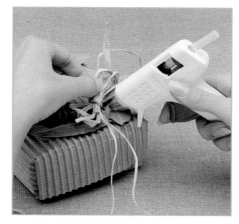

2 Bundle three sprigs of fresh or dried lavender, then tie bundle together with a raffia bow. Hot-glue onto leaf on top of box.

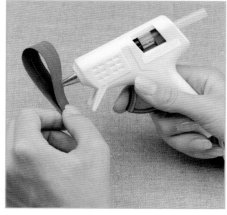

3 To make eucalyptus leaf bow, fold a leaf to make a loop and glue the ends together with hot glue. Make two of these loops.

4 Hold the two loops together and fold a third leaf around the joined loops and hot-glue. Trim end of third leaf. Glue two leaves to back of bow. Glue bow to box.

5 For small rectangular box, cut piece of green corrugated paper to fit lid; hot-glue paper to lid. Cut cinnamon sticks to fit lid and glue around edge of box.

6 Tie wire-edged ribbon into bow with long tails. Hot-glue blueberry spray under ribbon knot, then glue bow to corner of box top.

Sweetheart Boxes

These sweet feminine gift boxes are adorned with fresh flowers, greeting cards, and wonderful wire-edged ribbons. Honor a special friendship, a unique event, or even a family-oriented milestone by presenting a gift wrapped in one of these distinctive packages. Tuck a small gift into the special box to say "Thank You," "Happy Birthday," or just to let someone know that you care.

QUICK & EASY ALTERNATIVES

Option 1

An intimate gift of love from a sweetheart is even more personal presented in a golden box with a delightful bee imprinted on the ribbon and card. Coat a square papier-mâché box with metallic gold acrylic paint. Two coats may be necessary. Tie a 1½" (4cm)-wide ivory, multi-looped satin bow, then rubber-stamp each loop with a bee imprint using gold ink. Stamp another golden bee onto a pre-made, gilt-edged card, then write "Mine" in gold ink next to the stamped image.

Option 2

The key to this wrap is color-coordination—the brighter, the better! Choose a wrapping paper to suit the child's interests, such as sports, trains, dolls or animals. Tie a wide, coordinated ribbon around the package, then knot. Make a wrapped packet of jelly beans by piling a few into a square of cellophane, then pulling up and twisting the corners. Tie the jelly beans, a nosegay of bright balloons. and curled ribbons onto the knot of the wide ribbon with a bit of curled ribbon.

Option 3

A girl's sixteenth birthday is significant. Present a gift for the birthday girl in this charming blue box stenciled with the magic number. A papier-mâché box with several sides yields the greatest number of surfaces for imprinting. Coat box with blue acrylic paint. When paint is dry, stencil numbers with a sponge and yellow acrylic paint. Top box lid with a yellow, wire-edged, multi-looped bow. Cut a few of the loops into tails. Fold two tails under the box lid, and hot-glue. Trim remaining tails.

Materials You'll Need

- Round papier-mâché box
- White acrylic paint
- Foam brush
- Decorative greeting card
- Pencil
- Scissors
- Craft glue
- Pink-and-white striped ribbon
- Glue gun & glue sticks
- Fresh flowers

1 Coat papier-mâché box with white paint. Two coats may be necessary to achieve desired effect.

2 Trace box lid onto back of decorative greeting card. To make this easier, select a card size and configuration that will lend itself to the shape of the box.

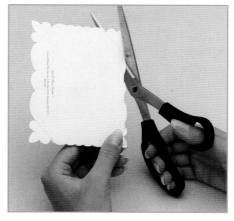

3 Use scissors to trim the card to fit onto top of box lid. Follow the traced line, as well as the design of the card, to determine where to cut.

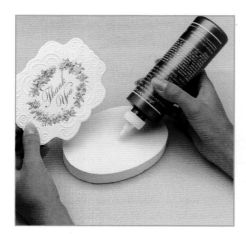

4 Use craft glue to affix card to box lid top. Spread smoothly with a small piece of cardboard, and then press the card to the lid with your fingertips.

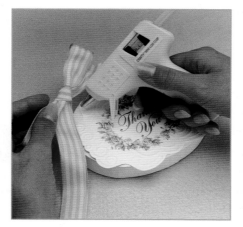

5 Tie striped ribbon into a bow. Hot-glue bow onto the left-hand corner of the box lid, or position it to coordinate with image on the greeting card.

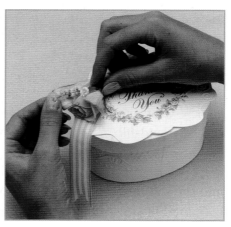

6 Tuck a fresh rose or another flower into the ribbon knot to add a finishing touch.

Mother's Day Bouquet Bag

R emember Mom's special day with a bouquet of roses in a beautifully decorated gift bag. A plain white bag embellished with a pastel plaid card, coordinating envelope, and a white lace doily combine to make a delicate and feminine presentation. An organza bow completes the package, ready to give to Mom with the beautiful bouquet of flowers.

QUICK & EASY ALTERNATIVES

Option 1

Rustic burlap and bold sunflowers look terrific paired together. Cut a piece of burlap to cover a quart-sized (1 litre) canning jar, adding 2" (5cm) all around. Place jar in center of burlap, then pull sides up and secure to neck of jar with a rubber band. Cut a 2" (5cm)-wide strip of fabric using pinking shears. Wrap the fabric around the jar to cover the rubber band and tie into a bow. Wrap twine around the fabric, tie into a bow, then glue painted wooden stars to the tails. Add water, sunflowers, and American flag.

Option 2

Autumn-hued mums and copper-hued leaves fill a hollowed pumpkin with fall splendor. Hollow out a pumpkin, then insert a block of fully saturated floral foam. Arrange mums and preserved leaves decoratively. Add a woven straw bow, securing it to pumpkin with a corsage pin. Pumpkins in all sizes, along with many other flat-bottomed winter squashes and gourds, will easily adapt to this design. Vary the flowers, then give as a gift for an autumn centerpiece.

Option 3

Displaying a vibrant, red poinsettia is a tradition in many homes during the holiday season. It's a gift that is always welcomed, especially when thoughtfully presented in a gaily wrapped box covered with holiday paper. Select a box strong enough to hold a potted poinsettia, then cover with paper, making sure edges are neatly folded. Fold paper down inside box to a depth of 2" (5cm) or more. Wrap the box with ribbon, tie into a bow, and glue to back of box. Insert the potted poinsettia.

Materials You'll Need

- White gift bag with handle
- Tape
- Mother's Day card with pastel envelope
- Two rectangular paper lace doilies
- Organza ribbon
- Florist's wire
- Roses & baby's breath
- Vase

1 Tape the pastel envelope slightly off-center and to the right on the front of the bag.

2 Tape paper lace doilies on top of pastel envelope slightly off-center to left. If using small doilies, overlap them to create a complete rectangle.

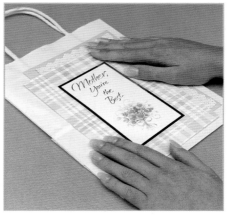

3 Tape the Mother's Day card on top of the doilies, slightly off-center to the left.

4 Fashion a multi-looped bow, wiring the center with florist's wire. Leave 3" (7.5cm)-long wire ends after making bow.

5 Wire the organza bow to the left front handle of the decorated bag. Trim excess wire.

6 Insert the bouquet of roses along with an assortment of baby's breath into the bag. A vase with water can be inserted into bag, if desired.

Paper Doily and Ribbon Basket

Delicate, white paper lace doilies and a ruffled strip of wire-edged ribbon transform a plain straw basket into a delightful container for chocolates, home-baked cookies, holiday cakes, and just about any delectable kitchen favorite. Presented to cheer up an ailing friend, to commemorate a special occasion, or to just show that you care, it's the perfect gift basket.

QUICK & EASY ALTERNATIVES

Option 1

Present the gift of a living plant in its own doily-decorated pot. Select a terra-cotta pot without a drain hole. Brush a coat of purple acrylic paint onto the pot, inside and out. Let dry completely. Fold doilies in half to find center, then cut in half. Overlap, then hot-glue doilies around lip of pot, lace side up, then fold down to cover lip. Wrap pot with matching ribbon and tie into a bow. Keeping plant in its nursery container, set it into pot.

Option 2

Fragrant spiced cookies and quick breads team up with a covered, papier-mâché box to present a total package of spiced and herbal delights. Cover the box base with herb or spice-themed self-adhesive paper, then select a compatible acrylic paint color, and brush a coat of paint onto the lid. Tie a matching ribbon bow and hot-glue it on the lid, securing the tails under the lid rim. Fill box with crumpled tissue paper, then add cookies and bread.

Option 3

What a delightful surprise—layers of candy in a glass jar that's trimmed with a perky doily. Select a square glass jar or canister with a lid, then cut three or more cardboard squares to fit into jar. Place first layer of candy in the jar, then top it with a cardboard square. Continue layering until jar is full. Top open jar with a square doily, then place lid on jar. Glue a multi-looped decorative bow to the top of the jar.

Materials You'll Need

- White basket
- Round paper lace doilies
- Glue gun & glue sticks
- Scissors
- Wire-edged ribbon
- Candies or cookies

1 Fold round white paper lace doilies to find center. Fold enough doilies to completely cover rim of basket.

2 Dab hot glue onto basket rim. Fold doily over rim, pressing onto glue; one half of the doily will be inside the basket.

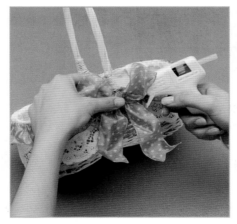

3 Cut ribbon length to one and one-half rim circumference. Expose wire on one end, and fold wire at the other end. Pull the exposed wire to ruffle the ribbon.

4 Gather ribbon to fit basket rim and then hot-glue it to top edge of basket, adjusting ruffles evenly around the rim.

5 Tie a matching ribbon bow, then hot-glue bow onto ruffled ribbon below handle.

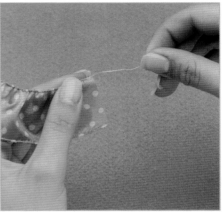

6 Complete presentation by placing a large doily into the basket before adding candies or cookies.

Stenciled Springtime Gift Bag

Match gift wrap to the seasons by stenciling plain white bags with colorful floral designs. For spring, a bouquet of pastel-colored pansies graces the gift bag and coordinates with the crisp tissue spilling from the inside. Stencils are easy to use and come in a wide variety of reusable motifs. Stencil flowers, leaves, ribbons, and even sweet sayings to personalize the bag.

QUICK & EASY ALTERNATIVES

Option 1

Beautifully stenciled yellow roses adorn the white gift bag topped with a matching enclosure of yellow card stock. Lay the bag flat and stencil with a pattern of yellow roses and green leaves. Cut card stock to fit the width of the bag. Glue a paper doily on top of the card stock, fold, then cut a slot for the handle. Place a gift in the bag, then insert the doily over the handle, and tie a yellow-and-white checked wire-edged ribbon bow onto the handle.

Option 2

A cute little bag stenciled with a bunny can be used to collect Easter eggs or hold candies and treats for an Easter party. The design is so charming, it's suitable for both children and adults. Select stencils and paints at a craft store. Choose traditional Easter colors, or select hues to match a party theme or special color scheme. Lay bag flat to stencil. After stenciling, place contents in bag. Add matching tissue, then tie a colorful bow to the handle.

Option 3

Create very unique bags with the addition of the name and color-copied picture of the recipient. Or, if using the bags as party favors, use the photo of the honoree. The white bag is stenciled in a two-color pattern to coordinate with a fabric square highlighting the framed photo. A strip of matching fabric, tied in a bow, graces the handle. Glue fabric square onto the stamped bag. Use a hand-cut, heart-shaped mat to frame the photocopy, then glue framed image to bag.

Materials You'll Need

- White gift bags
- Stencils
- Stencil paint
- Stencil brush
- Colored tissue
- Narrow ribbon
- Yellow card stock
- Square paper doily
- Scissors
- Wide ribbon
- Color copy of photograph
- Printed fabric
- Colored paper
- Glue stick

1 For springtime bag, lay bag flat and position stencil. With a stencil brush, use a "pouncing" motion to paint the cut-out area of stencil.

2 Tie narrow ribbon to one side of handle; select a ribbon that matches the one used on the stenciled bouquet. Add colored tissue and bag contents.

3 For rose-stenciled bag, cut yellow card stock, glue a square doily on top, then cut a slot for the handle loops.

4 Add bag contents, then slip paper doily over handle loops to close bag. Complete by tying a ribbon bow onto one of the loops.

5 For personalized bag, color-copy photo to fit bag size, then cut a heart-shaped mat from colored paper and frame the photo.

6 Stencil name and hearts in a diagonal pattern on front of bag. Glue a square of coordinating fabric, then matted photo, offsetting slightly. Tie bow to handle.

Gift-Wrapped Jars

QUICK & EASY ALTERNATIVES

Option 1

Present a jar of delicious, ready-made gourmet food costumed in an equally terrific covering. A beautiful cloth dinner napkin wraps this jar and is tied with a ribbon. Place the jar in the center of the napkin, draw the sides up above the lid, and secure them with a rubber band. Conceal the rubber band with wire-edged rose and light green ribbons. Wrap and tie the two ribbons together to make a bow. Arrange the folds of the napkin attractively.

Option 2

Evoke memories of the sea with a collection of perfumed soaps in a wide-mouth canister with a shell-adorned label. Make the label from white paper using fancy-edged scissors to create interesting edges. Write "Soap" on the front of the label and glue it to the jar. Glue one or more tiny seashells to the label in a decorative fashion. Wrap a length of thick ivory-colored cord around the neck of the jar, and finish with a bow. Fill jar with small, unwrapped bars of ivory and white soap.

Option 3

Festive, colorfully printed tissue paper becomes a beautiful topping for gifts of jam, jelly, preserves, and other ready-made gourmet delicacies. Match the tissue to the contents or choose a contrasting color. Either way, the result will be a terrific and inexpensive dress-up. Cut a square of tissue paper using fancy-edged scissors, then place it on top of the jar. Secure the tissue square by wrapping the neck of the jar with matching cotton cord. Tie the cord into a bow, then knot the tails.

Delightful fruit concoctions become beautiful gifts when packaged in sparkling glass jars. The ribbon wraps and decorative lids featured on this trio of glass jars enhance the contents and glorify the gift. Clusters of miniature artificial lemons, pears, and peaches top glass canning jars to identify the delicious fruit inside. Matching ribbon bows add a festive finishing touch. Buy fruits and then repackage them in these lovely jars.

Materials You'll Need

- Glass canisters
- Artificial fruit & leaves
- Glue gun & glue sticks
- Ribbon

- Jar of fruit
- Cloth dinner napkin
- Rubber band
- Pink & green wire-edged ribbons

1 For fruit-adorned canisters, use hot glue to affix small, whole artificial fruit to top of lid. Cluster tightly for prettiest effect.

2 Hot-glue small green leaves in between and under the artificial fruit.

3 Fill jar with desired fruit. Close lid and tie matching ribbon around neck of canister. Include storage instructions: Keep refrigerated and use within one week.

4 For napkin-wrapped gift jar, place jar in center of napkin and draw sides up.

5 Gather napkin corners at the top and wrap them securely with a rubber band.

6 Conceal rubber band with light green and pink wire-edged ribbons tied into a bow.

Baby's Keepsake Box

This sweet container for baby's early mementos is sure to be a hit at the baby shower. Personalized with a copy of a birth certificate and a baby's photo, the small wooden box can hold a hospital bracelet, lock of hair, and other precious keepsakes. Paint the box white and add a pink-checkered ribbon. Add a baby spoon to the lid for a handle. The result is a one-of-a-kind gift. Include the date and gift-giver's name inside the lid for a special touch.

QUICK & EASY ALTERNATIVES

Option 1

Purchase a small photo album. Open and place it on the wrong side of the white solid fabric and trace around with a pencil. Add 1" (2.5cm) all around and cut out. Wrap around album and glue to inside. Glue a copy of a photo to the center of the album cover. Then glue blue feather-edged ribbon along the border of the photo. Glue on buttons where ribbons intersect. Grandma will be delighted with her own special "brag book."

Option 2

Start with an acrylic glass double frame (available in variety or gift stores). Thread alphabet beads onto a narrow pink or blue ribbon, separating each with a white bead. Spell "baby," or the child's name. Use tape or craft glue to neatly affix ribbon to the back of the frame on each side, letting the beads hang down slightly. Tie two bows and glue to the front on each end of the ribbon and you have a perfect addition for Dad's desk.

Option 3

Make or buy a pretty white pillow. Have a favorite baby photo color-copied at a copy shop onto a sheet of transfer paper (available at craft stores). Iron the transfer onto coordinating fabric, then trim away the excess fabric. Glue or sew the fabric to the pillow top. Add white ribbon around the border of the photo. Sew white buttons at each corner. Finish with pink or blue ribbon and tie into a bow.

Materials You'll Need

- Wooden box
- Fine grit sandpaper
- Baby spoon
- Sponge brush

- White & pink acrylic paints
- Alphabet stencil
- Stencil brush
- Pink-checked ribbon

- Photocopy of birth certificate (reduced)
- Color copy of photo
- Craft glue
- Glue gun & glue sticks

1 Sand box lightly using a fine grit sandpaper. Wipe the box with a clean cloth.

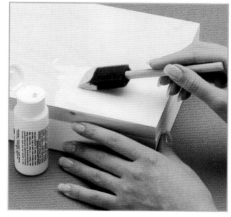

2 Add two coats of white acrylic paint using a sponge brush. Allow to dry.

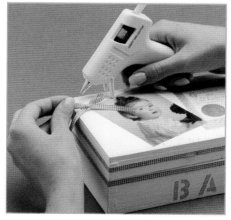

3 Tape on stencils. Dip stencil brush in pink paint and dab on a paper towel until the brush is almost dry. Stencil "Baby", the child's name, or your design choice to the box.

4 Glue the pink-checkered ribbon around the box as pictured. Glue birth certificate and copy of photo to top of box, overlapping them slightly.

5 Tie the remaining ribbon into a bow and glue to the top left corner of the box.

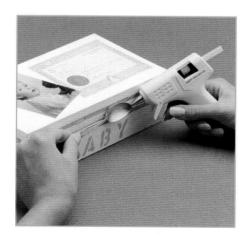

6 Hot-glue the keepsake baby spoon onto the front of the box lid to use as a handle.

Pinked-Edge Gift Bags

Sometimes the package is just as interesting as the gift inside. These gift bags typify that sentiment. With a pair of pinking shears, craft bags, and paper and ribbon trims, even a modest gift is glamourized. Once you receive compliments on unique gift bags such as these, purchased gift wrap will be a thing of the past.

QUICK & EASY ALTERNATIVES

Option 1

Fill this handsome handled bag with a man's gift, and watch his face light up! Start with a dark-colored bag, like this forest green one. Use pinking shears to trim the top edge. Use a hole punch to add holes 1" (2.5cm) apart and about 1" (2.5cm) down from the top edge. Thread the green-and-beige plaid ribbon through the holes and tie into a bow. Fill the bag with a contrasting tissue, letting it spill out of the top, and add an interesting assortment of masculine toiletries.

Option 2

Fill a white bag dotted with bright red polka dots with matching red tissue, and the gift contents might take second place! White craft bags are easy to find at craft or paper stores and, with the addition of polka dots painted with a sponge dauber and red acrylic paint, this bag couldn't be simpler. Adapt this design using a variety of colors, either changing the shade of the bag or the paint. Be creative, and make the design of the bag coordinate with the gift inside.

Option 3

This clever buttoned envelope is a gift bag for sweets. Select a sturdy bag in a luscious hue, then use pinking shears to trim away the front and both sides 2" (5cm) down from the top, leaving the back panel intact. Fold the back panel over the front. Then cut it to form a pointed flap. Add a large button. Pull a piece of ½"x6" (1.5x15cm) ribbon or fabric strip through button hole, knot, then hot-glue button onto the front of the flap.

Materials You'll Need

- Forest green bag with handle
- Scissors
- Pinking shears
- Corrugated paper
- Craft glue
- Raffia
- Glue gun & glue sticks
- Brass button
- Coordinating tissue paper

1 To prepare the bags, use scissors to carefully remove the craft handles. Discard the handles.

2 Cut the top edge all around the bag ¼" (6mm) from the top, using pinking shears.

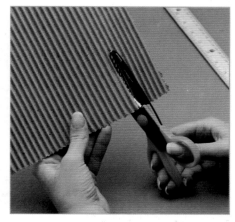

3 Cut small square of corrugated paper to fit bag, approximately 1" (2.5cm) smaller than bag front. Use craft glue to affix paper to front of bag.

4 Tie a length of raffia into a bow and hot-glue it to the top of the corrugated paper.

5 Hot-glue a burnished metal button to the center of the raffia bow.

6 Wrap contents of gift bag in coordinating green-checkered tissue paper, and place in the bag.

Crepe Paper Gift Bags

Goody bags are popular at children's birthday parties, but favor bags can be an unexpected surprise for adult guests attending a shower or dinner party. These beautiful handmade gift bags can hold shower game prizes or any small gift. Colorful crepe paper has a unique, delicate texture, yet is sturdy enough to create the lovely ribbon and flower designs that put the finishing touch on these delightful bags.

QUICK & EASY ALTERNATIVES

Option 1

For festive and fun favors, measure length of small cardboard cylinder and add 6" (15cm). Measure diameter, double this figure, and add 1" (2.5cm). Cut crepe paper to fit with pinking shears. Fold in half. Center cylinder (with gift inside) on paper and roll from one edge to the other, securing overlap with white glue. Cut two pieces of crepe paper 2"x18" (5x25cm). Twist and use crepe paper as ribbons to tie ends of favor. Glue on fancy-cut strips and holes punched from the different colors of paper.

Option 2

Cut colorful crepe paper streamers into strips to fit gift. Fold all strips in half widthwise. Set two strips aside and glue remaining strips to secure fold. Line up the horizontal strips and glue each end to the inside of an unglued strip. Weave strips one at a time. Trim edges and glue inside second unglued strip. Fold in half and glue to form bag. Punch holes in top and thread a crepe paper ribbon through. Tie a bow, and with end of a small paintbrush, dot bow with white paint.

Option 3

For Easter or anytime—cut a circle of yellow and blue crepe paper, each large enough to gather around a plastic cup and form ruffle. Gather up both circles, securing to cup with a rubber band. Trim top ends with scallop scissors. Cut a 2" (5cm)-wide piece of blue paper for ribbon. Fold widthwise and glue ends. Dip pencil eraser in yellow acrylic paint to add dots. Wrap around cup and tie into a bow. Repeat with smaller piece and glue a handle on cup. Fill with candy for party favor.

Materials You'll Need

- Crepe paper, assorted colors
- Scissors
- Ruler
- White glue
- White florist's wire
- Small perfume or nail polish bottle
- Artificial stamens
- Florist's tape

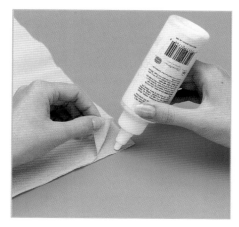

1 Cut a piece of crepe paper into a 14"x12" (35x30cm) rectangle. Fold in half so bag measures 7"x12" (18x30cm) and glue sides together. Place gift in bag.

2 To make ribbon, cut a strip of different colored crepe paper 2"x18" (5x45cm). Fold in half lengthwise and glue edges together. When dry, gather bag at top, tie ribbon around, and form bow.

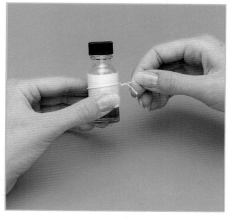

3 Wrap a piece of florist's wire around a small bottle to form a flower petal. Twist ends, leaving one long end for "stem."

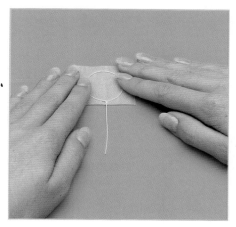

4 Cut squares of crepe paper. Slide wire off bottle and dip one side in white glue, then lay in center of square and dry.

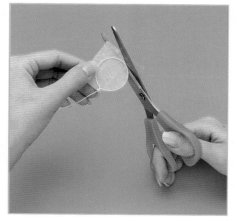

5 Cut excess paper around wire. Repeat Steps 3–5 to create several flower petals.

6 Gather five or six stamens together and arrange petals around them. Tape stamen and petal stems together with florist's tape. Trim stems, then glue flower to bow or slip stem inside.

Handy Canisters for the Golfer

Avid golfers never have enough golf balls, so they will truly appreciate a large canister filled to the brim with these much-needed accessories. With its exterior decorated with colorful, golf-themed papers, there's no mistaking the contents of this container! Make this terrific canister from a potato chip container. As a companion gift, cut down another chip container to one-third its original size to create a handy tee holder.

QUICK & EASY ALTERNATIVES

Option 1

The tennis player on your gift list will appreciate a fresh can of tennis balls wrapped in colorful, polka-dotted paper and tied with a head-band bow. Simply place the canister of balls in the center of a piece of tissue paper, draw the sides up, and secure the paper near the top of the canister with a rubber band. Add a special accent to the wrapping by concealing the rubber band with a terry cloth headband tied into a bow. An elastic wristband could also be used to cleverly wrap this can.

Option 2

New fishing tackle will make the fisherman want to start planning his next trip to the lake or stream. And once the tackle is safely stored in his tackle box, the boat will remind him of your thoughtful-ness. Purchase the little boat at a craft store and brush the sides and bottom with a coat of blue acrylic paint. Locate tackle at a tackle or bait store, then arrange the contents in the boat. As an option, personalize the boat by stenciling it with the name of his real boat!

Option 3

A bona fide do-it-yourself enthusi-ast takes pride in his or her care-fully packaged screws, washers, nuts, bolts, and nails. Surprise one of these meticulous folks with two cleverly labeled jars contain-ing their favorite home-repair accessories. Spray jar lids with metallic paint. Choose the contents for each jar, then glue one item to each of two tags. Spray tags with metallic paint. Fill the jars, then affix an identifying tag to each jar with metallic cord.

Materials You'll Need

- Potato chip container
- Measuring tape
- Wrapping paper
- Scissors
- Craft glue
- Blue, red & yellow ribbons, each a different width
- Golf balls

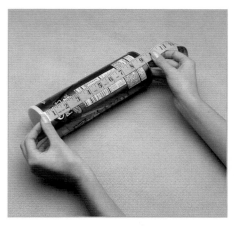

1 Measure the height and circumference of a potato chip can. Add ½" (1.5cm) to the circumference.

2 Cut the golf-themed wrapping paper to fit the measurements of the can.

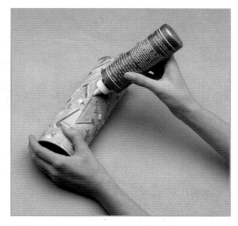

3 Wrap paper around can. Use craft glue to affix paper to side of can, overlapping slightly. Gently smooth down seam with fingers.

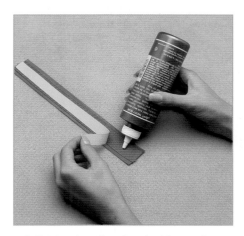

4 Cut two lengths of each ribbon to fit circumference of can, adding ½" (1.5cm) for an overlap. Glue ribbons together with widest ribbon on the bottom.

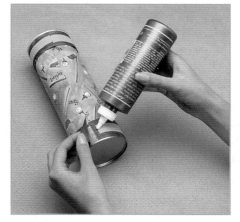

5 Glue assembled ribbon strips onto each end of can, butting up to the rim. Overlap each strip.

6 Let canister cover dry completely, then fill with a selection of favorite golf balls.

Keepsake Gift Box

QUICK & EASY ALTERNATIVES

Option 1

Mother-of-pearl and some wooden and ivory-hued buttons top this gold-painted cardboard box. The result is a small, elegant keepsake container for rings, tiny trinkets, or even more buttons. Paint a 3" (7.5cm) papier mâché heart box with a coat of acrylic metallic silver. Let the paint dry, and then sponge on metallic gold. Load an old toothbrush with black acrylic and flick the paint onto the gold. Hot-glue buttons to the lid, overlapping and stacking them to achieve a pleasing effect.

Option 2

Lovely lilacs are découpaged onto the lid of this round container. Start by painting a 4" (10cm) round papier-mâché box with cream-colored acrylic paint. Let dry. Brush on umber stain, and then rub most of it off to achieve an antiqued effect. Use découpage medium to add lilac flower print. When dry, coat entire lid and bottom with découpage medium. Hot-glue a 1" (2.5cm) wide, green velvet ribbon around the box bottom. Make a 3" (7.5cm) flat bow. Hot-glue bow to cover ribbon seam.

Option 3

Commemorate a special gathering of friends or coworkers with a memento of the event. This plain papier-mâché keepsake box is 4"x4"x2" (10x10x5cm). Cap it with a color copy of a photo of the well-wishers by gluing it to a slightly larger piece of black construction paper. Use a glue stick to affix photo and black paper to box lid. Add four metallic gold photo corners to add shine and interest. This box is so special that everyone in the photo will be requesting one!

M ost people keep the mementos of their life experiences tucked away somewhere. Here are some lovely and useful containers for those bits and pieces too precious to lose. Use a favorite portrait to personalize the lid. Add pieces of decorative trim to suit the individual. Lace, buttons, small charms, and ribbons all add intriguing charm.

Materials You'll Need

- White cookie tin
- Large white doily
- Glue gun & glue sticks
- Wavy-edged scissors
- Color copy of a photo
- Black paper
- Glue stick
- Gold photo corners
- Laces & braids
- Buttons
- Pearl & pearl string

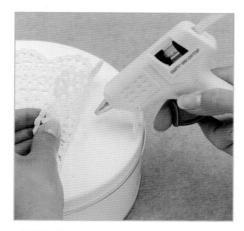

1 Hot-glue a new or antique crocheted doily to the lid. A doily with a scalloped edge works well.

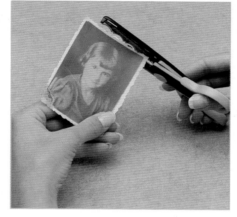

2 Use wavy-edged scissors to cut the photo. Leave a narrow white border. Cut black paper slightly larger than photo.

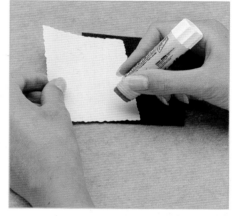

3 Use a glue stick to affix photo to black paper. Add enough glue to ensure sufficient adhesion.

4 Place the gold photo corners on each corner of the black paper. Then glue photograph to tin.

5 Arrange laces and braids and then attach to box with hot glue. Fold a piece of ivory lace into a fan, and glue to lid. Hot-glue buttons and pearls.

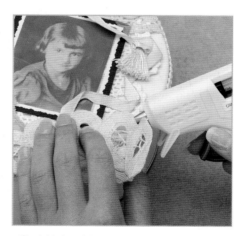

6 Add the ribbons over the top of the trims, weaving in and out around the box. Hot-glue the final piece of lace over the ribbon. Overlap the trims for best effect.

Jasmine Tea

QUICK & EASY ALTERNATIVES

Option 1

Give your daughter a decorative kitchen gift with exotic flavor! Purchase a glass jar with a round, wooden lid. Cover lid with white acrylic paint and let dry. Dip the tip of a paintbrush handle in dark green paint and create a polka-dotted pattern on lid. Set aside to dry. Combine 5 tablespoons loose green tea with 8 tablespoons Moroccan spearmint leaves (or other mint tea). Pour tea in container and replace lid. Tie a length of green satin ribbon around neck of jar and form bow.

Option 2

For one who has trouble falling asleep, this relaxing blend of rose petals, cinnamon sticks, and exotic extras will help her get some rest. Combine 5 tablespoons rose petals, 2 tablespoons jasmine, and 1 cup (230g) green tea. Add 2 cinnamon sticks, 1 mugwort leaf, a small clary sage floret and 1 tablespoon lecithin (found in health food stores). Pour into a glass spice jar and replace lid. Tie a few strands of raffia around neck of jar, forming a bow. Tuck a dried rosebud into the bow.

Option 3

An unusual mix of sweet and spicy flavors creates a delicious brew for an iced tea lover. Combine 5 tablespoons loose, orange pekoe tea, 6 cloves, 3 vanilla beans, 3 sticks cinnamon and 15 to 20 green cardamom pods. Add 3 inch (2.5cm)-long pieces fresh ginger root, 9 tablespoons sugar and 4 to 5 marigold flowers. Pour mixture into glass jar. Tie two pieces of yellow ribbon around neck of jar and form a bow. Glue a dried orange slice in center.

Jasmine means "amiability" in the language of flowers, and a hand-made blend of aromatic jasmine tea is certainly an agreeable gift. Whether sipped hot on a chilly day or iced when the sun is beaming, flavorful tea is the ultimate refreshment for many, and peaceful jasmine offers a calm respite. This jar displays pretty blooms enhancing a tasty mixture to brew and enjoy together.

Materials You'll Need

- Spoon & measuring cup
- Loose tea & small bowl
- Fresh jasmine blossoms (or dried jasmine flowers can be used)
- Lemon & lemon zester
- Computer or pen
- Card stock: white & pink
- Pinking shears
- White glue
- Hole punch
- Ribbon
- Airtight jar

1 Place 1 cup (230g) of loose tea (such as English breakfast or oolong) in a small bowl.

2 Add 1 tablespoon of cleaned, fresh jasmine blossoms to the loose tea.

3 Use a lemon zester to peel small strips from the skin of a fresh lemon. Add 1 tablespoon lemon zest to tea and jasmine mixture.

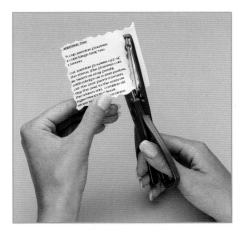

4 Print tea recipe and the following instructions on white card: Add 1 teaspoon of tea to tea ball. Fill cup with boiling water; let tea steep, three to five minutes.

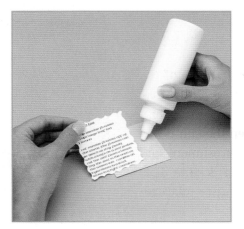

5 Trim card edges with pinking shears. Glue recipe card to pink card stock that is cut ⅛" (3mm) larger. Punch a hole in the corner of card and thread a ribbon through.

6 Put tea mixture in glass jar. Wrap a pink ribbon around jar and tie a bow on the front. Glue a small jasmine blossom to the bow. Tie the recipe card onto the jar.

Bathroom and kitchen projects

When it comes to making homes look beautiful, kitchens and bathrooms are not always given the attention they deserve. Yet these rooms really benefit from a personal touch.

The delightful decorations and accessories shown in this chapter will add a welcome splash of individuality to any-one's kitchen décor and will help turn even the most drab and dreary bathroom into a cozy and intimate retreat.

Summer Shower Curtains

Every day is sunny when it begins with a shower in this summer garden. Colorful flowers stretch tall on slender stalks, spreading petals wide to greet the day. Several sizes of a photocopied flower were arranged as a template to create this pretty scene. A see-through curtain was laid on top and painted using dimensional paint. To bathe behind this cheery curtain is to view the world through its "rose-colored" perspective.

QUICK & EASY ALTERNATIVES

Option 1

Cut pictures of fish from a magazine, or from enlarged computer clip art. Position cut-outs of fish into desired arrangement on a large flat work surface. Tape in place. Lay a clear, vinyl shower curtain over the fish. Using dimensional paint, outline the fish in various colors. Add eyes, fins, stripes, and bubbles. Use a sponge brush to paint simple wide lines at the bottom of the shower curtain to represent seaweed.

Option 2

These flowers will appear to float in your mother's bathroom. Make enlarged copies of pictures of various flowers. Position the copies in the shape of a square on a large, flat work surface. Tape in position. Lay a clear, vinyl shower curtain over the copies. Outline flowers onto the curtain using black dimensional paint. Write the name of each flower in block lettering underneath each flower. Color in flowers using air-dry enamel paint.

Option 3

For a classy curtain, fold a clear, vinyl shower curtain in half lengthwise. Then fold in half again (to divide into fourths). Make a pattern by placing paper on one fold and drawing a triangle about 14" (35cm) long. Place curtain over pattern and follow the outline with gold dimensional paint to simulate a valance. Use brush to paint green and yellow lines for the plaid design. Glue tassels to each point.

Materials You'll Need

- Patterns of a flower enlarged to various sizes
- Surface covering
- Transparent tape
- Clear, vinyl shower curtain
- Dimensional paint: orange, yellow & green
- Plate
- Large sheet of paper
- Pen
- Ruler
- Scissors

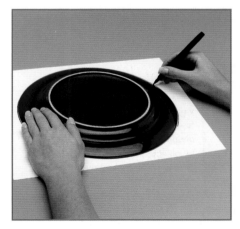

1 Lay pattern of flower on a large work surface and tape flat. Place a clear, vinyl shower curtain over the top of the pattern.

2 Using bright colors of dimensional paint, outline all around the flower pattern.

3 Paint stems and leaves on the flowers with green dimensional paint. Paint blades of grass around the flowers.

4 Add a sun to the top right-hand corner. To create a pattern for the sun design, trace with a pen around a large plate onto paper.

5 For rays of the sun, use a ruler and pen to draw a long slender triangle on paper, then cut out.

6 Arrange the circular pattern under the shower curtain. Outline it in yellow. Outline the triangle in several positions around the sun to represent the rays.

Rope Bathroom Accessories

A well-placed strand of beads can make all the difference to an otherwise Spartan room, but it's not always easy to slip such decorative touches into Dad's territory. This attractive bathroom accessory gains passage through creative interplay of texture: thick wooden beads accent coils of rough rope. The design is shaped on a terra-cotta pot and is attached with hot glue—creating a "strong, silent type" of style!

QUICK & EASY ALTERNATIVES

Option 1

Not only will this soap dish add flair to his bathroom, a ring of rope will remind him that "the soap stops here!" Select a white, oval-shaped, ceramic soap dish. Measure the lip of the dish with rope and cut rope to that length. Using an epoxy kit, mix epoxy according to manufacturer's instructions. Apply epoxy with mixing stick around lip of soap dish. Lay rope on the epoxy and hold firmly in place until epoxy has set according to the package directions.

Option 2

These "treasures of the sea" play off a favorite seaside photo. Purchase a frame with a distressed finish. Position a scallop shell, starfish, and small conch shell in the lower right corner of the frame. Secure with hot glue. Select rope to fit thickness of frame. Cut to fit top and bottom of frame, and glue in place. Cut rope to cover vertical sides of frame, including the ends of rope already in place. Glue rope to sides and tack securely at corners.

Option 3

A young explorer will recognize immediately that this chest is vital to his quest! Purchase a small wooden treasure box decorated in antique-style brass trim. Use rope to measure perimeter of a rounded rectangle around the top of the box. Cut the rope to required length, and use hot glue to secure in place. Measure and cut rope to form a smaller rectangle inside the first and glue in place. Repeat to add two consecutively smaller rectangles.

Materials You'll Need

- Hemp rope
- Pencil or paintbrush
- Glue gun & glue sticks
- Rough-surfaced terra-cotta pot
- Strand of wooden beads
- Scissors

1 Coil a length of hemp rope around a pencil or paintbrush. Allow the rope to remain in this position for a time to prepare it for shaping curves.

2 Place a dab of hot glue onto a terra-cotta pot. Press one end of the rope firmly into the glue. (If desired, roughly draw a penciled line on pot as a guideline.)

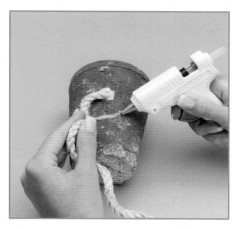

3 Coil the rope loosely into curves against the surface of the pot. As you shape the curves, secure with a line of hot glue underneath the rope. Trim ends.

4 To prevent beads from falling off, remove some beads from the end of the strand and wrap the twine back around the first bead.

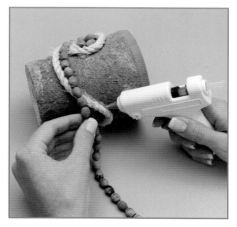

5 Arrange the strand of beads to compliment the curves of the rope. Attach the beads with hot glue. Repeat Step 4 to secure the other end of the beads.

6 When design with rope and bead curves is complete, hot-glue individual beads to fill in the curves of rope.

After-Sun Moisturizer

A lotion bottle is bathed in sponge-painted sunshine as a gift for your favorite sunbather. The swirls and triangles of a stylized sun are stenciled to the sun-drenched backdrop, reaffirming the bottle's "sol" purpose. A therapeutic balm fills the bottle, its fresh tangerine scent rich with summer. Soothing, cooling, aloe vera gel is scented with essential oil, ready at the pump to revitalize parched skin.

QUICK & EASY ALTERNATIVES

Option 1

This gentle treatment will leave skin feeling fresh and rejuvenated. Machine-stitch trim to a facecloth. Dab pepper-mint essential oil on the cloth. Roll the facecloth to fit a small basket and place inside. Cut a square of card stock, and punch a hole in the corner. Using a fine-tipped marker, write: "Moisten with cool water and apply after exposure to the sun." Thread ribbon through tag and tie to handle of basket.

Option 2

When your best friend spends her days in the sun attentively cheering the soccer team, her skin will appreciate this attention in the evening. Apply rub-on decals to a glass jar with lid. Combine 1 cup (230g) each baking soda and cornstarch in a bowl. Add several drops of a favorite essential oil, sift well, and add to the jar. Shape card stock into a tag. Add a decal to center and a border drawn with colored marker. Write recipe inside tag and title it "Soothing After-Sun Powder."

Option 3

A "steep" in a bath of tea will do wonders for her sunburn. Purchase a fancy sachet pouch as a gift container. Attach satin roses with hot glue to the front of the pouch. Cut small squares of muslin and machine-stitch them closed on three sides. Fill the muslin pouches with loose black tea, then tie a 12" (30cm) piece of string around bag to close. Fill fabric pouch with several tea bags. Attach gift tag with instructions: "To ease sunburn, tie a tea bag to faucet with string so running water flows over it."

Materials You'll Need

- Small sea sponge
- Glass paint: yellow, orange & red
- Lotion dispenser bottle
- Manila tag
- Sun stencil
- Small glass bowl
- Spoon
- Aloe vera gel
- Tangerine essential oil
- Funnel
- Fine-tipped marker
- Orange-&-red plaid ribbon

1 Using a small sponge and yellow glass paint, cover a lotion dispenser bottle and a manila tag.

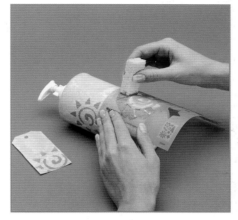

2 When paint has dried, stencil a sun in orange in two places on the bottle. Stencil the corner of the tag with a partial sun.

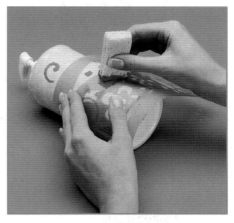

3 Using red glass paint and a sponge, stencil swirls and triangles randomly over the dispenser.

4 In a small glass bowl, mix aloe vera gel with drops of tangerine essential oil. Use a funnel to pour the mixture into the dispenser.

5 Write "Aloe Vera After-Sun Gel" on the front of the tag. Add the recipe to back: In a bowl, mix 16 oz. (450g) aloe vera gel and 2 or 3 drops tangerine essential oil. Use funnel to pour into dispenser.

6 Thread the tag with orange-and-red plaid ribbon, and tie it to the top of the dispenser.

Decorated Wash Mitt

A decorated wash mitt is a wonderfully unique gift to add to any bathroom decor. Use children's handprints to create an entire theme for their bathroom and make a fun family project at the same time! Customizing the colors and embellishments allows for personalization in a wide range of colors and themes.

QUICK & EASY ALTERNATIVES

Option 1

Here's a gift your son is sure to use and appreciate. Cut two pieces of a washcloth to 6"x10" (15x25cm), leaving selvages (finished edge) on the 6" (15cm) edge. On one piece of the washcloth, stitch a wide, coordinating grosgrain ribbon just above the selvage. Place the two pieces with right sides together, and machine-stitch along three sides to form a mitt, leaving the selvage end open. Clip seams of the mitt and turn right-side out. Enclose a bar of favorite soap in the mitt.

Option 2

Make a bath mitt that will appeal to the teen in your life. Bold checks or stripes will compliment his or her style. Cut checked or striped washcloths to two 6"x10" (15x25cm) pieces. Leave the webbed and finished edge on one piece and finished edge on the other piece, both on the 6" (15cm) side. Stitch matching ribbon across the bottom of webbed selvage side. With right sides together, pin and machine-stitch three sides to create mitt. Leave selvage edge open. Clip seams and turn right-side out.

Option 3

Pretty toile fabric makes this washcloth a favorite with Mom. The toile print is reminiscent of a more relaxed and elegant time and will make Mom feel so special when she uses it. Cut heavy toile fabric to 6"x10" (15x25cm). On the 6"(15cm) edge turn over ¼" (6mm) and then ¼" (6mm) again. Cut coordinating washcloth to 6"x10" (15x25cm). Put right side of toile to right side of washcloth and pin. Stitch together on three sides, leaving hemmed edge open.

Materials You'll Need

- Scissors
- Two short-pile white washcloths
- Ruler
- Blue fabric paint
- Sponge brush
- Pins
- Sewing machine
- Needle & thread
- Yellow ribbon
- Daisy appliqués

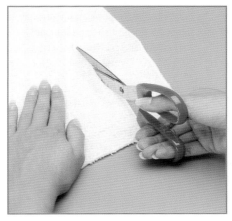

1 Cut washcloths into two 6"x10" (15x25cm) pieces leaving the webbed and finished edge intact on one 6" (15cm) side.

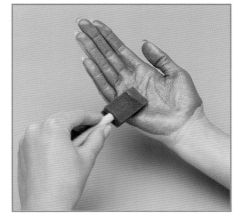

2 On one of the washcloth pieces, make a handprint by painting a thick coat of fabric paint onto palm.

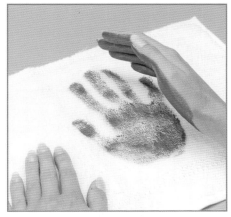

3 Imprint firmly on washcloth. Allow to dry. Place right sides of the washcloths together and pin three sides, leaving the finished sides open.

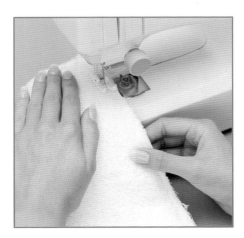

4 Using a sewing machine, stitch three sides to form a mitt, leaving finished edge open.

5 With a sponge brush and the same paint, fill in any areas that were not covered previously. Follow manufacturer's instructions to permanently set paint.

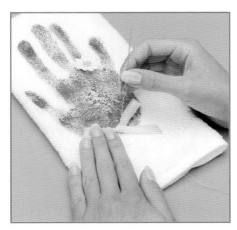

6 Using a needle and thread, stitch on a pretty bow of yellow ribbon and the daisy appliqué onto the ring finger.

Hand Cream for an Aunt

A boxed bottle of fragrant hand cream becomes an unforgettable gift for an aunt: The gift is wrapped in a handwritten letter. Words of respect and admiration are priceless, and the stationery, embellished with lovely dried flowers and pretty ribbon makes a beautiful presentation. There's no need to buy an expensive birthday present for your aunt when the gift wrap is this special.

QUICK & EASY ALTERNATIVES

Option 1

Your sister will love this gift box. Trace lid of papier-mâché box on the wrong side of handmade paper. Measure lid depth and add 1" (2.5cm) to the measurement. Tear paper for a ragged edge. Spray adhesive on wrong side of paper and place lid top down on center. Clip longer edges of paper ⅛" (3mm) in from corners and fold edges up and around. Fill box with excelsior and a bottle of essential oil. Tie with raffia and tuck in two stems of lavender.

Option 2

Let her bathe in the aroma of delicious herbal tea. Cut a sheet of lightweight interfacing and a sheet of rice paper to 5"x11" (13x27.5cm). Place interfacing on rice paper and fold in half. Stitch a ¼" (6mm) seam on each side, leaving top open. Turn inside out, spoon blend of herbs and herbal tea into bag, and sew top closed with ¼" (6mm) seam. Fold top down 1" (2.5cm) to form a flap. Punch two holes 1" (2.5cm) apart through flap and bag. Thread ribbon through holes and tie into a bow.

Option 3

Soap wrapped in paper embossed with your daughter's initial will add an elegant touch to her powder room. Use a ruler to tear medium-weight drawing paper into strips long enough to go around the individual soaps. With a light table, stylus (available at craft or art supply stores), and an embossing stencil, emboss her initial into each strip of paper. Wrap the paper strip around each soap, tearing ends and adhering them together with craft glue. Place soaps in a basket.

166

Materials You'll Need

- Pen with dark ink
- 8½"x11" (22x27.5cm) sheet of stationery with border
- Boxed hand cream
- Spray adhesive
- Scissors
- Craft glue
- Ribbon
- Dried flowers

1 With pen, and in your best handwriting, write a loving letter to your aunt or other gift recipient on pretty bordered stationery.

2 Remove hand cream from small rectangular box. Carefully unfold box so it is completely flat and spray the exterior with adhesive.

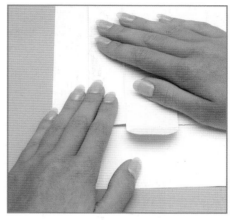

3 Press the sticky side of the flattened box to the middle of the wrong side of your letter. Smooth with your fingertips to ensure adhesion.

4 Use scissors to trim excess stationery, so that your letter becomes the exact shape of the box.

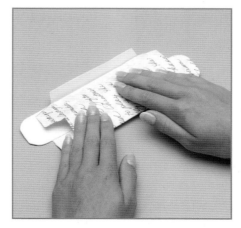

5 Refold the box along fold lines until original shape is formed. Long edge and one end of box will remain open.

6 Secure the long edges of the box together using craft glue. When dry, insert hand cream in box. Tie a ribbon bow and add dried flowers.

Luxurious Shaving Soap

There's something romantic about the vintage method of shaving—using an old-fashioned bar of shaving soap and a brush. A soft-bristle shaving brush dipped in water whips up mounds of luxurious foam. Present a rustically wrapped bar of shaving soap with a brush in a mug and give it to your husband as a gift. Pamper him with this original gift for a birthday or Father's Day.

QUICK & EASY ALTERNATIVES

Option 1

What could be more soothing and relaxing than a back scrubber for the bath? Present a wooden back scrubber to a special family member. Tightly roll up a plush facecloth. Secure roll with a rubber band. Tie secured facecloth onto the scrubber handle using wire-edged ribbon. Tie on ribbon so it covers up rubber band. Place a few sprigs of aromatic lavender underneath the ribbon knot. Attach a note wishing the recipient a relaxing day.

Option 2

You'll have as much fun hunting for body care products as you will in giving this gift to a loved one. Visit a bath and body store and purchase a loofah bath mitt as well as several other bath care products. Choose items such as body gels, a nail brush, pumice stone, polishing lotion, or a jasmine-scented body lotion. Fill the mitt with all the bath items. Enclose a card and place in mitt. While you're making the selections, add a few items for yourself!

Option 3

Turn a silver-plated mint julep cup into a soap-filled container for the bath. If you don't have a mint julep cup, use a silver cup purchased at an antique shop or flea market. Place a bit of crumpled tissue paper in the bottom of the cup. Fill the cup with an assortment of small scented soaps (available at bath and body shops). Add a sprig of fresh mint to the cup for a fragrant and cooling touch. Present the cup of soaps with a card containing a greeting and a recipe for relaxation.

Materials You'll Need

- Bar of shaving soap
- Handmade paper
- Raffia
- Distinctive mug
- Spray adhesive
- Card stock
- Scissors
- Hole punch
- Shaving brush

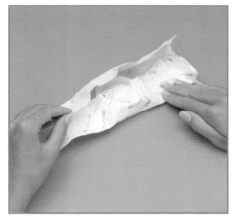

1 Wrap the bar of shaving soap in a large square of interesting handmade paper.

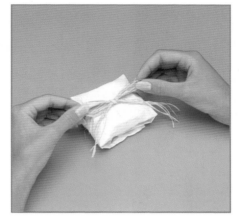

2 Secure the gift by wrapping with strands of raffia and tying into a bow. Place wrapped soap in the mug.

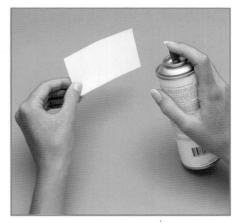

3 Spray one side of the card stock with spray adhesive for the gift tag. Press the sprayed side to a piece of handmade paper trimmed the same size as the gift tag.

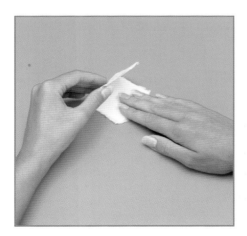

4 When the glue has dried, fold the card in half. Crease the fold with your fingertips.

5 Using the hole punch, punch a hole in upper corner (when card is folded) of the gift tag.

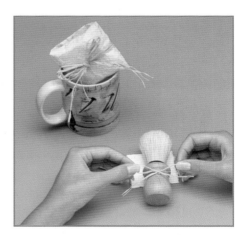

6 Thread raffia through the card and tie to the shaving brush. Place in mug.

Decorative Bottle of Aftershave

A custom-designed container filled with a favorite aftershave will surely please the man in your life. This handsome bottle—adorned with colorful cord, a homemade label, and the stylish addition of a bay leaf—is the perfect gift for a man's birthday, Father's Day, Valentine's Day, anniversary, or Christmas. Take his aftershave to new heights with this elegant container he'll be proud to keep on display.

QUICK & EASY ALTERNATIVES

Option 1

This bath crate is a great complement to any bathroom, whether it be a country or beach motif. In keeping with the rustic nature of the crate, tear fabric to create rough, torn edges, which add character. The fabric will serve as the bedding to protect the items in the crate. Add a loofah, pumice stone, and bath sponge, all available at most specialty bath stores. Make a gift tag from handmade paper and tie to the crate with strands of raffia.

Option 2

Nothing is as nice as a long soak in the tub after a hard workday. You can contribute to this relaxing activity by making some scented soaking salts. In a bowl, add a few drops of a scented oil to ½ cup (110g) Epsom salts. Write fragrance name on adhesive label and press onto a glass jar. Spoon scented salts into jar. Cut a square of gauze fabric a bit larger than jar. Stretch fabric over jar and hold in place with a rubber band. Tie twine around the gauze, then remove the rubber band.

Option 3

Pamper a man by giving him his own scented soaps, available at most specialty bath or gift shops. Tear shirting fabric into squares that are slightly larger than the bars of soap. Wrap each bar in a fabric square. Using natural twine, secure each soap package and then tie into a rough bow on the front. Use a piece of shirting fabric to line the basket. Place the wrapped soaps into the basket and, if desired, tie a gift tag to the basket handle.

Materials You'll Need

- Decorative glass bottle with cork
- Purchased aftershave
- Funnel
- Melted paraffin
- Small container
- Square of gingham paper
- Craft glue
- Calligraphy pen
- Handmade paper
- Bay leaf
- Glue gun & glue sticks
- Cord

1 Purchase a favorite aftershave and pour it into a new container using a funnel.

2 Cork the bottle and then seal the cork by dipping it in melted paraffin.

3 Affix the square of gingham paper to the front of the bottle using craft glue.

4 Write "Aftershave" on a square of hand-made paper with a calligraphy pen. Glue label to the gingham paper.

5 Using a hot-glue gun, affix the bay leaf to the upper left-hand corner of the label.

6 Wrap the blue cord around the neck of the bottle, knot the ends, and slightly fringe them.

Colorful Homemade Soaps

What a wonderful treat for the entire family! In sparkling jewel-like tones or soft, muted pastels, these colorful hand-made soaps are both fragrant and useful. Be creative when making these soaps. Add a marbleizing effect, or simply color them to match a bathroom color scheme. Mound them in a clear glass bowl, or present them wrapped individually. This project is so easy you'll want to make some for yourself.

QUICK & EASY ALTERNATIVES

Option 1

Handmade paper sprinkled with rose petals adds a distinctive touch. Measure the circumference of the soap, and then cut the paper. Tear the long edges of the paper about 1" (2.5cm) shorter than the length of the soap. A torn edge gives a more handcrafted appearance. Wrap the paper around the soap and glue it in the back. Tie a soft silk ribbon around the soap, then tie it into a bow. Tuck in a single dried rosebud. Glue rosebud to secure firmly in place.

Option 2

Beautiful paper, glistening wire, and handsome beads make this wrapped soap special. Trace the soap shape on a small piece of hand-made paper or tissue. Add 2" (5cm) all around, then cut paper. Wrap paper around the soap as you would a small gift. Wrap wire around soap in random design, adding beads at each intersection, as desired. A suitable gift for a man or a woman, you can vary the paper, wire, and bead colors to suit the recipient.

Option 3

Cut a piece of corrugated paper to fit the soap. Punch a hole at each edge with a hole punch. Weave ribbon through holes, then tie or glue to back of soap. Light sealing wax and drip it on the center of the corrugated paper. Then use an alphabet seal to personalize this handcrafted gift. Seals are available in many styles and designs, and this very sophisticated wrapped soap package can be embellished in a number of creative ways to add even more panache!

Materials You'll Need

- Soap molds (or use milk cartons or small cans)
- Spray vegetable oil
- Glycerine soap (unscented, clear)
- Chopping block
- Knife
- Measuring cup
- Microwave oven
- Soap coloring
- Toothpicks

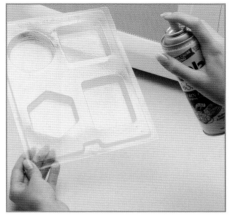

1 Lightly spray mold with unflavored vegetable oil, spraying about 6" (15cm) away from the mold.

2 Using a sharp knife, cut the glycerine into small cubes to approximately 1" (2.5cm) square.

3 Place cubes in a measuring cup and heat in a microwave oven on high until glycerine is melted. This usually takes about one minute. (Microwave ovens may vary.)

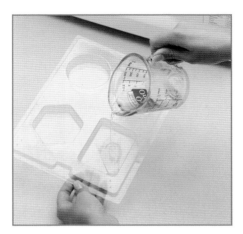

4 Using a potholder, pour the melted glycerine into the mold, milk carton, or tin.

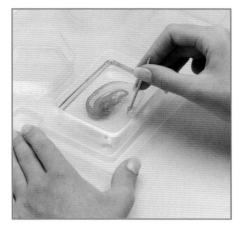

5 Swirl one drop of soap coloring in center of mold with a toothpick for marbleized effect. Let soap cool 30 minutes.

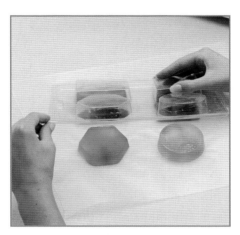

6 Turn mold onto waxed paper to release soap. For milk carton mold, cut sides to release soap. For tin can mold, cut bottom with opener and push soap out.

Herbed Butter

There are times when your family members are so happy to be getting together, the hostess will insist that the only thing to bring along is yourself. This is often when your desire to show your love and appreciation is at its strongest. The solution to such a dilemma is found in an elegantly simple offering of irresistible rosemary, chive, and garlic butter wrapped in parchment and rolled in a pretty reed mat.

QUICK & EASY ALTERNATIVES

Option 1

Your little gift of honey butter will positively glow on the table with all the warmth and sweetness of thoughtful giving. Long after the last scone has been buttered, she will cherish the lovely antique sugar bowl. Soften ½ lb. (225g) of butter (two sticks) to room temperature. When soft, stir in 1 tablespoon of honey and mix well. Spoon mixture into small pot and add a fancy spoon. Find a coordinating ribbon and tie it to the handle of the pot. Keep refrigerated.

Option 2

Your family will marvel that you've "done it again!" when you present this delightful contribution at a family potluck. Soften ½ lb. (225g) butter to room temperature. Spoon onto a parchment-lined plate and chill until firm. Using your hands, shape each spoonful into a ball, then roll each into chopped chives. Re-chill on plate before placing balls carefully in jar. Add a ribbon and flowering chive as garnish. Keep refrigerated.

Option 3

For those occasions when you'd like to bring along a little something, consider a specialty butter log seasoned with herbs. It's easy to prepare and is a simple way to add love and flavor to any family meal. Soften butter in bowl. Stir in chopped tarragon and parsley to taste. Transfer to parchment paper and roll into log. Twist ends, tie with raffia, and cut edges with scallop-edged scissors. Add a gift tag. Keep refrigerated.

Materials You'll Need

- ½ lb. (225g) butter
- Mixing bowl
- Knife
- Cutting board
- Garlic

- Rosemary
- Flowering chives
- Spoon
- Parchment paper
- Raffia

- Reed mat (available at Asian markets)
- Kraft paper
- Double-sided tape

1 Set butter in mixing bowl to soften. Chop herbs and garlic, reserving a sprig of rosemary for garnish, and stir into butter.

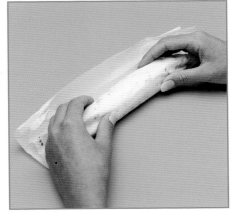

2 Spoon butter onto parchment paper and roll into log the same length as the rolled-up reed mat. Put butter log in freezer to firm.

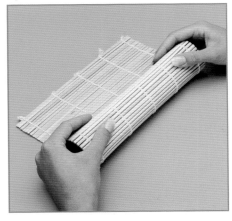

3 When butter mixture has chilled and holds its shape, roll it up in the reed mat.

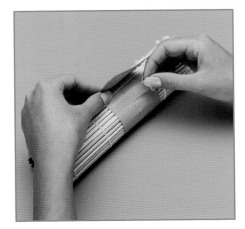

4 Wrap a 3"x 6" (7.5x15cm) strip of kraft paper around center of mat. Secure with double-sided tape.

5 Secure rolled mat and paper with length of raffia and fashion an attractive bow.

6 Slip the reserved sprig of rosemary between the bow and the paper to garnish the gift. Keep refrigerated.

Silverware Caddy

The hostess of an informal dinner party will appreciate your thoughtfulness when you present her with this sunny plaid silverware caddy. Not only will the caddy keep all the dinner utensils and napkins organized, but the colorful design will decorate the tables as well. The blue plaid design is achieved using a textured sponge roller and the bright yellow dots are created with a pencil eraser. Tuck in some flowers to finish this handy gift.

QUICK & EASY ALTERNATIVES

Option 1

A long, narrow wooden box is the perfect container for a tableware caddy to use during a family brunch. Add the fruits along the bottom edge of the caddy, using yellow acrylic paint, a stencil with a citrus design, and a stencil brush. Use sunny yellow organza ribbon to accent the upper edge of the box. Tie the ribbon in a pretty bow on the front. Tie the same ribbon around matching napkins, plates, and tableware, and add to the caddy.

Option 2

The bottom half of a shallow, square papier-mâché box can become a wonderful napkin holder for a patio barbecue. Affix a miniature picket fence around the outside of the box using hot glue. Paint the inside of tiny flowerpots brown and glue miniature carrots into each one. Glue pots to front of fence along with a miniature watering can. Add napkins and tie a ribbon around the box to secure them. Decorate with a tiny bunch of carrots.

Option 3

Bring adventure to a youngster's birthday party by using a small painted wooden wagon as the tableware caddy. Find the wagon at a craft store and, if needed, paint the rails red using a sponge brush and red acrylic paint. Let the wagon dry thoroughly. Then assemble the plates, napkins, and forks in the wagon. Keeping with the red theme, use red plates and a red-checkered tablecloth for an extra-special party decoration.

Materials You'll Need

- Sponge brush
- Acrylic paint: white, blue, & yellow
- Wooden carpenter's tote
- Sponge rollers with three stripes
- Pencil
- Silverware, napkins, & plates
- Flowers

1 Use a sponge brush and white acrylic paint to cover the carpenter's tote. Two coats may be necessary. Let dry.

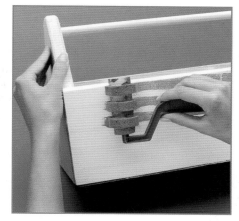

2 Roll on blue lines laterally, using the stripe sponge roller and blue acrylic paint. Allow to dry thoroughly.

3 Repeat Step 2, this time rolling on the lines vertically, creating the plaid pattern.

4 Make yellow dots in between the lines by using the eraser end of a pencil dipped in paint.

5 Roll the tableware in blue cloth napkins to form individual utensil place settings.

6 Insert the tableware, the plates, and the flowers into the plaid painted caddy.

Painted Tiles

D oes your daughter love the look of faux-finished walls and natural, stone surfaces? Created with matching squares of ceramic floor tile, this simple wall art will fit right in with her decor. Using earth-toned paint and an antiquing glaze, the center tile is stamped with a pretty, fleur-de-lis design and edged with a sponge. Accenting her beautiful painted wall, this textured piece is perfectly at home.

QUICK & EASY ALTERNATIVES

Option 1

This sophisticated faux-finished frame is a perfect way to set off a pretty tile! Create a work of art to help decorate a loved one's new home. Spray an unfinished shadow-box frame with primer. Allow to dry. Brush light tan, acrylic paint on frame and let dry. Dampen a sponge and apply light green glaze, followed by a light application of black glaze. Let frame dry completely. Use industrial-strength glue to affix purchased, painted tile inside the frame.

Option 2

Your friend of family member gets a new photo and a distinctive home accent! Select a 6" (15cm) square tile with a painted border design. Make a color copy of a photograph. Cut image to fit in bordered center of tile. Using découpage medium and a sponge brush, affix photo onto a piece of colored lightweight paper, matching tile paint. Cut around photo, leaving a small border of paper. Affix paper in center of tile using more découpage medium. Present tile on a table easel or affix hangers on back.

Option 3

A book lover will appreciate the gift of unique bookends for his or her library. Purchase a set of acrylic book stands and select two identical 6"x6" (15x15cm) tiles painted with an attractive design (available in home improvement stores). Select an acrylic paint that matches one of the colors of the tile. Use a paintbrush to cover the outer edge of the tiles with paint, creating a finished look. Let dry. With industrial-strength glue, affix a tile to the outside of each bookend.

Materials You'll Need

- Paintbrushes: medium & small
- Tan acrylic paint
- Foam fleur-de-lis stamp

- 6"x6" (15x15cm) floor or counter tile
- Antique-white glaze
- Small piece of sponge

- Paper towel
- 12"x12" (30x30cm) floor tile
- Industrial-strength glue
- Mirror hangers

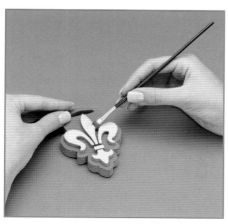

1 Using a medium artist's brush, apply tan acrylic paint to a foam stamp with a fleur-de-lis or other simple design.

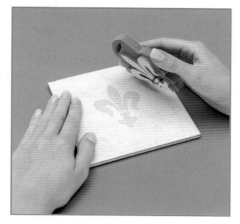

2 Stamp the fleur-de-lis design in the center of a 6" (15cm) square, ivory, textured tile.

3 Fill in any area of design that did not stamp evenly by painting with artist's brush. Let dry.

4 Using a small brush, highlight center areas of design with antique-white glaze. Let dry.

5 Dampen sponge piece with water, then dip it into tan paint. Dab sponge onto a paper towel to blot excess paint. Sponge-paint edges of tile, then allow to dry.

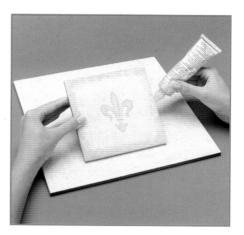

6 Center painted tile on a matching 12" (30cm) square tile. Affix with industrial-strength glue. Use mirror hangers to hang tile.

Découpaged Napkin Plates

Sometimes you come across a thing that is just too pretty to use for its intended purpose. Why settle for a brief encounter with the loveliest blend of colors and the most sumptuous of styling? With some découpage and good old-fashioned initiative, a gorgeous paper napkin is easily transformed into a lasting work of art. Meet the newest family heirloom…a tribute to tenacious ingenuity!

QUICK & EASY ALTERNATIVES

Option 1

This pretty plaid fruit plate will cheer up her kitchen. Select paper cocktail napkins in four pastel shades. Open napkins and press with a warm iron. Separate the two layers of each napkin. Paint the back of a square, clear glass plate with découpage medium. Place one color of the napkins onto each corner of the plate and overlap the others to create a plaid effect. Cover plate with two coats of découpage medium. Trim the excess edges.

Option 2

Set Sis up with this fancy dinner ensemble. Cut a floral napkin to fit center of a clear glass salad plate. Paint back center of plate with découpage medium and apply round napkin piece. Brush on another coat of medium and apply a solid paper napkin over the top. Trim edges, then apply another coat or two of medium. Découpage a matching printed napkin to the back of a clear glass dinner plate. Repeat to make a set of four.

Option 3

This fancy plate looks fabulous. Use a warm iron to press five coordinating colors and patterns of paper napkins. Paint the back of a clear glass plate with découpage medium. Lay pieces of narrow ribbon diagonally across the plate, spacing them in equal intervals. Cut the napkins into strips to fill the area between the ribbons. Lay strips one at a time, applying medium to each strip. Apply additional coats of medium. Trim edges.

Materials You'll Need

- Two printed paper napkins with scalloped edges
- Iron & ironing board
- Paper napkin in coordinating print
- Scissors or craft knife
- Clear glass plate
- Découpage medium
- Sponge brush

1 Use a warm iron to press the creases from two scallop-edged, printed paper napkins and a paper napkin in a coordinating print.

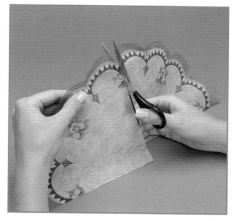

2 Cut one of the scalloped napkins into quarters, and cut the second scalloped napkin in half.

3 Use a sponge brush to apply découpage medium to the back of a clear glass plate.

4 Smooth napkins facedown into the wet medium, overlapping them into a pleasing design. Apply découpage medium carefully over the top of the napkins.

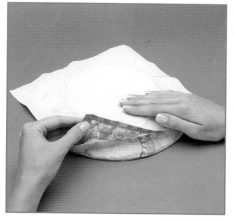

5 Place the napkin with the print face-down over the scalloped layers while the previous coat of medium is still wet. Smooth the napkin down with your fingertips.

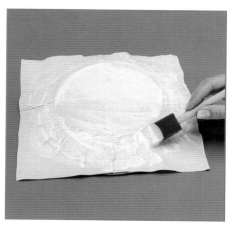

6 Apply two more coats of découpage medium to back of the plate. Let dry completely, then trim excess paper using scissors or a craft knife.

Clever Coasters

W hen the "Gone fishing" sign is removed from the door, Granddad will find great solace in these cheery coasters. They set just the right tone for his latest version of "the one that got away"—three fish caught in a single haul. Reeled through a sea of blue fabric, each fish at the end of the fishing line is a magnificent specimen. Fusible webbing is used to join the layers of fabric for Granddad's "fabric"-ation.

QUICK & EASY ALTERNATIVES

Option 1

A set of ladybug coasters makes a perfect springtime gift. To make a set of four coasters, cut the background fabrics, following Step 1 on opposite page. Follow Steps 2-6 to construct coasters. To create the ladybug designs, iron fusible webbing to back of red and black fabric. Cut both fabrics in the same-size circles. Cut red fabric in half for wings. Peel off backing paper and iron on pieces (as shown) onto the coaster. Draw dots on wings using a black marker.

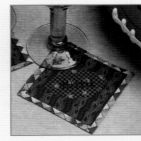

Option 2

Score points with Dad with these cool U.S. football coasters. He'll love using them as he watches the big game. To make a set of four coasters, cut background fabrics as in Step 1 on opposite page. Then follow Steps 2-6 to construct the coasters. Iron fusible webbing to back of brown print fabric. Cut the fabric in the shape of a football. Peel off the backing paper and iron the football onto the coaster. Draw on the black lacing of football using a felt marker.

Option 3

Design these tulips for your guests' juleps! What better way to entertain them during a Sunday afternoon sports event? To make a set of these four floral coasters, cut the fabric as instructed in Step 1 on the opposite page. Follow Steps 2-6 to construct the coasters. For the tulip designs, iron fusible webbing to the various print fabrics used for the flowers and the stems. Cut out the tulips and stems; peel off backing paper. Iron the three tulips onto the coasters.

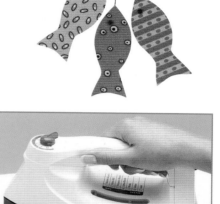

Materials You'll Need

- ¼ yd. (23cm) background fabric
- Scissors
- 1 yd. (91cm) fusible webbing
- Iron
- ¼ yd. (23cm) coordinating fabric
- Scraps of three different fabrics for fish
- Fish pattern
- Fine-tipped black marker

1 Measure eight 4" (10cm) squares on the fabric selected as the background fabric. Cut out the squares.

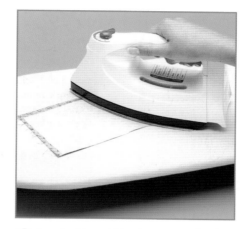

2 Iron fusible webbing to wrong side of four squares, following manufacturer's directions.

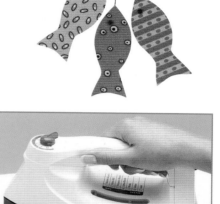

3 Peel the backing paper off the squares. Place the squares, adhesive-side down, onto the wrong side of the other squares of fabric. Iron fabric together.

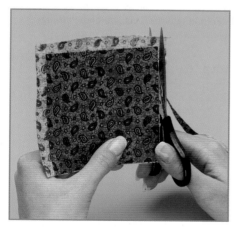

4 Trim any excess fabric from around the 4" (10cm) square. Repeat Steps 3 and 4 for each 4" square.

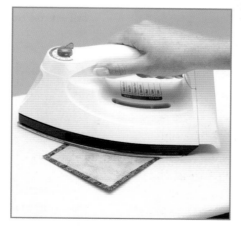

5 Iron fusible webbing to the wrong side of a coordinating fabric. Measure and cut four 3" (7.5cm) squares and iron these to the top center of the 4" (10cm) squares.

6 Iron fusible webbing to three different print fabrics. Cut four fish shapes from each color of fabric. Iron to the coasters. Add fishing line and eyes with black marker.

Painted Frosted Glassware

P resent your sister with this delightful, hand-painted serving ensemble. The gift is served to her with the same picturesque charm as the tray of lemonade she'll serve to thirsty summertime guests. A set of frosty glasses is arranged on a serving tray alongside a crisp napkin. Twin cherries dance on the tumblers, painted from a pattern once taped inside the glass. The cherry design is so cheery, you'll want to paint the linens to match.

QUICK & EASY ALTERNATIVES

Option 1

Frosted glass lends a taste-tempting "chill" to these berries. Make several photocopies of a picture of a strawberry. Cut out the copies and tape them in an attractive arrangement to the inside of a frosted bowl. With the copies as a guide, paint the strawberries on outside of bowl using red glass paint. Paint the stems and leaves with green glass paint. Dip a toothpick into black glass paint and dot "seeds" onto the berries. Repeat same process on the second bowl.

Option 2

The thrill we experience at the sight of a hot fudge sundae is captured in the enthusiastic design on these sundae dishes. Perky polka dots seem to tap out the exquisite anticipation of that first mouthful. A scattering of boldly painted stars explodes with the thrilling sensation of cold, sweet taste. Paint the wavy rim of a frosted dish with dots of red using the end of a small paintbrush. Or use red dimensional paint to add the dots. Paint simple free-hand stars onto the body of the dish using a small brush or fine-tipped dimensional paint.

Option 3

This pretty plate is a natural for serving, what else…watermelon! It's a perfect summertime gift. Invert a frosted glass plate onto a paper-lined work surface. Paint a ring of "seeds" in the center of the plate with black glass paint. Paint the outer edge of the plate in dark green and paint 1" (2.5cm) border inside the edge with light green glass paint. When the other colors of paint have dried, paint the center of the plate red, over the seeds and up to light green edge.

Materials You'll Need

- Photocopied picture or drawing of cherries
- Scissors
- Transparent tape
- Tall, frosted glasses
- Dauber sponges
- Glass paint: red & green
- Small paintbrush
- White linen napkins
- Fabric paint: red & green
- Serving tray

1 Photocopy or draw a picture of cherries. Cut out and tape to the inside of a tall frosted glass.

2 Dip a dauber sponge into red glass paint. Paint cherries onto the glass using the taped picture as a guide.

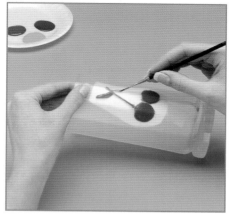

3 Using a small paintbrush, paint the stems and leaves of the cherries with green glass paint.

4 Using a second dauber sponge and red fabric paint, add cherries on each corner of a white napkin. Repeat the design on the desired amount of napkins.

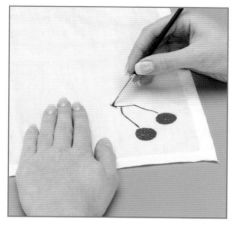

5 Paint leaves and stems of the cherries with green fabric paint onto the napkin.

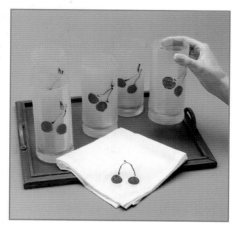

6 When the paint has dried, arrange glasses on the tray with the painted napkins.

Themed Candle Jars

If your mother's a legendary cook, she has likely made her share of tempting, homemade fruit jams and compotes. This unique, decorative gift pays tribute to her blue-ribbon efforts and adds "freshly canned" charm to her warm, country kitchen. Faux strawberries and cherries are "gelled" inside a canning jar, with a tie-on gift tag adding authentic flavor. Topped with a floating candle, this aromatic gift is useful, too.

QUICK & EASY ALTERNATIVES

Option 1

Here's a creative way to pay tribute to Dad's favorite pastime. Select a tall, glass cylinder or vase, an assortment of golf balls, multi-colored golf tees, and a floating candle. Fill the cylinder with the golf tees and balls, stopping 1" (2.5cm) to 2" (5cm) from the top edge. Intersperse so balls are spaced among the tees for the length of the vase. Use a skewer or long knife to arrange the golf items. Add water and 1 tablespoon of bleach, filling until items are completely submerged, then place candle on top.

Option 2

When the family beach lover finally fulfills her dream to live near the seashore, here's a great apartment or house-warming gift idea to help her celebrate. Select a large round glass container, an assortment of pretty seashells, and three floating candles. Fill the clear container to 1" (2.5cm) to 2" (5cm) from top edge with shells, arranging according to type, size, and shape. Pour water into the container until there's more than enough to submerge the shells. Arrange three floating candles on top.

Option 3

Help fulfill your daughter's aspirations for a home filled with beauty and light. Inexpensive and so easy to put together, this creative home accent gift will impress all who encounter it. Select white silk flowers with leaves along with ivy leaves for a lush, green look. Fill a clear glass vase to about 1" (2.5cm) or 2" (5cm) from top rim with the flowers and leaves. Arrange the flowers using a skewer. Pour water into vase completely covering flowers and leaves, then place a white floating candle on top.

Materials You'll Need

- Gel candle base
- Canning jar
- Plastic fruit
- Skewer
- Fancy-edged scissors
- Card stock, white
- Stamp ink pad
- Rubber stamp with jar design
- Hole punch
- Checkered ribbon
- Water
- Floating candle

1 Add some gel candle base to canning jar, filling it ½" (1.5cm) from bottom. Place plastic strawberries or chosen fruits in jar, using a skewer to push pieces into gel.

2 Add more gel to cover fruit and continue layering fruit and gel until you reach spot about 2" (5cm) from top of jar.

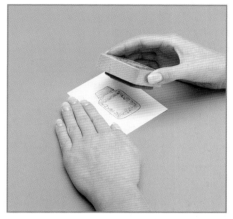

3 Cut a square of card stock for a tag. Use a stamp ink pad and rubber stamp with a jar design to decorate. If desired, personalize the label using recipient's name.

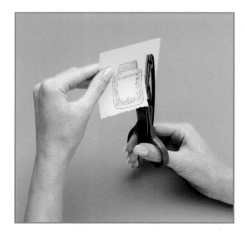

4 Cut around edge of tag with fancy-edged scissors. Punch a hole in upper corner.

5 Cut a length of ribbon and thread through hole. Tie ribbon and tag around rim of jar, forming a pretty bow.

6 Replace jar lid, leaving out center piece. Place floating candle on top.

Painted Plates for the Family Dining Table

Today's popular home furnishings stores carry a variety of hand-painted glass and ceramic dinnerware items. Since hand-decorated plates tend to be somewhat costly, an option to consider is purchasing plain ones to paint yourself. The plate and drinking glass shown here were decorated with a colorful, painted dot pattern. A versatile service set for the dinner table, this is a wonderful gift idea for a grown daughter or son.

QUICK & EASY ALTERNATIVES

Option 1

Plain white plates become country charmers with this easy design. Wash and dry plates. Prepare center surface with conditioner, according to paint manufacturer's directions. Cut a 2" (5cm) square of paper. Place it in the center of a plate and paint a black dot at each point with non-toxic glass paint. Remove paper. Form a tree in the area between the dots, with a brown stroke for the trunk and dotted green for foliage. Apply a topcoat to seal the design.

Option 2

Enhanced with a paintbrush, plain blue, provincial border plates will set a beautiful table for Mom. Wash and dry plates. Prepare surface of plate border with conditioner recommended by non-toxic glass paint manufacturer. When dry, form daisies using white and yellow glass paint and a small, pointed brush or squeeze bottle. Paint five small, white dots in a circle around a yellow center dot. Allow to dry, apply topcoat, and dry completely.

Option 3

A family member who already owns nice everyday dishes can still use a set like this for holidays and parties. Wash and dry blue, black, or white ceramic or glass plates. Apply conditioner recommended by glass paint manufacturer to plate borders. Use a purchased star stencil or make one from card stock. Stencil evenly spaced stars around plate borders with non-toxic gold glass paint and a stencil brush. Apply topcoat.

Materials You'll Need

- Dishwashing detergent
- Paper towels
- Glass plates and glasses
- Surface conditioner

- Small paintbrushes
- Non-toxic glass paint (air dry): blue, red, yellow, white & green
- Topcoat

1 Wash and dry all plates and glasses until thoroughly clean and dry.

2 To help paint adhere, apply surface conditioner to underneath of plates and outside of glasses with paper towel, according to paint manufacturer's directions.

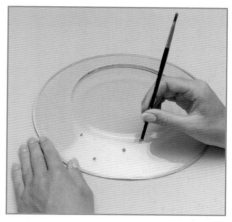

3 Dip end of paintbrush into blue paint and dot on back of plates at well-spaced intervals. Decorate border of plates only. Dot paint on lower outside of glasses.

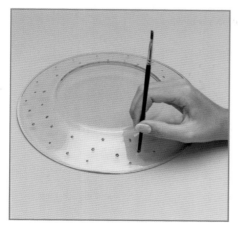

4 Repeat above process using red paint. Create random dots, with plenty of space between each.

5 Continue to decorate plates and glasses with colored dots, using yellow, white, and green paint.

6 When paint is dry, apply two coats of topcoat over design with paintbrush, following manufacturer's directions.

Frames and mirrors projects

Whether you want to make a special setting for a favorite photo or picture, or create a stunning piece of art from scratch, the projects in this chapter will show you how.

With over fifty different projects and variations to choose from, ranging from rose petal frames to mirrored house key holders, this chapter is sure to provide you with plenty of inspiring and exciting ideas.

House Key Mirror

When searching for a way to add interest to a decorative gift, take a look at a mirror or two. Craft store mirrors come in all shapes and sizes, and add a quality touch to a wall hanging or tabletop gift. This key holder features a painted bird house with a braid-trimmed mirror embellishment forming the circular "entrance." Charming on the kitchen wall, this gift is also useful—no more misplaced keys for Mom!

QUICK & EASY ALTERNATIVES

Option 1

This bureau top box will collect pocket items and always remind Dad of you. Using acrylics, paint exterior of a small, round box blue with a red interior. Sponge-paint to add red design on top of the blue exterior. When the box is dry, adhere a round mirror to the center of the lid with industrial-strength glue. With a toothpick, apply a thin line of glue around the mirror edge. Glue red satin craft cord in place, trimming excess with scissors.

Option 2

Boost your girl's confidence with this golden, glittery mirror, and let her know she'll always be a superstar to you. Hot-glue a metal picture hanger to the back of a medium-sized wooden star (so that a single point will face upward). Apply a very thick coat of gold acrylic paint to star. While paint is wet, sprinkle gold and crystal glitter on top. Allow to dry. Hot-glue a square mirror with a beveled edge diagonally to center of star front. A teenager will love hanging this mirror in her bedroom or bath.

Option 3

Here's a lovely gift for a china lover. Purchase a pretty china saucer at a flea market and a round mirror to fit the center. Glue the mirror to the center of the plate using industrial-strength glue. Cut a 6" (15cm) piece of matching wire-edged ribbon. Form a bow and secure center with a twist tie. Tie another long piece of the same ribbon to the bow center, leaving flowing streamers. Hot-glue metal picture hanger to back of bow, then glue saucer to streamers about 3" (7.5cm) below bow. Trim streamers.

Materials You'll Need

- Small wooden bird house
- Paintbrush
- Light green & terra-cotta acrylic paint
- Twine
- Scissors
- Glue gun & glue sticks
- Small round mirror
- Two mug hooks
- Nail, hammer & hanger

1 Paint wooden bird house light green, leaving the roof unpainted. Set aside to dry.

2 When completely dry, cover bird house roof with terra-cotta paint. Allow to dry.

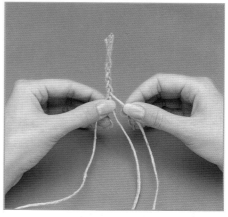

3 Cut three long pieces of twine of equal lengths. Braid the three pieces together to form one strip.

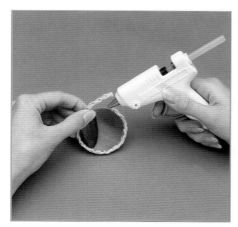

4 Using hot-glue gun, attach braided twine around edge of round mirror. Trim any excess length before securing end.

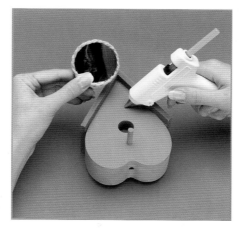

5 Apply hot glue to bird house, making a circle around entry hole. Press mirror to glued area.

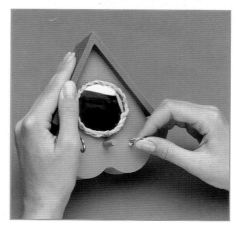

6 Screw a mug hook on either side of perch on front of bird house to create three evenly spaced key holders. Nail a metal picture hanger to back.

Pearl Button Mat

I sn't it so often the unusual that catches the eye? The unexpected flourish, taking us by surprise, delights with a charm all its own. Consider the case of pearl buttons. On a photo mat they're positively arresting! Glued to bands of ribbon, the buttons add a subtle flair and distinction to this framed photograph for Mother. She'll find herself drawn to its alluring "Je ne sais quoi."

QUICK & EASY ALTERNATIVES

Option 1

Despite what they say about "snaps and snails and puppy dog tails," he is still as cute as a button! Purchase a textured white double mat to fit a black frame. If inner mat is a color other than black, use small paintbrush and black acrylic paint to paint the exposed portion of the mat. Allow paint to dry. Arrange black buttons—in an assortment of shapes and sizes—to form a border around the inner mat. Secure buttons with tiny dabs of hot glue.

Option 2

Resembling little fingerprints, this painted design features a delicate "touch." Dip a stencil brush into blue acrylic paint and dab off excess paint onto a paper towel. "Pounce" paint onto a white frame. When blue paint is dry, repeat to apply red, green, and yellow paint, drying between applications. Use hot glue to attach a big blue button to one corner, and a red, green, and yellow button to each remaining corner. Insert photos in mat.

Option 3

Dad looks so good in plaid, it's no wonder it's his favorite "color!" Place a pre-cut mat onto plaid fabric. Mark fabric in pen 1" (2.5cm) out from all four sides of the mat. Mark fabric 1" (2.5cm) out from the inside of the mat, and cut fabric along markings. Replace mat on fabric and snip corners of fabric diagonally to edges of the mat. Fold fabric to back of the mat, securing with hot glue. Glue a border of matching buttons around opening of the mat. Tape photo to back of mat.

Materials You'll Need

- Picture frame
- Ruler
- Mat board
- Craft knife
- Photograph
- Pencil
- 1"(2.5cm)-wide ribbon
- Scissors
- Craft glue
- Pearl buttons
- Tape

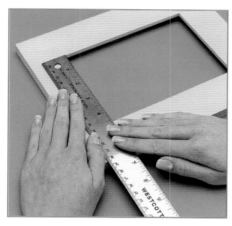

1 Measure length and width of inside of frame. Cut mat board to that measurement using a ruler and craft knife.

2 For center opening, measure picture and subtract ¼" (6mm) from all four sides. Pencil measurements on back of mat board.

3 Lay a ruler along lines drawn on back of mat. Cut out opening using a craft knife.

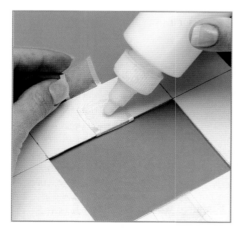

4 Wrap the ribbon through opening and around center top of mat. Secure with craft glue at back of mat. Repeat for a band of ribbon around center bottom.

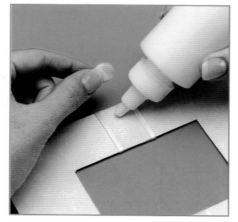

5 Use craft glue to attach pearl buttons in a row along both bands of ribbon.

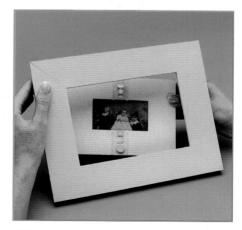

6 Using tape, mount picture to the back of the mat. Place mat in frame.

Wooden Appliqué Frame

S pinning straw into gold is the stuff of fairy tales, but turning wood into gold is easy, modern-day magic! A gilded frame, worthy of a masterpiece, enters the story as a humble wooden craft piece. Carved wooden appliqués cast the first spell, beginning the transformation with a flourish, while the glowing gold-leaf paint completes the pretty picture!

QUICK & EASY ALTERNATIVES

Option 1

These cleverly applied paints mimic the rustic appeal of verdigris on antique ironwork. To replicate this finish, spray a wooden frame and appliqués with primer and allow to dry. Attach appliqués to frame with wood glue. When glue has dried, apply metallic copper paint to frame using a 1" (2.5cm) soft-bristle paintbrush. Allow to dry. Using sea sponge, apply darker green acrylic paint to frame. Dry, then sponge on light green paint. When paint is dry, spray with varnish.

Option 2

Corner-shaped appliqués decorates a frame for a classic, artsy look. Spray a wooden frame and wooden corner appliqués with primer and allow to dry. Use wood glue to attach appliqués to frame. When glue has dried, apply liquid silver leaf paint to frame and appliqués using a 1" (2.5cm) soft-bristle paintbrush. Allow to dry. Using new paintbrush, apply antiquing gel to frame. Wipe gel off with soft cloth as directed on label. When dry, spray frame with a coat of varnish.

Option 3

Choose bold and elaborate appliqués to decorate this frame for the office. Spray a wooden frame and wooden appliqués with primer and allow to dry. Use wood glue to attach appliqués to frame. When glue has dried, apply metallic copper paint to frame using a 1" (2.5cm) soft-bristle paintbrush. Allow to dry. Using new paintbrush, apply antiquing gel to frame. Wipe gel off with soft cloth as directed on label. When dry, spray frame with a coat of varnish.

Materials You'll Need

- Wooden frame
- Wooden appliqués (available in craft or home improvement stores)
- Spray primer
- Wood glue
- Liquid gold-leaf paint
- 1" (2.5cm) soft-bristle paintbrushes
- Antiquing gel
- Soft cloth
- Spray varnish

1 To prepare a wooden frame and wooden appliqués for painting, first spray with primer and allow to dry.

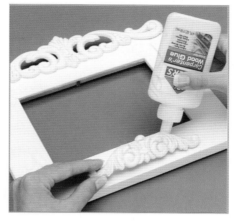

2 Use wood glue to attach appliqués to frame according to directions on label.

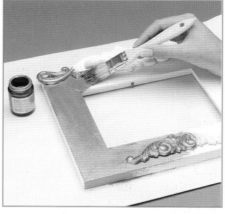

3 When glue has dried, apply liquid gold-leaf paint to frame and appliqués, using a soft-bristle paintbrush. Allow to dry.

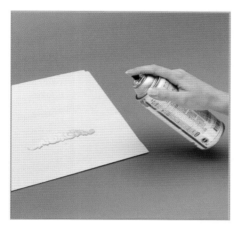

4 Using a clean paintbrush, apply the antiquing gel to the frame and appliqués.

5 Follow manufacturer's instructions to remove antiquing gel by wiping off with a soft cloth.

6 If desired, when antiquing gel has dried, spray frame (in a well-ventilated area) with a coat of varnish.

Windowpane Memo Board

If your daughter is into an eclectic style of decorating, here's a gift that will surely put a gleam in her eye. Perfect for the bare walls of her new home or apartment, this clever photo board will display her favorites with style. A hammer, nails, and rope turn a weathered windowpane find into this decorative treasure. Old drawer pulls add more flair, and function as key holders. It's handy...it's chic...she'll love it!

QUICK & EASY ALTERNATIVES

Option 1

This offers all the benefits of a cork board with added charm! Cut five pieces of white foam board 3"x8" (7.5x20.5cm) and two 1"x17" (2.5x43cm) strips using craft knife. Cut one short side of each 3"x8" (7.5x20.5cm) piece into a point. Roll out thin cork and outline foam core shapes using pencil. Cut cork with craft knife, then hot-glue cork to foam board. Lay cork strips on a flat surface and hot glue the pickets to the strips. Glue a variety of cute buttons onto thumbtacks.

Option 2

Black button tacks add the dots on this cute ladybug. Using an awl, make two antenna holes in outer edge of an oval, wood plaque. Curl one end of a 5" (13cm) piece of 16-gauge wire. Hot-glue a black bead to the end, then glue other end into hole. Repeat for second antenna. Trace plaque onto scrap paper and cut out. Fold paper in half lengthwise and cut off top third. Cut remaining piece in half lengthwise. Use these as templates to cut out red foam core wings. Hot-glue wings to plaque. Glue black buttons to thumbtacks.

Option 3

Make a wall board for family pictures. Measure bottom of a straw tray and cut thin cork to fit. Affix cork with hot glue. Measure from bottom to top diagonally at five evenly spaced points. Cut two pieces of grosgrain ribbon to fit each measurement. Hot-glue first layer of ribbons in place, then glue ends only of second layer, crisscrossing the bottom layer. Hot-glue rope around the inner edge of board, covering ribbon ends.

Materials You'll Need

- Hammer
- 1" (2.5cm) nails
- Old window frame
- 10 yds. (9 meters) sisal rope
- Epoxy glue
- Four drawer pulls
- Photographs

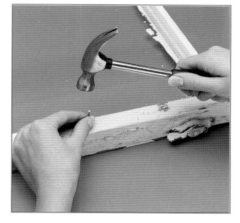

1 Using hammer, drive nails into each corner of window frame, then in the middle of each side. Drive another nail between each nail already in place.

2 Tie sisal rope to one bottom corner nail, forming a knot. Stretch rope up and over first nail above, then down to center nail near knotted rope on bottom.

3 Weave rope around nails back and forth so it stretches diagonally across window frame in one direction.

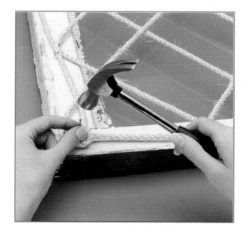

4 Reverse rope's direction and weave in the same pattern, crisscrossing the other rope diagonally. Secure at corners with a nail when necessary.

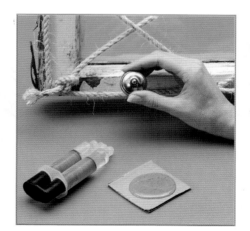

5 Follow manufacturer's directions to mix epoxy glue. Glue four metal drawer pulls along bottom of frame, spacing them evenly across the window.

6 Insert photographs at criss-crossed points of rope, securing between the two layers.

199

Tooling Foil Frame

L et's get down to brass tacks! Your parents would love nothing more than a gift you've made yourself...especially when it includes a photo of their grandchildren. This wooden frame is transformed with handcrafted silver. Aluminum tooling foil has been cut with scalloped edges, then embossed with a galaxy of shooting stars. Reface the frame with personality by attaching the artwork with—you guessed it—brass tacks.

QUICK & EASY ALTERNATIVES

Option 1

Give Grandpa a gift etched with his monogram and a dose of family pride! Cut aluminum tooling foil ½" (1.5cm) smaller than lid of a wooden box. Using a rubber stamp with a scroll design, stamp a border around foil edges with black ink stamp pad. Trace over the design with a stylus. Stamp the center of box with a monogram, emboss the letter, and dot the background with the tip of the stylus. Hammer a silver tack through foil at each corner of the box and all around the monogram.

Option 2

This design of two joined hearts is perfect on a gift for your sister. Cut copper tooling foil ½" (1.5cm) smaller than a notebook. Stamp a checkerboard pattern onto foil with black ink stamp pad. Scratch the first black square vertically with a stylus, then scratch the next square horizontally. Repeat this pattern. Stamp two hearts in the center of the foil and emboss with stylus adding some texture. Rub off excess ink. Attach foil to notebook with industrial-strength glue.

Option 3

This embossed copper cylinder transforms a flower-filled jar into an elegant arrangement. Cut a piece of copper tooling foil to wrap around a small jar. Stamp the foil in a random pattern using a rubber stamp with a leaf design and black ink stamp pad. Trace over the design using a stylus. Rub off excess ink allowing some to stay in the grooves. Secure foil on the jar using industrial strength glue. Fill jar with a small flower arrangement.

Materials You'll Need

- Wood picture frame
- Aluminum tooling foil
- Felt pen
- Gloves
- Scissors
- Star stencils
- Double-edged metal stylus
- Foam board
- Awl
- Tack hammer

1 Place a wood frame on a sheet of aluminum tooling foil and trace around both borders with a felt pen.

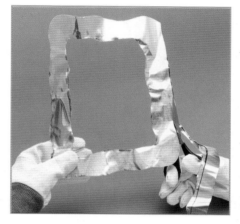

2 Wearing gloves, use scissors to cut the foil with scalloped edges, just inside the traced line.

3 Lay the foil over a stencil of stars. Trace stars randomly onto the foil using a stylus.

4 Turn the foil over and this time with the stencil on top, fill in randomly placed stars making "scribble" lines with a stylus.

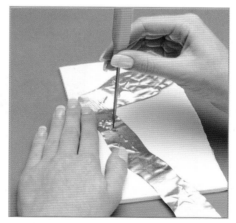

5 Turn the foil back over and lay it on a piece of foam board. Using a metal awl, poke holes through the foil in curving lines behind the stars.

6 Using a tack hammer, tap the brass tacks in various places around the frame, attaching the foil to the frame as you go.

Silver "Tiles" Frame

An avid shutterbug is never at a loss for gift ideas to please family and friends. Set off by a dazzling, hand-embellished frame, this portrait of a loving mother and son is a beautiful one-of-a-kind gift. Coated with silver paint, the border is then texturized with decorative, square "tiles" created from pliable, metallic film. The frame shines a shimmering spotlight on the picture, now a precious family jewel.

QUICK & EASY ALTERNATIVES

Option 1

This study in gleaming contrasts is ideal for a sibling photo. Select a small square frame. Spray frame with silver paint and let dry. Cut sheets of metallic gold and metallic silver corrugated paper into 1½" (4cm) strips, longer than needed to cross frame diagonally. With craft glue, attach the strips diagonally to frame, overlapping photo opening, and frame edges. Use a craft knife to cut strips away from opening and trim excess at edges. Insert photo and use the same paper for backing.

Option 2

What could be dreamier for a romance-minded girl than a heart-shaped frame decorated with shiny, silver and pink foil? Cut foil paper into random shapes and sizes to fit border of heart frame. Rub a glue stick on the back of each shape before attaching it to frame. Begin on one side and decorate frame without overlapping foil pieces to achieve mosaic design effect. Trim foil shapes as needed on the edges of the frame. Insert the photograph, then back frame with a piece of the foil.

Option 3

Gleaming red "diamonds" decorate a frame that's sure to catch the eye. Spray frame and the back of a sheet of metallic silver tissue paper with adhesive. Place tissue face down and lay frame face down on top. Wrap paper around to back of frame. Turn frame over and cut out opening, leaving ½" (1.5cm) of paper around edges to fold to back of frame. Trace a diamond pattern on red foil paper and cut out. Attach to frame with glue stick. Add strips of silver and red foil across diamond design.

Materials You'll Need

- Wooden picture frame
- Covered work surface
- Silver spray paint
- Poster board
- Spray adhesive

- Metallic silver polyester film
- Scissors
- Craft glue
- Photo

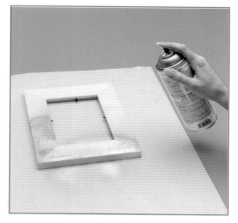

1 Place wooden frame on a covered work surface and spray with silver paint. Set aside to dry.

2 Using covered work surface, spray one side of poster board with adhesive.

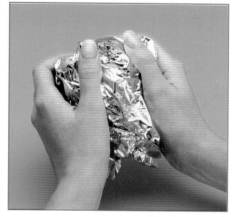

3 With your hands, crunch a large piece of polyester film into a ball to wrinkle surface. Pull sheet apart to former shape.

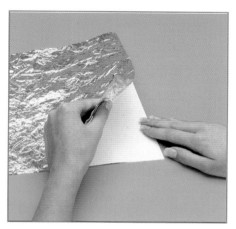

4 Cover poster board with polyester film. Press lightly to affix without smoothing out wrinkles.

5 Cut through film and poster board to form squares sized to fit border of frame. Cut enough "tiles" to cover frame.

6 Affix squares all around border of frame using white glue. Insert photo in frame and use silver foil or decorative paper for frame backing.

Decorated Picture Mats

Some photos work best as a two-some, parallel partners in a double-cut mat. Exhibit such a pair inside the elegant haven of this stenciled mat. Its border is enhanced with floral flourishes of pink and green. The two photographs are centered within oval openings cut from green card stock, presented to their best advantage, side-by-side, in this harmonious and beautiful display.

QUICK & EASY ALTERNATIVES

Option 1

Because they work so beautifully together, plaids and florals often find themselves in each other's company. Lay mat board onto plaid paper. Trace around the edges of the mat—including the cut-out. Using a ruler, expand traced lines by 1" (2.5cm) outside both borders. Cut out along expanded lines. Make a small diagonal cut from each of the eight corners to the corners of the original traced lines. Wrap the mat and glue the paper to the back of the mat mitering the corners. Tape print in back.

Option 2

This cute mat board is the "purr-fect" accent for a photo of a cat. It appears to have been decorated by the photographed kitty itself—along with help from an ink stamp pad and some fancy footwork! Choose a complementary mat board to fit a favorite photo of a kitty. Place sticker of cats in lower left corner of mat. Using a stamp with paw print design and black ink stamp pad, add paw prints randomly over mat board. Tape photo to back of mat and place in frame.

Option 3

Create this "ivy league" ensemble to add a pretty touch to a garden room wall. Choose a mat board to fit a print of climbing ivy. Tape ivy stencil over mat using masking tape. Dip stencil brush lightly into dark green acrylic paint, removing excess paint onto paper towel. Stencil corners and long sides of mat. Change brushes, and continue stenciling with light green paint. When paint has dried, tape the print to the back of the mat and place into frame.

Materials You'll Need

- Double-cut mat with inner mat
- Stencils: small flowers with leaves & oval
- Acrylic paint: green & pink

- Stencil brush
- Sponge brush
- Glue gun & glue sticks
- Green card stock

- Pencil
- Cutting board
- Craft knife
- Photos

1 Separate inner mat from outer mat. Use flower stencil and green acrylic paint to stencil leaves onto the corners and then the sides of the outer mat.

2 When green paint has dried, stencil flowers over the leaves using pink acrylic paint.

3 Set outside mat aside to dry. Paint top of inner mat pink using a sponge brush.

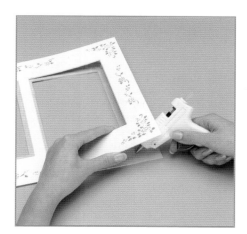

4 When both mats have dried, use hot glue to attach stenciled outer mat over pink inner mat.

5 Place mats over a sheet of green card stock. Trace an oval shape into each opening using oval stencil. Place green paper on cutting board and cut out ovals.

6 Using glue gun and glue stick, attach the green paper with the cut-out ovals to back of mats. Insert photographs and place the assembled mat in frame.

Embossed Wallpaper Mirror

No one will know that this metallic-looking frame was actually created using embossed wallpaper and a little paint. It's the texture that counts. Choose wallpaper embossed with the right "feel" and stand back for an amazing transformation. Its border is snipped and restructured, glued to a plain wooden frame with mirror, and made barely recognizable in a blaze of burnished copper.

QUICK & EASY ALTERNATIVES

Option 1

Design this elegant mirror for Grandmother's shelf. It will sparkle with the reflection of her knickknacks and treasures. Follow instruction Steps 1–5 on the opposite page to cover the frame with embossed wallpaper. Spray the frame with gold spray paint. When the paint has dried, paint a thin border around the inside edge of frame using a small paintbrush and silver acrylic paint. Insert a mirror into frame and secure. If desired, cover the back with decorative paper.

Option 2

The border of embossed wallpaper creates an elegant, somewhat formal effect. For a more spontaneous "framework" on this mirrored gift, choose wallpaper patterned in a soft, floral style. Follow step-by-step instructions on opposite page to cover frame with embossed wallpaper. Use silver leaf glaze to paint this frame. Apply glaze to frame with a medium-sized paintbrush. Insert a mirror into the frame and secure in the back. Glue on kraft paper as backing.

Option 3

To make a faux-verdigris frame, trace outline and opening of wooden frame on back of embossed wallpaper. Measure depth of frame. Extend outline by that distance so paper will cover sides. Cut out with a craft knife. Cut each corner diagonally from extended outline to outline of frame. Glue wallpaper to front and sides of frame. Spray with light green paint. When dry, sponge on dark green, teal, and copper acrylic paint, then insert mirror.

Materials You'll Need

- Ruler
- Wooden frame
- Scissors
- Embossed wallpaper
- Craft glue
- Cutting board
- Craft knife
- Surface covering
- Copper spray paint
- Mirror to fit frame

1 Measure width and length of sides of wooden frame. With scissors or a craft knife, cut four strips of wallpaper border to fit the molding of the frame.

2 Apply craft glue to middle of one side of frame as far as inside corners. Attach first strip of wallpaper.

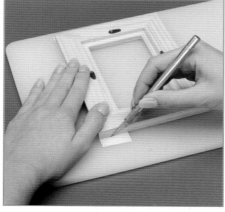

3 Turn frame over onto cutting board and trim edges of wallpaper with craft knife.

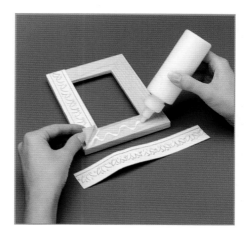

4 Glue second strip of wallpaper to frame as in Step 2. Lift lower edge of first strip, and overlap wallpaper. Trim excess wallpaper. Repeat for each side of frame.

5 To miter corners, lay ruler from inside corner to outside corner of frame. Cut along edge with craft knife, and remove excess wallpaper. Repeat for each corner.

6 Place frame on surface covering, and in a well-ventilated area, spray with copper spray paint. When dry, insert mirror into back of frame and secure.

Family Placemat

This memory placemat is a special reminder for family members who live far away. Trimmed in beautiful ribbon and laminated, the placemat is a practical as well as functional gift. Dinnertime conversations can be centered around the photographs and the memories enclosed. The placemat will be a warm, loving reminder to adults and children alike. What a nice way to share family memories.

QUICK & EASY ALTERNATIVES

Option 1

A collage of Dad's pictures as he grew up makes for a sentimental placemat for a daughter. Make photocopies of pictures of Dad at various ages. Measure and cut medium to heavyweight paper to 12"x18" (30x45cm) to form the placemat base. Place the photographs and space them as desired. Use craft glue to affix black ribbon and striped ribbon strips down each 12" (30cm) side of the paper. Affix photocopies on paper using a glue stick. Let dry, then laminate the placemat at a copy shop.

Option 2

Your son will enjoy seeing photos of himself and his puppy on his own placemat. Make color copies of the photos and trim with scissors. Measure and cut medium to heavy-weight paper to 12"x18" (30x45cm) for placemat base. Measure in 2" (5cm) from each side. Draw lines with a brown marker to form center section. Affix photos inside the border. Stamp paw prints in brown ink around the border and between photos. Have placemat laminated at a copy shop.

Option 3

Grandchildren will appreciate a placemat adorned with photographs of their grandparents. Make color copies of grandparents' photographs. Measure and cut medium to heavy-weight pink paper to 12"x18" (30x45cm) for placemat base. Measure in 2" (5cm) from all four sides and draw a line to form a border. Affix flower border stickers along lines. Use a glue stick to affix photos to completely cover the center. Have the placemat laminated at a copy shop.

Materials You'll Need

- Ruler
- Medium to heavyweight paper
- Scissors
- Ribbon, 2 yards (180cm) of 2" (5cm)-wide floral
- Cutting mat
- Rotary cutter
- Craft glue
- Photocopies of family photos
- Photograph mounting corners

1 Measure the paper to 12"x18" (30x45cm), then use scissors to cut to that measurement.

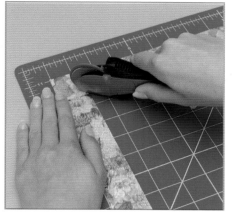

2 Measure the ribbon. On a cutting mat and using a rotary cutter, cut the ribbon into four pieces. Miter the ends of ribbon.

3 Use craft glue to affix the ribbon to the edges of the paper to form a frame around the mat.

4 Use a small, sharp scissors to cut out the photocopies of the family photographs.

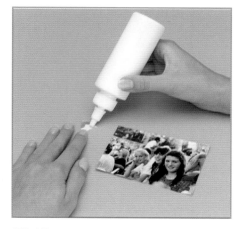

5 Affix mounting corners to all the photocopies before placing them on the paper.

6 Use craft glue to affix photos to the placemat in the desired design. Have the placemat laminated at a copy shop.

Rose Petal Frame

Few events are as exciting as the birth of a brand-new baby, and caring family members will want to present a special gift to commemorate the occasion. A beautiful frame for the little one's sweet photo will help decorate the nursery and warm the hearts of the proud parents. This frame is strewn with delicate silk rose petals, an ideal accompaniment to your wishes for a baby's "rosy" future.

QUICK & EASY ALTERNATIVES

Option 1

How your granddaughter will love this frame! Choose cloth ribbon the same width as the wooden frame. Cut into four lengths to fit frame. With iron, press back one corner at each end of ribbon strips, creating mitered edges to fit together on frame. Apply a thin layer of craft glue to the front of the frame and smooth on the ribbon strips. Glue two large, silk leaves on one corner. Tie twine around sunflower stem and form bow, then hot-glue sunflower on leaves.

Option 2

Create a special gift for your niece, adding "floating" blossoms to beautifully frame her baby photo. Purchase a panoramic, glass photo frame hinged together at the bottom. Snip silk flower blossoms from stems with wire cutters. Place photo in center of frame, then hold open and sprinkle a few blossoms on either side. Form small bow from piece of narrow ribbon and hot-glue it along top of frame.

Option 3

Displaying prints of her children in a natural setting, this frame is a perfect Mother's Day gift. The flower petals add just the right amount of color and contrast to set off the artistic black- and-white photos. Purchase a pewter double-sided picture frame. With wire cutters, clip blossoms from silk hydrangeas. Use a hot-glue gun to attach the flowers and individual petals at various points around the frame edges.

Materials You'll Need

- Wire cutters
- Four yellow silk rose heads
- Scissors
- White wooden frame

- Glue gun & glue sticks
- Blue-and-white wire-edged ribbon
- Photo

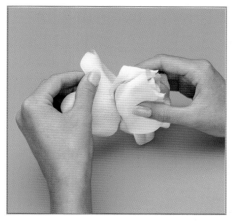

1 Clip rose heads from stems with wire cutters. Set one aside, then pull petals from remaining heads by hand.

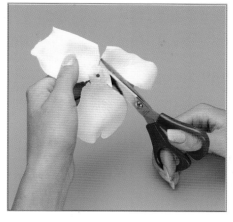

2 Use scissors to clip the individual petals from the separated rose heads.

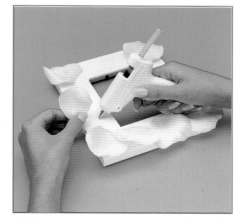

3 Beginning on outside corners of frame and working toward center, hot-glue petals, overlapping until entire frame is covered.

4 Cut a piece of wire-edged ribbon and tie into a bow with long streamers.

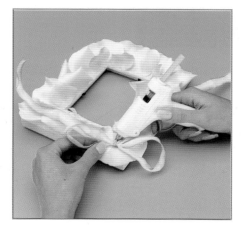

5 With glue gun, attach bow to one of the corners of the frame. Arrange streamers to weave among petals.

6 Insert the photograph of baby. Hot-glue the rose head (set aside previously) on top of the bow on corner of frame. Edges of bow loops should be visible.

Twig Picture Frame

A rustic, natural twig frame makes an ideal desktop gift for Dad. The moss green color is reminiscent of a soft forest carpet, growing beneath giant redwoods. Accented with slender twigs and bay leaves, the woodsy frame can hold a favorite print of Dad's, such as an antique bird lithograph. Or frame a photograph of the family on a recent camping trip to the mountains. He'll love either one.

QUICK & EASY ALTERNATIVES

Option 1

Miniature pinecones decorate a frame holding a favorite photo for Grandpa. Using a hot-glue gun, affix miniature pinecones (available in craft stores) to the front and sides of a small wooden frame. Tie a small bow of green-and-white gingham ribbon. Hot-glue the bow to the top center of the frame, over the pinecones. Insert the photograph in the frame. Trim a piece of decorative paper or kraft paper to fit and affix to the back of the frame using craft glue.

Option 2

This pretty picture frame holds a special photograph from a family wedding. Cover a small wooden frame with peach acrylic paint. While the frame dries, make two mini bouquets of small dried flowers such as strawflowers, statice or baby's breath. Hot-glue the bouquets to the frame in corners (as shown). Form two small bows of peach satin ribbon and hot-glue to the bouquets. Place wedding photo in the frame and secure with tape.

Option 3

Smooth, multi-colored pebbles frame a special vacation photograph. Apply white glue to the outer edges of a small rectangular picture frame. Wrap with twine to cover edges. Using a hot-glue gun or industrial strength glue, affix pebbles all over the frame, alternating the colors, shapes, and textures. Make a small bow using three strands of twine and hot-glue it to the front of the frame. Place the photo in the frame and tape to secure.

Materials You'll Need

- Paper surface
- Rectangular wooden frame
- Paintbrush
- Moss green acrylic paint

- Glue gun & glue sticks
- Twigs
- Scissors
- Several bay leaves

1 On a covered surface, paint a rectangular wooden frame using a paintbrush and moss green acrylic paint. Let dry.

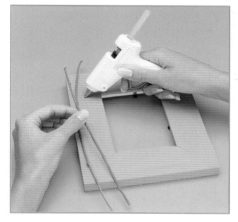

2 Using a hot-glue gun, affix two slender twigs to outer edges of the frame.

3 If twigs extend past the frame edges, trim them with scissors so that they are even with frame.

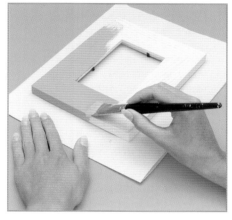

4 Cut four of the twigs to fit diagonally across the corners on the frame.

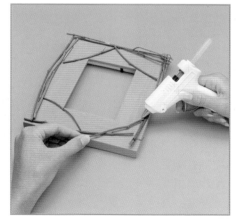

5 Affix the short twigs to each corner as shown, using a hot-glue gun.

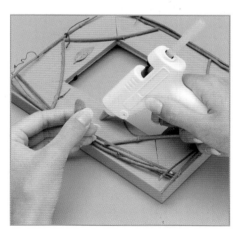

6 Hot-glue the bay leaves to the inside areas created by the corner twigs. Insert photo or print into the frame and cover with a paper backing.

Grandma's Photo Tote Bag

Grandma won't need a brag book when she's toting this clever bag adorned with photos of all her grandchildren. Her grandkids are her pride and joy and whenever she's using this handy bag, she can keep them close to her to remind her of how much she's loved. Every trip to the library or store will give passersby the opportunity to see her "little darlings."

QUICK & EASY ALTERNATIVES

Option 1

Your favorite cousin will enjoy this sweet lamp shade you've made for her room. Draw a 5" (13cm)-wide daisy pattern on paper and cut out. Trace this pattern onto a sheet of pink vinyl and cut out. Make a color photocopy of a favorite picture. Cut the photocopy and another piece of pink vinyl into a circle and affix with craft glue to daisy center. Using glue, affix daisy to lamp shade. With a round stencil dauber and pink fabric paint, apply dots randomly over the lamp shade.

Option 2

A sister heading off to college will love this fur pillow with a favorite family photo on it. Cut out two 10"x10" (25x25cm) squares of faux fur fabric. Have a color copy made of the photo. Cut the photocopy and yellow vinyl into a heart shape. Machine-stitch yellow vinyl over photocopy onto one square of the fur. Pin right sides of fur together and machine-sew three sides. Turn inside out. Stuff batting-wrapped pillow form into the opening and hand-stitch the opening closed.

Option 3

Give a family member a framed picture of yourself surrounded with colorful vinyl. Cut eight ¾" (2cm)-wide strips of aqua vinyl, an irregular pink vinyl square (that needs to be slightly larger than photo), and smaller chips of pink vinyl. Randomly overlap the strips on a white 8"x10" (20.5x25cm) sheet of paper so that it resembles a plaid design. Place the irregular pink square in the center of the paper. Glue photo on top of it, then surround the design with pink vinyl chips.

Materials You'll Need

- Photocopies of grand-children
- Scissors
- Square & star templates

- Vinyl: pink, yellow, aqua & purple
- Ruler
- White canvas tote bag
- Tape

- Tear-away stabilizer
- Sewing machine & thread
- Fabric glue
- Jumbo blue rickrack

1 Have two photocopies of grandchildren made at a print shop and cut them into 4"x4" (10x10cm) squares.

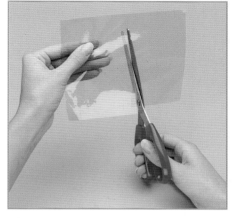

2 Trace the square template onto the vinyl pieces and cut 4"x4" (10x10cm) squares of the different colors.

3 Place the star template on the colored vinyl and trace, then cut out two stars.

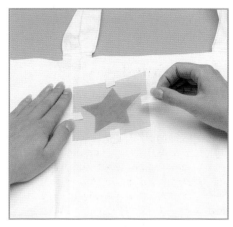

4 Determine position of squares with photo and stars under them and place them ½" (1.5cm) apart in center of bag. Tape one down at a time.

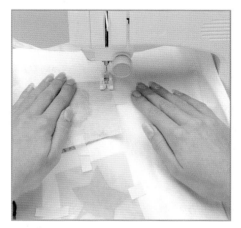

5 Place stabilizer over vinyl square to prevent the machine foot from sticking, and sew on the squares one at a time. Tear stabilizer away when finished.

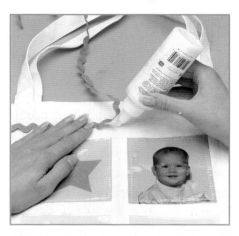

6 Using fabric glue, affix rickrack about 2" (5cm) below upper edge of tote bag. Design can be repeated on the other side of bag if more photos are to be included.

Glass and Flower Frame

Flowers and photographs are forever preserved when pressed between two pieces of glass. The combination of a favorite photograph enhanced with an assortment of pressed flowers and leaves is simply stunning. The edge of the frame is painted with an antique gold for a striking finishing touch. A family member will treasure this very special gift.

QUICK & EASY ALTERNATIVES

Option 1

Frame a treasured autumn photo of the children in a glass frame with pressed maple leaves. Remove the plastic edging from a glass float frame. Spray this with antique copper paint. Let dry. Remove top piece of glass. Using the double-sided tape disk provided with the frame, place photograph in the center of the glass. Arrange maple leaves around photo. Replace the glass. Place the painted edging around edges of glass.

Option 2

Tapestry fabric lends an antique look and feel to this photo of your great grandmother. Remove the plastic sides of a float frame. Place the piece of glass on the tapestry fabric and trace around it with a fabric marker. Cut the fabric along this mark. Cut a piece of decorative paper ⅛" (3mm) larger than photo on all sides. Affix photo to center of paper with glue. Place the ensemble on the center of tapestry fabric. Replace the top glass piece and plastic sides.

Option 3

Handmade paper is the key to this unique photo display. Wet an assortment of handmade paper by running under tap for a few seconds. Tear into various small sizes and shapes. Lay on a flat surface and dry thoroughly. Remove the plastic sides of the frame. Lay photo on bottom piece of glass. Use tape provided in frame to secure photo. Arrange dried paper pieces around the photo. Replace top glass and frame sides, being careful not to shift papers.

Materials You'll Need

- Glass float frame
- Newspaper
- Antique gold spray paint
- Scissors

- Decorative handmade paper
- Copy of photograph
- White glue
- Assorted pressed flowers & leaves

1 Remove plastic sides from the float frame. Place on newspaper or blank newsprint and spray with antique gold paint. Let dry.

2 For backing, cut decorative handmade paper ⅛" (3mm) larger than the photograph on all sides.

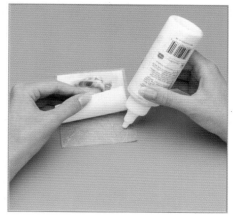

3 Using white glue, affix photograph to the paper, centering the picture.

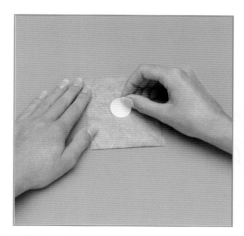

4 Using the tape disk supplied with the frame, secure to back of paper, then place picture ensemble to the back piece of glass.

5 Add pressed flowers and leaves to the frame in a random pattern surrounding the picture.

6 After all the flowers and leaves are placed in frame, replace the top glass and the plastic sides.

Saucer Picture Frames

You can create a whole new look for family photographs by framing them on saucers embellished with silk flowers and leaves. Display one or several on plate racks mounted on a wall, or sitting on a tabletop. Don't throw away those mismatched saucers that have lost cup mates. Save them and turn them into pictorial memory keepers. Display family and pet photos on the saucers and then trim the saucer rims.

QUICK & EASY ALTERNATIVES

Option 1

Preserve an old photo by making a color photocopy of it. For an antique look, soak a doily in a mixture of water and tea. Let sit in mix for a half hour. Wring out and dry well. Cut out the center when dry. Using a glue stick, affix photocopy to lightweight cardboard. Cut circle out and affix to saucer center using hot glue, framing the picture. Spread glue on back of doily and affix to saucer. Embellish with pearls and buttons to decorate doily edges.

Option 2

Your sister will cherish this picture of her kitty displayed in a saucer frame. Make a photocopy of a cat picture. Using a glue stick, mount color copy onto a lightweight piece of cardboard. Allow to dry, then cut a circle of the picture. Glue circle to center of saucer. Using hot glue, affix twine around photo. Also affix twine in looping pattern around saucer rim. Paint wooden birds red and yellow, adding eyes and beaks. Using hot glue, affix wooden birds to saucer.

Option 3

Preserve a treasured outdoor memory for a brother by creating this frame. Make a color photocopy of a picture. Glue copy to a lightweight piece of cardboard. Let dry thoroughly, then cut out picture in a circle shape. Glue picture to saucer center. Using hot glue, affix dried green moss around photo and cover entire saucer. Trim edges with scissors. Tie raffia into a bow and hot-glue to saucer top. Hot-glue acorns to the bottom right.

Materials You'll Need

- Color photo of children
- Glue stick
- Lightweight cardboard
- Mug
- Pen
- Scissors
- Glue gun & glue sticks
- Cup saucer
- Wire cutters
- Silk hydrangea leaves & blossoms

1 Find a favorite picture and make a color photocopy of it. Using a glue stick, affix photocopy to lightweight cardboard.

2 Trace a circle pattern onto the copy. You can do this with a mug and pen, or with a circle cutter.

3 Using sharp scissors, cut right inside the line of the circle on the copy, so the line doesn't show.

4 Hot-glue the cut color copy to the center of the saucer. Use saucers from home that have lost their cups or find them at garage sales or thrift shops.

5 Cut the leaves off of the hydrangea blossom using wire cutters and hot-glue the leaves all around the outside edge of the saucer.

6 Cut the petals from the hydrangea blossom and glue them over the leaves, framing the photocopy.

Antique Keys Frame

A ntique keys find new life on this frame for Grandfather. At one time, these skeleton keys turned many a lock, and today they can unlock a flood of memories. Grandfather can reminisce about bygone days every time he gazes at the decorated frame. He is sure to be delighted with this timely, thoughtful gift.

QUICK & EASY ALTERNATIVES

Option 1

Lilac-colored ribbon adorns this special frame for Mom. Gluing one end of lilac, wire-edged ribbon to frame that is at least 1" (2.5cm) wide, wrap ribbon diagonally around the perimeter of the frame. The frame should not show through ribbon. Secure remaining end of ribbon to frame back with a dot of hot glue; trim off excess. Glue navy tassel to upper left corner of frame. Add a small bunch of flowers with hot glue to the tassel to form a floral bouquet.

Option 2

Dad will appreciate this special frame created for him from crossword puzzles. Remove the white cardboard interior of an acrylic box frame. Cut out a selection of both finished and unsolved crossword puzzles from a book. Hot-glue the puzzles to the cardboard, covering the front and edges. Place a photograph in the center of the puzzle collage and secure with craft glue. When dry, place acrylic frame over the collage and give this interesting gift to Dad.

Option 3

Your aunt will feel pretty special when you present her with this artful frame. Color-wash the frame by first dampening the wood with water and a sponge. Then mix a small amount of aqua acrylic paint with three times as much water and apply to frame with a sponge brush; allow to dry. Hot-glue three mini baskets to the frame. Fill and glue silk flowers and greens in each basket. Insert a floral print in the frame, and it's ready for gift-giving.

Materials You'll Need

- Wooden frame
- Sandpaper
- Teal acrylic paint
- Sponge brush
- Matte acrylic varnish
- Paintbrush
- Three antique keys
- Glue gun & glue sticks
- Double mat
- Tape
- Illustration
- Kraft paper

1 Sand the frame using a fine grade of sandpaper. Wipe off any residue after sanding.

2 Using a sponge brush, paint the frame with the teal acrylic paint. Two coats may be needed.

3 Apply a clear coat of the acrylic varnish to the painted area of the frame. Allow to dry.

4 Using a glue gun, affix the keys to three corners of the frame. (See photo on opposite page for exact placement of keys.)

5 Tape an illustration (such as a house plan from an old book) to the double mat.

6 Insert the mat in the back of the frame. Cover the back with a piece of kraft paper.

Gilded Flowers and Leaves Frame

A treasured family photo deserves a special frame. Surprise a mother or grandmother on her birthday with her own likeness showcased in this beautiful gilded leaf frame. Made of painted leaves, flowers, and berries, this is a unique picture frame that lends an aura of richness to any photo it graces. She'll treasure it always.

QUICK & EASY ALTERNATIVES

Option 1

Here's a simple way to turn an ordinary picture frame into something special. The whimsical charm of this shoelace frame will be appreciated by a grandmother. Paint a wooden frame with acrylic paint. Use two sets of shoelaces in different colors or patterns. Cut three laces in half. Starting at cut edge of one shoelace, roll it into a coil; hot-glue coil to frame. Repeat with the other five pieces, gluing coils to bottom, corners, and sides. Make a bow with a whole shoelace; glue bow to top of frame.

Option 2

If your parents or grandparents will be celebrating a fiftieth wedding anniversary, you'll need a special way to mark this momentous occasion. To make this gift, cut metallic gold and gold-printed wrapping paper into assorted sizes. Overlap the cut pieces on a wooden frame; affix pieces to frame using découpage medium and a sponge brush. Tie a white organza ribbon into a bow. Affix a "50" gold charm to center of bow, then glue the bow to top of frame. Insert a photo of the couple's wedding day into the frame.

Option 3

Here's the ideal frame for a sea-loving family member—a great gift for birthdays, Father's Day, or any occasion. Paint a wooden frame with red acrylic paint and allow to dry. Using small pieces of cord, tie nautical knots and hot-glue them to the top and bottom of the frame. Glue single pieces of the cord to the sides of the frame, as shown. Affix starfish and sand dollars on the alternate corners to complete the frame. Add a photograph of a favorite boat or the "ship's" captain.

Materials You'll Need

- Oval picture frame
- Silk leaves
- Silk flowers
- Artificial berries

- Glue gun & glue sticks
- Gold spray paint
- Newspapers

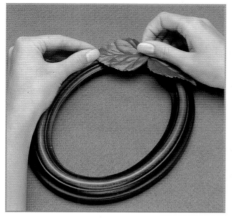

1 Arrange the artificial leaves, flowers, and berries around an oval picture frame.

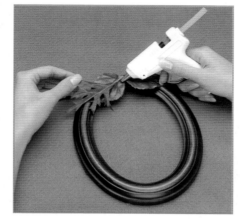

2 Hot-glue leaves to top of frame, allowing them to extend beyond the frame's edges.

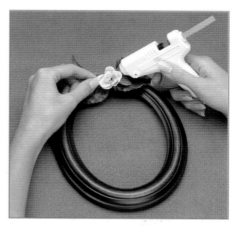

3 Use hot glue to attach a silk flower to the center of the leaves clustered at top of frame.

4 Glue artificial berries to each side of leaf cluster. Continue to add leaves, silk flowers, and berry clusters in this same manner until frame is covered.

5 Place frame on newspaper in a well-ventilated area. Holding the can a few inches away, spray-paint the frame gold.

6 When the front is dry, spray around the frame's outside edges to cover it completely with gold paint.

Silk-Flower Photo Album

Presenting family memories in a beautifully bound photo album is a gift that will be cherished for generations. Not only will the recipient appreciate this thoughtful album, but so will all other family members who take the time to stop and browse through its pages of family treasures. Embellished with silk flowers, leaves, and ribbon, this keepsake gift will keep on giving for years to come.

QUICK & EASY ALTERNATIVES

Option 1

Every teenage girl loves to write in her own private diary. To make this feminine gift, lay a purchased journal on the wrong side of floral fabric and trace around it, adding 1½" (4cm) to all sides. Cut out. Glue a piece of thin batting to the front cover. Wrap fabric around journal. Notch at spine; tuck notches into the spine and glue. Hot-glue fabric to inside covers, mitering corners. Slightly flatten the nosegay holder and glue to front of journal. Make a small bouquet with a bow and glue to the front of the diary.

Option 2

Mom will prize this address book, especially if it's filled with important family numbers. To make, lay a square address book on top of kraft paper and trace around book, adding 1½" (4cm) all around. Cover the address book with the paper, gluing excess to the inside covers and mitering the corners. Form a bouquet of small artificial flowers. Wrap a piece of narrow ribbon around the stems and tie into a bow. Hot-glue the bouquet to center of the cover.

Option 3

Grandma will be taking this special book out at every opportunity. Place the opened album on a piece of handmade paper and trace around it, adding 1½" (4cm) all around. Cover the photo album with handmade paper, gluing the excess to the inside covers and mitering the corners. Remove centers from artificial daisies, then hot-glue flowers and leaves to the front cover of the book. Cut out photos of children or have them color-copied and glue them to the centers of the flowers.

Materials You'll Need

- Photo album
- Thin batting
- Glue gun & glue sticks
- Green linen fabric
- Handmade paper

- Wire-edged ribbon
- Florist's wire
- Green satin ribbon
- Silk hydrangea blooms & leaves

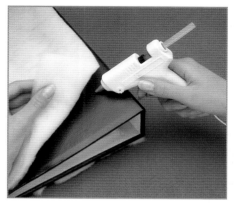

1 Cut the thin batting to the size of the photo album cover. Hot-glue the batting to the cover.

2 Lay album on fabric, batting side down. Cut top and bottom 1½" (4cm) wider than the album and sides 2" (5cm) wider. Notch fabric at top and bottom of the spine. Tuck under at spine and glue.

3 Close album to allow the fabric to stretch. Reopen and glue fabric to the inside cover, mitering the corners. Glue handmade paper to cover raw edges of the fabric.

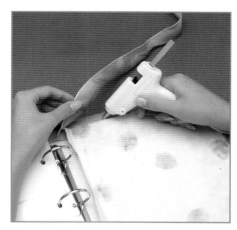

4 Hot-glue the wire-edged ribbon around the paper edge on the inside front and back covers.

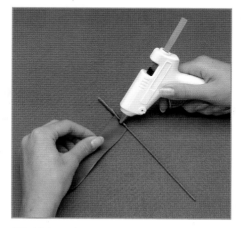

5 Make a flower stem for the cover by gluing and wrapping florist's wire with the green satin ribbon, then curving the end.

6 Affix the stem to the cover. Hot-glue individual hydrangea florets to form the flower. Glue a large leaf to each side of the stem.

Victorian-Inspired Picture Frames

Victorian-inspired frames decorate a wall with such drama and elegance that no one will believe just how easy they were to create. By adding charms, silk cord, a string of inexpensive pearls, and a coat of gold spray paint, these wooden frames have been transformed into glowing replicas of that bygone era. Add lovely sepia-toned photographs of family members for a meaningful gift that a grandparent will treasure.

QUICK & EASY ALTERNATIVES

Option 1

Golden highlights and ornate trims are the hallmarks of Victorian decoration, so this frame lavishly trimmed with gold buttons is right in style. Search through your button collection for unusual and attractive gold buttons, then randomly arrange them on top of a ready-made frame. Use hot glue to secure each button into position, making sure some of the buttons overlap for an opulent appearance. Find buttons at tag sales, antique shops, and fabric stores.

Option 2

A crackled paint surface typically means that the wood beneath it has aged well. Today, however, an antique finish is easy to achieve with a variety of kits. A crackle finish on a frame serves to enhance a colorful vintage print and makes a perfect addition to almost any decor. Buy an unfinished frame with a wide molding, then sand it smooth. Finish the frame surface according to the kit instructions, add gold filigree trims, then slip the print and mat into frame.

Option 3

Enhance a vintage rose print with a velvet, rosebud-decorated mat. Place mat on the wrong side of the velvet, then trace around the mat with a marker. Cut velvet around traced image, adding a 1" (2.5cm) border to the perimeter and around oval opening. Clip inside border to within ⅛" (3mm) of oval opening at 1" (2.5cm) intervals, then fold velvet to back of mat and glue. Fold outside edges of velvet to back, mitering corners, then glue securely. Place print and velvet mat in frame, then glue rosebuds around oval.

Materials You'll Need

- Wooden frames with backings & hangers
- Filigree corner charms
- Epoxy glue
- Newspaper
- Gold spray paint
- Gold cord
- String of pearls

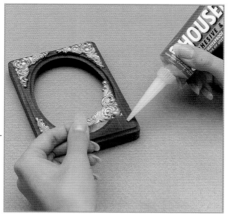

1 For rectangular wooden frame, affix filigree charms to corners with epoxy glue.

2 Line work area with newspaper. Spray entire frame with metallic gold paint, making sure to cover all surfaces. Be sure to spray in a well-ventilated area.

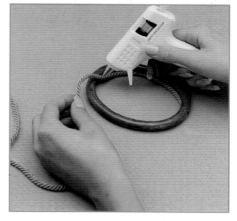

3 For oval frame, use hot glue to affix gold cord around inside of frame, starting at the bottom of the oval.

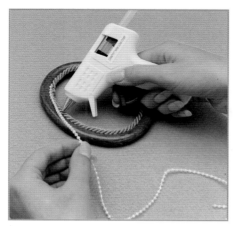

4 Starting at the bottom, hot-glue string of pearls around outside of gold cord.

5 Use epoxy glue to affix filigree charms to the top and bottom of the frame.

6 Spray entire frame with metallic gold paint, making sure to cover all surfaces. Insert vintage photograph and backing.

227

Grandpa's Memento Picture Frame

Family photographs document sentimental events and depict special moments for all family members to enjoy. Especially treasured are framed photos of grandchildren—keepsakes that grandparents can proudly display on their desktops, mantelpieces, and family-history walls. Beautifully and imaginatively framed photos of kids and their parents remind Grandpa how quickly his little ones grow.

QUICK & EASY ALTERNATIVES

Option 1

Select memorable items from a child's early years to add to this framed portrait. Use an acrylic box frame, then remove back side of cardboard frame insert. Place a pink mat into back of insert, then line sides of box insert with ruffled ribbon. Glue photo on mat, then hot-glue spoon and fork to mat. Place shoe in position, trail narrow ribbon around box, and tie ends in a bow. Place acrylic box frame onto completed insert.

Option 2

Fashion this attractive display with ribbon and three inexpensive gold-tone frames. Make two double, flat bows, one smaller than the other. Wrap and glue a strip of ribbon around the larger bow to form a knot. Glue smaller bow behind large bow to form a cross. Cut a large ribbon strip long enough to extend beyond the frames. Use a needle and thread to gather one end, then glue gathered end to the back of the bows. Place children's photos in frames, then evenly space them along the long ribbon strip. Trim tails in an inverted "V."

Option 3

A frame displaying a photo with the names of their grandkids makes a wonderful gift for proud grandparents. A purchased frame is used to display the photograph, which is then embellished with flat marbles that magnify letters placed beneath them. Use computer-printed letters or cut letters from a magazine. Coat front of each letter with découpage medium; press letters onto backs of flat-backed marbles (available at craft stores). Glue the marbles to the frame.

Materials You'll Need

- Photographs
- Scissors
- Découpage medium
- Sponge brush
- Cotton swab
- Acrylic box frame with cardboard insert
- Craft knife
- Corrugated mat & matching paper strips
- Craft glue & soft cloth

1 Have color photocopies made for the outside of the frame. Enlarge or reduce as necessary to fit frame corners, then trim carefully with pointed scissors.

2 Brush découpage medium on back and front of each photo and rub down firmly with fingers. Remove medium from around photos with a moist cotton swab.

3 Carefully cut away and remove the back of the box insert, leaving the rest intact.

4 Cut strips of corrugated paper to fit sides of insert and glue into place.

5 Place corrugated mat over portrait photo, secure to back of photo with tape, then place matted photo into cardboard insert.

6 Place the front of the acrylic frame piece over the insert with the matted photo. Remove any fingerprints with a soft cloth.

Baby Photo Holder

A proud new Mom is rarely without her camera, and always on the lookout for ways to display her growing baby-picture bounty. Any new mom will be thrilled with this loving gift, a montage of photos mounted onto colorful alphabet blocks to spell out her little girl's name. This desktop or baby's room accessory can be arranged in a variety of ways. The new mom will love the gift as well as the friend who knew just how to touch her heart.

QUICK & EASY ALTERNATIVES

Option 1

A baby's own gently worn shoe becomes a useful, decorative keepsake for her parents. Follow the directions on the opposite page for the wire coiling instructions. Use 18-gauge coiling wire and coil it for the photo holder, using pliers and a 1" (2.5cm) marker or dowel. Cut the wire to the desired length. Prepare plaster of Paris as directed on package. Pour plaster into shoe. insert wire in the center. Cut a piece of card stock ¼" (6mm) larger all around than photo and affix to photo with double-sided tape. When plaster is set, place picture in coiled wire.

Option 2

How her sprouts are blossoming! Fill a milk pitcher with dry florist's foam, pushing firmly to secure. Cover foam with Spanish moss. Form wire photo holders, as described on back of this card. Affix bright flower stickers and a bee sticker onto pieces of card stock, then cut out shapes. Cut out faces to fit on each flower, then affix using double-sided tape or glue stick. Insert flowers into wire holders and push into foam in pitcher. Hot-glue bee to a wire, then insert in pitcher. Finish with a bow.

Option 3

Great in a child's or teen's bedroom, this display can hold his sports photos or some friendly faces. With a hot-glue gun, attach small plastic sports balls to a box lid or flat piece of painted wood. Follow directions on the opposite page to make wire picture holders to insert in each ball. Pierce balls with an awl, then insert wire holders into balls. Cut card stock ¼" (6mm) larger all around than selected photos. Attach photos to card stock backgrounds with double-sided tape, then insert into wire holders.

Materials You'll Need

- Needlenose pliers
- Coiling wire, 18-gauge
- 1"(2.5cm)-round marking pen or dowel
- Wooden alphabet blocks
- Awl

- Glue gun & glue sticks
- Scissors
- Baby photos
- Card stock, several colors
- Glue stick

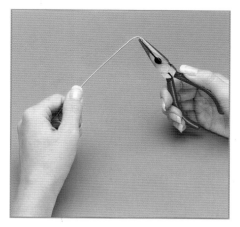

1 Use needlenose pliers to form a small hook on one end of the coiling wire.

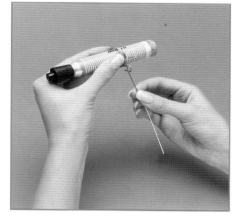

2 Wrap hooked end of wire around marking pen or dowel twice. Bend to bring wire straight down below loop. Cut wire to desired length.

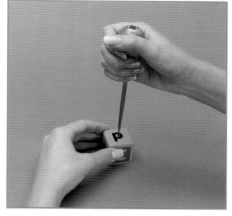

3 Position block so desired letter is on the front, then use awl to form a hole in the center top of block.

4 Cut baby photos into varied shapes. Cut colorful card stock into matching shapes, ¼" (6mm) larger all around than each photo. Attach the photos to card stock shapes using a glue stick.

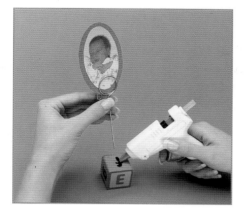

5 Dab hot glue into hole and insert straight end of wire firmly inside. Repeat steps for each block until baby's name is spelled out. Cut the wire in varying lengths to add interest.

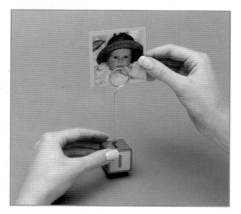

6 Insert a mounted picture between double-wire loops at top of each alphabet block.

Candles and lamps projects

Soothing, relaxing and romantic—it's no wonder candles make such a popular gift. The warm light of a candle or the glow of a pretty bedside lamp will help add atmosphere and ambience to any room.

But why stick with regular candles and lamps when it is so easy to make a gift that really looks like it has come from the heart? The decorated lanterns, lamp shades and candles in this chapter are sure to inspire you to make your own special gifts.

233

Simple Holiday Lamp Shades

Show Mom your appreciation by making her a special Valentine lamp shade. Each year that she displays it on Valentine's Day, it will be a thoughtful reminder of how much you love her. Adorned with vintage Valentine cards and a gold, rope-shaped trim and tassel, this shade is dressed in the cheerful red color of the day of hearts. This Victorian lamp shade is so lovely that she'll want to use it all year long.

QUICK & EASY ALTERNATIVES

Option 1

Your niece will love this adorable lamp shade as an Easter gift, but she'll want to use it all year long. Stamp the Easter patterns in black ink along the bottom edge of a small white lamp shade. Use a variety of paintbrushes and pastel-hued acrylic paints to color in the stamped designs. Use green acrylic paint and a small paintbrush to add short strokes of "grass" along the bottom edge of the stamped designs. Use a hot-glue gun to affix rainbow-hued rickrack to the top edge of shade. Overlap slightly and trim.

Option 2

When the family is celebrating New Year's Eve together, you'll want to decorate the whole house—even the lamps! Make a festive lamp shade to complete the party decorations. Press a "Happy New Year!" stamp onto a black ink pad, then randomly stamp the greeting onto the white shade. Add New Year's stickers to the shade. Use a hot-glue gun to affix silver-and-black cord to the shade edges. Make a bow from the cord and glue it to the top edge of the shade.

Option 3

Since you have your sister's name in the holiday gift exchange, make her a Christmas lamp shade that she can use each year. Paint the lamp shade green, using acrylic paint and sponge brush. Let the shade dry. Use white ink to stamp "Merry Christmas!" randomly all over shade. Add snowflakes to the lamp shade by painting white "wheel spokes" between the stamped greetings. Use the end of a paintbrush to dot the end of each spoke with white paint. Add white dots between the snowflakes.

Materials You'll Need

- Large paintbrush
- White, textured vinyl lamp shade
- Red acrylic paint
- Gold-and-red trim
- Glue gun & glue sticks
- Color photocopies of vintage Valentines
- Scissors
- Découpage medium
- 1" (2.5cm)-wide sponge brush
- Gold heart button

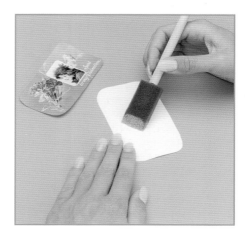

1 Cover a white, textured vinyl lamp shade, using a large paint-brush and red acrylic paint. Allow to dry thoroughly.

2 Affix the gold-and-red trim to the top and bottom of the lamp shade, using a hot-glue gun.

3 Have color copies of vintage valentines made at a print shop. Cut around the designs to create oval and rectangular shapes.

4 Using a sponge brush, apply découpage medium to the backs of the cut-outs. Press them onto the lamp shade, smoothing them with your fingertips.

5 Cut a length of trim to form a bow, then glue the bow to the bottom edge of the shade.

6 Glue a gold, heart-shaped brass button to the middle of the bow.

Bamboo Lantern

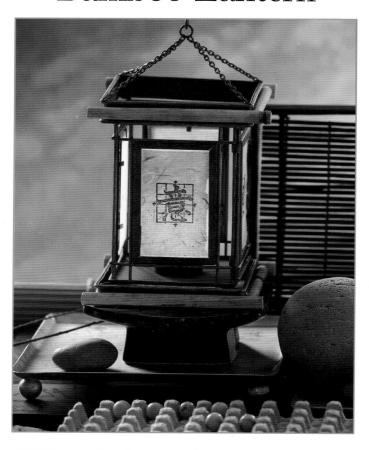

Tranquil reflection and ordered simplicity are the hallmarks of a traditional Japanese garden. Some say one who tends such an oasis is certain to find peace. This embellished hanging lantern is an exquisite gift for a family member who loves to linger in his Asian-inspired retreat. It's hand-trimmed with authentic bamboo and symbol-stamped rice paper, imparting harmony, wisdom, and of course, illumination.

QUICK & EASY ALTERNATIVES

Option 1

An Asian-inspired housewarming gift. Cut slim bamboo sticks into eight 4" (10cm) pieces. Using a ruler, tear rice paper into four 3"x3" (7.5x7.5cm) squares. Wrap one edge of first square around center of bamboo stick and hot-glue. Wrap opposite edge around another stick and glue. Repeat to make four "scrolls." Glue pieces together to form a square, overlapping bamboo at corners. Place around a small votive candle (a safe distance from flame).

Option 2

Make a table screen for an elegant gift. To make frame, lash two 7" (18cm) and two 9" (23cm) bamboo sticks together with raffia as shown. Then lash another two 7" (18cm) sticks and one 9" (23cm) stick onto this as shown in photo. Using a ruler, tear rice paper to 7"x14" (18x35cm) to fit openings in screen. Fold paper in half. Stamp Asian characters on center of each half of the paper using a black ink stamp pad. Glue paper to the back of the bamboo screen at sides and center.

Option 3

Create arresting wall art for Mom. Cut two pieces of bamboo 9" (23cm). Cut a piece of rice paper 7"x10" (18x25cm). Cover fresh bamboo leaves with green paint and stamp on rice paper. When dry, use a green marker to loosely draw an outline around the leaves and branches (as shown). Attach rice paper to bamboo sticks at top and bottom using hot glue. Roll the paper once more on bamboo stick and glue again. Cut a 22" (55cm) length of twine and tie at both sides of top bamboo stick for a hanger.

Materials You'll Need

- Clippers
- Bamboo
- Garden lantern
- Ruler & tape measure
- Glue gun & glue sticks
- Pencil
- Rice paper
- Oriental symbol rubber stamp
- Black ink stamp pad
- Spray adhesive

1 Using garden clippers, cut four pieces of bamboo to fit sides of lantern and another four pieces 1" (2.5cm) longer.

2 Hot-glue two short pieces to opposite sides of top rim of lantern, then repeat on bottom. Glue longer pieces to remaining sides of lantern, top and bottom.

3 Measure glass and draw light pencil guidelines on rice paper to help in tearing pieces to fit the panes of lantern.

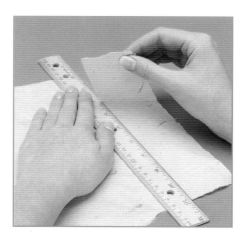

4 Use straight-edge ruler to help form straight lines, and tear out four pieces of rice paper.

5 Using a rubber stamp and ink pad, stamp symbol in the center of each piece of paper. Let dry.

6 In a well-ventilated area, spray back of rice paper with adhesive, and smooth each piece onto a pane of glass.

Frosted Glass and Leaf Votive

Rose leaves, cast in gold, lend a lovely touch to an enchanted candle. The frosted glass of the plain votive lends an air of ethereal mystery to the presentation. Gold leafing was applied to natural rose leaves to preserve their delicate nature. Grouped and fanned out on the votive, the resulting look is timeless in its beauty, the perfect accessory for a truly romantic evening.

QUICK & EASY ALTERNATIVES

Option 1

Pressed flowers create a Victorian look on a pastel-colored votive. Use craft glue to affix a pressed-flower blossom and its leaves onto a glass votive. In a well-ventilated area, spray the back of a sheet of vellum paper with spray adhesive. Wrap the sticky side around the votive, smoothing out any air bubbles with your fingertips. Trim the edges of the paper to align with the votive. Wrap a pretty, sheer ribbon around base of candle, and tie into a bow.

Option 2

This votive is beautiful and simple to make. An ivy leaf was used here, though any sturdy leaf could have been used as the stencil to create this beautiful design. Put small pieces of double-sided tape on the top side of the leaf, at each leaf tip. Press the leaf onto a glass votive, getting it as flat as possible on the glass. Use transparent glass spray paint to spray the votive and leaf. Be sure to spray only in a well-ventilated area. Let dry thoroughly, then carefully remove the leaf. The light of the candle will glow through the image.

Option 3

The long, slender leaves of agapanthus are perfect for this project, but any long, narrow leaves will work. Spray a straight-sided glass votive with adhesive in a well-ventilated area. Press the leaves onto the votive, overlapping slightly. Continue this process around the entire votive until it is completely covered with leaves. Trim the leaves so that they are even with the votive, top and bottom. Wrap with two or three strands of natural raffia, and tie into a knot.

Materials You'll Need

- Paintbrush
- Three rose leaves
- Gold leaf sizing
- Gold leaf
- Soft make-up brush
- Spray adhesive
- Paper
- Frosted glass candle votive

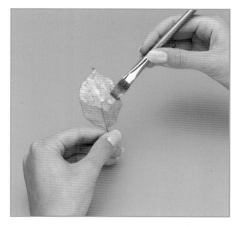

1 Use paintbrush to paint the top of the rose leaves with the gold leaf sizing. Let dry thoroughly, according to manufacturer's instructions.

2 After drying, lay the rose leaves face down on top of a sheet of gold leaf. Lift the gold-covered leaf, reserving the remaining sheet.

3 Use a soft make-up brush to carefully brush the gold leaf onto the leaves.

4 Spray the backs of the three leaves with adhesive. Spray in a well-ventilated area, following manufacturer's instructions.

5 Gently press each leaf onto the votive surface. Overlap and fan the leaves as you press.

6 If there are any air pockets, gently smooth the leaves using your fingertips.

Painted Candles

Option 1

Traditional birthday candles enjoy only a brief moment in the spotlight before they are extinguished in a puff of breath and a wish. Meanwhile, this candle continues to light the birthday festivities! Purchase a lavender candle 4" (10cm) in diameter. Using a stencil with 2" (5cm) numbers and light green candle paint, stencil candle with the person's age. When the paint is dry, paint orange dots down the centers of the numbers using the end of a medium-sized paintbrush, then place on a candle dish.

Option 2

When turquoise combines with lime green, the colors practically pop off the candle! Purchase a lime green pillar candle 3" (7.5cm) in diameter. Using turquoise candle paint and a ½" (1.5cm)-wide paintbrush, add ½" (1.5cm) vertical stripes down the length of the candle. When paint has dried, paint small yellow dots on the candle using the end of small paintbrush. Allow paint to dry. Using red candle paint, make a series of smaller dots around the yellow dots to create the tiny flowers. Place candle on a candleholder.

Option 3

This candle takes a whole new approach to quilting! Trace a quilt design from a stencil onto paper. Place a clear laminate sheet over the traced quilt pattern and cut out sections of the design with a craft knife. Peel off the back of the laminate pieces and reassemble the design onto a light blue candle 4" (10cm) in diameter. Using a kitchen sponge, apply dark blue candle paint over the entire candle. When the paint has dried, peel off the laminate pieces to reveal the design. Place the sponged candle on a plate.

Wouldn't this "bee" a great gift for your "honey"? (And the kids will get a kick out of it too!) It features three industrious chenille bumblebees, somersaulting from their hive, on a quest for nectar. A sheet of beeswax is rolled around a wick to shape the candle and then decorated with black candle paint into "bee-coming" stripes. Lit during dinner, the whole family will enjoy this playful reference to their busy lives.

Materials You'll Need

- Ruler
- Pen
- Standard 8"x16" (20.5x40cm) sheet of beeswax
- Scissors
- Candlewick
- Medium paintbrush
- Black candle paint
- Chenille bumblebees with wired stems
- Pencil

1 Using a ruler and a pen, mark the halfway points on opposite ends of the short end of an 8"x16" (20.5x40cm) sheet of beeswax.

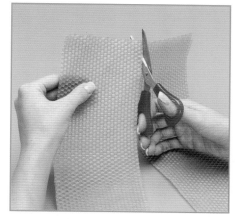

2 Cut the sheet of beeswax along the row between the two marked halfway points.

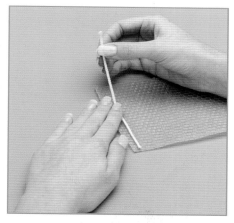

3 Lay a candlewick across one end of one of the half sheets. Starting at that end, roll the beeswax evenly forward.

4 When the first half-sheet of beeswax is rolled, add the second half-sheet and continue rolling.

5 Using a medium paintbrush, fill the first four rows with dots of black candle paint. Skip the next four rows, and paint the next four. Repeat the length of the candle.

6 Curl the wired stem of three chenille bumblebees by wrapping each one around a pencil. Insert the ends of the bees into the top of the candle.

241

Bridal Shower Candles

Delight a bride at her shower with a beautiful candlelit centerpiece. Pastel candles in a variety of heights, wrapped with paper lace doilies and ribbons, light up the bridal shower table. A bowl of fresh, pink roses encircling a single white candle is the focal point. Softly glowing and wonderfully fragrant, the memorable centerpiece will be a gift the bride will long remember.

QUICK & EASY ALTERNATIVES

Option 1

Each guest who attends the wedding can take home a fragrant, ribbon-bedecked candle. Select short, square pillar candles to match the table decorations or wedding theme. Measure the ribbon to accommodate a bow, then inscribe the ribbon tails with the names of the bride and groom, and date of wedding in gold ink. Wrap each candle with the satin ribbon, tie into a bow on the front, and secure at the back of the candle with hot glue. Place the candles by each place setting and at the head table.

Option 2

Honor the engaged couple with a touching poem-adorned candle. Découpage medium is used to embellish this white double-wicked candle. Brush the back of the poem with découpage medium, then press it onto the candle. Allow medium to dry thoroughly, then wrap the candle base with a sheer white ribbon and tie it into a bow. Place the flower blossom into the candle above the bow with a corsage pin. Place on a pretty plate surrounded with fresh roses.

Option 3

Present this metallic candle to the guests of honor at an anniversary celebration. Choose colors to coincide with traditional anniversaries if appropriate. Purchase a large cubed candle in the color of your choice. Fold gold florist's foil into a narrow strip, then wrap it around the candle, tacking it into place with pearl-headed boutonniere pins that have been clipped to ½" (1.5cm). Place numerals onto candle using craft glue.

Materials You'll Need

- Deep basin
- Water
- Round florist's foam block & holder
- White candle
- White paper doily
- Craft glue
- Narrow green ribbon
- Variegated greenery
- Pink roses
- Waterproof saucer
- Gold painted terra-cotta saucer

1 Completely submerge round florist's foam in water until saturated. When bubbles cease to rise to the surface, foam is ready to be removed.

2 Remove the florist's foam from the water and place onto the plastic holder.

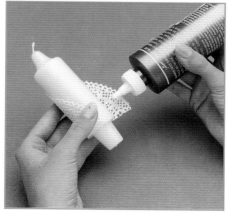

3 Cut the lace paper doily into a half-circle. Use craft glue to affix doily to candle.

4 Wrap a narrow ribbon around the candle and tie into a bow. Insert candle into the center of florist's foam.

5 Cover lower portion of florist's foam with a single row of variegated greenery by inserting stems into the foam.

6 Trim stems of roses and insert into the foam starting with the bottom row and building up. When finished, place into the gold painted terra-cotta saucer.

Candle Bobeches for a Cozy Get-Together

Decorations can be quickly fabricated to embellish candles for special occasions. Create ambience at a cozy get-together or wedding reception with charming little candle bobeches. Though many bobeches merely serve to protect surfaces from melting candle wax, these miniature garlands of greenery, enhanced with berries and silk flowers, provide beautiful touches to candles in a centerpiece or grouped alone on a table.

QUICK & EASY ALTERNATIVES

Option 1

Brighten a spring brunch table with glowing candles tied with jaunty floral bows. Add a bird house and complete the springtime effect. To make this delightful candle bobeche, place a white pillar candle into a small grape-vine wreath, then wrap the candle with a wire-edged ribbon and tie into a crisp bow. Use hot glue to secure a brightly painted, miniature birdhouse behind the bow. Select candle color, ribbons, and birdhouse to match the spring brunch theme or table decor.

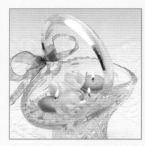

Option 2

Cluster fragrant, fresh roses with floating candles in a water-filled crystal basket to beautify a bridal shower. Purchase disc-shaped floating candles at a craft or candle shop. Remove the stems from the roses just beneath the flower heads. Fill a crystal basket with water, then float roses and candles on top. Select a ribbon to match the candle color, then tie it into a bow on the basket handle. Place the basket on a buffet or gift table and light the candles.

Option 3

Celebrate the accomplishments of a graduate with candles emblazoned with a collection of shiny gold stars. To make this creative candle decoration for a graduation celebration, cut a 6" (15cm) cardboard square, then brush it with a coat of black acrylic paint. Hot-glue the string of a black tassel to the center of the black-painted square. Apply metallic gold star stickers in various sizes to the candle in an attractive pattern, then place candle on center of black "mortarboard."

Materials You'll Need

- Lightweight white cardboard
- Scissors
- Craft knife
- Artificial leaves & greenery
- Artificial flowers & berries
- Glue gun & glue sticks
- White taper candles
- Candleholders

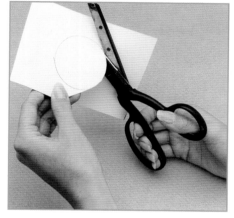

1 Draw a 2" (5cm) circle onto the lightweight white cardboard. Cut out the circle.

2 Cut an "X" shape in the middle of the circle with a craft knife, then fold back the corners.

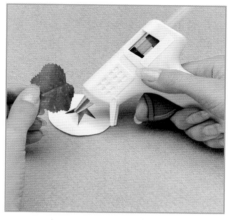

3 For bobeche with pink blossoms, hot-glue flat leaves to circle. Overlap leaves slightly; make sure they don't obscure the center "X" opening.

4 Glue individual pink blossoms to tops of leaves, covering circle completely. Do not cover center "X" opening.

5 For berry-topped bobeche, follow Steps 1 and 2, then hot-glue greenery to circle. Hot-glue small berry bunches to top of greenery.

6 Place white taper candle into candle-holder, then slip decorated bobeche over top of candle. Slide bobeche down candle and position on top of candleholder.

Gilded Pillar Candles

Even a minor event can become a glorious celebration when illuminated by glowing, metallic gold candles. Simply use gold leaf and dramatic, wire-edged ribbons to transform plain candles into chic and stylish golden accessories. Delight a special friend or the hostess of a holiday party with a collection of these dazzling, festive pillar candles. For added visual interest, use an assortment of candle shapes and sizes.

QUICK & EASY ALTERNATIVES

Option 1

A pale beige skeleton leaf against a forest green candle is a lovely study in contrasts. To create this beautiful candle, sponge découp-age medium on the back of the leaf, before applying it to the side of the candle. Carefully press the leaf down with your fingertips. When dry, apply another coat of découpage medium over the leaf; cover the entire candle with medium, then let dry completely. Finish by tying a bow of gold cord around the candle. Find skeleton leaves at craft, art, and paper stores.

Option 2

This elegantly beaded candle is perfect for a bathroom or bedside table. Iridescent glass beads reflect the candle's firelight and seem to shimmer. Select a candle in any size to make this gift. To determine final length, first wind dark green, 26-gauge wire around candle in as many rows as desired. Cut wire and remove it from candle. String beads onto candle (tying a knot after each one to secure it) until wire is full. Wrap candle and twist wire to secure ends.

Option 3

For an instant party decoration, create candles to match any theme by adorning them with colorful napkins. Select candles that coordinate with the napkin colors, then cut an appropriate portion of the napkin, and lay it on the can-dle. Use an embossing gun to heat the surface of the napkin-covered area. The heat from the embossing gun will melt the candle wax, causing the paper nap-kin to adhere to the surface. Arrange napkins in different ways to vary the design.

Materials You'll Need

- Solid-colored candles in a variety of sizes
- Gold leaf adhesive size
- Disposable paintbrush
- Gold leaf
- Soft-bristled brush
- Gold wire-edged ribbon
- Glue gun & glue sticks

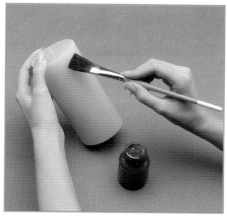

1 Paint each of the pillar candles with the adhesive size and allow it to dry according to the manufacturer's directions.

2 Apply a sheet of gold leaf to the sides of the candle by gently smoothing it on with the soft-bristled brush.

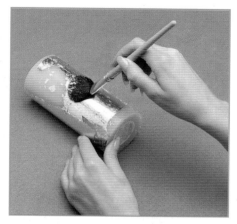

3 Gently rub the gold leaf with the brush, allowing it to tear away in places and reveal the candle color underneath.

4 Allow some of the gold leaf to fold over the top edge of the candle.

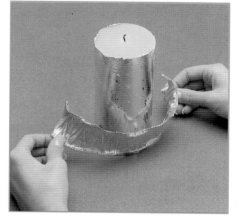

5 Wrap the base of the candle with a band of gold wire-edged ribbon. Use hot glue to secure ribbon ends.

6 Create a multi-looped bow, then hot-glue it to the base of the candle.

Carved Candles

The unusual designs on these candles are striking. Present the pair as a special gift to a good friend for a birthday or anniversary. Using twice-dipped candles, the design process removes the top layer of wax to reveal a lighter layer underneath, which becomes your design. Designs can be applied using a stencil, stylus, and cutting tool. The results are exquisite and would look great with any decor.

QUICK & EASY ALTERNATIVES

Option 1

A dotted pattern is applied to this unique candle with the use of hot-glue gun. To make the candle, you will need a three-wick, twice-dipped candle in the color of your choice. Heat a glue gun without glue sticks in it. While heating, take a large nail and randomly poke holes in the candle. With the heated tip of the glue gun, press deep into each nail hole on the candle. The polka-dot pattern emerges as the color layer melts away to reveal the white layer underneath.

Option 2

The floral design achieved on this candle was made with graduated sizes of the same shape cookie cutter. Using a twice-dipped candle, press smallest cookie cutter in candle center. Using craft knife, trace around design, making a ⅛" (3mm)-deep impression. Position the larger cookie cutter over the smaller impression. Trace around edge with a craft knife, leaving ⅛" (3mm) impression. Carve out center dot. Using craft knife, carve area between small and larger impressions. Remove excess wax with a paintbrush.

Option 3

The wavy effects on the sides of this candle are created using a kitchen fork. Lay the candle on its side. Create the swerving design by carving from top to bottom in a wavy pattern with a fork. Apply enough pressure so that the second layer of candle wax is exposed. Continue the technique until the candle is covered with several wavy designs. Brush off excess wax with a dry, flat paintbrush. Mount candle in a coordinating candle holder. Experiment with various kitchen implements to create other unique carved designs.

Materials You'll Need

- Stencil
- Twice-dipped candle
- Tape
- Pen or stylus
- Craft knife
- Paintbrush
- Bowl of warm water

1 Position the stencil on the candle so that the main part of the design is on front center.

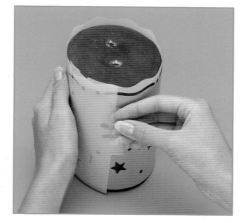

2 After the stencil is in position, secure the ends with tape, overlapping slightly.

3 Using a pen or stylus, trace around all stencil openings. Press stylus deeply into candle to leave an impression.

4 With the craft knife, carefully carve out the traced designs deep enough to expose the white layer of the candle.

5 As you're carving the design, brush away any excess wax with a clean, dry paintbrush.

6 When carving is complete, dip paintbrush into warm water and clean up any messy areas.

Eggshell Votives

Candles add beauty to all settings—especially holiday celebrations. They can bring ambience to a dinner table or add a soft glow to a coffee table. Complement Easter table decorations with a collection of pastel-hued votive candles in natural eggshell containers. Place candles in a colorful glass bowl of florist's marbles to enhance the flickering candlelight. Present this gift of color and light to someone special for Easter.

QUICK & EASY ALTERNATIVES

Option 1

Shiny little tin pails and washtubs are perfect containers for glowing candles. Use them for a touch of country sparkle and ambient light. Birthday candles create wicks for these colorful candles. Cut paraffin into cubes, then place cubes along with crayon shavings in a glass measuring cup. Microwave on high for six minutes or until paraffin is melted. Pour melted colored paraffin into pails. When almost hard, cut birthday candles to fit depth of pails, and insert into cooling paraffin.

Option 2

Glass flowerpots make perfect receptacles for candles. As it burns, the candle's heat releases perfumed oils from the rosemary (around the base) into the air. Cut paraffin into cubes, then place paraffin along with crayon shavings in a glass measuring cup. Microwave on high for six minutes or until paraffin is melted; pour melted paraffin into pot. When almost hard, cut a birthday candle to fit depth of pot, and insert into cooling paraffin. Glue fresh rosemary around sides of glass flowerpot.

Option 3

These candles are easy to make in a basin of wet sand. Cut paraffin into cubes, then place cubes along with crayon shavings in a glass measuring cup. Microwave on high for six minutes or until paraffin is melted. Make a mold in wet sand with a plastic foam ball, then pour melted colored paraffin into indentation. When almost hard, cut birthday candles to fit depth of candle, and insert into cooling paraffin. Carefully lift hardened candles from sand.

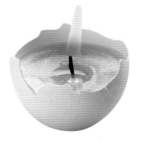

Materials You'll Need

- Fresh eggs & carton
- Bowl
- Paraffin
- Cutting board & knife
- Crayons
- Glass measuring cup
- Birthday candles

1 Break eggs into a bowl, then wash eggshells, let dry, and place into egg carton. Reserve raw eggs for cooking.

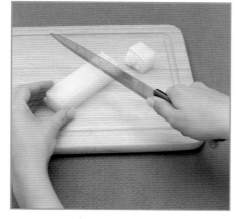

2 Use a cutting board and sharp knife to cut the paraffin block into 1" (2.5cm) cubes.

3 Cut shavings from crayon in desired color. Less shavings will produce a pastel candle; more shavings will yield a deeper hue.

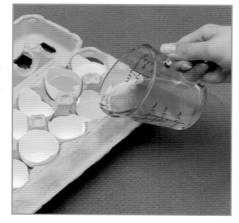

4 Place paraffin cubes into a glass measuring cup. Add cut shavings. To reach desired color, begin with small amount of crayon shavings, adding more as necessary.

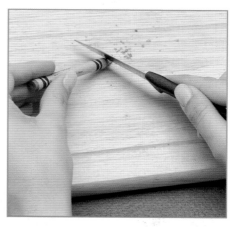

5 Pour melted paraffin into dry eggshells, filling each almost to the rim of the shell.

6 When paraffin is almost hard, cut birthday candles to fit depth of candle. Insert candles into cooling paraffin.

Natural Accents Candleholder

Natural botanicals beautifully enhance these white candles. Tall tapers wrapped in bright green agapanthus leaves, short pillars with perfectly matched rose leaves on their base, and stately tall pillars with a gathering of twigs are innovative and easy to make. Fresh greenery, seasonal conifers or holly, and raffia add color. Imaginative and useful, these candle gifts suit all types of decor, any time of the year.

QUICK & EASY ALTERNATIVES

Option 1

Four pastel votive candles embellished with tiny blossoms glow in a bed of reflective glass pebbles. Whether in a cluster or individually placed, their beauty will shine. Make these simple beauties by brushing a small amount of découpage medium onto the sides of the candle, then pressing a dried flower over the damp medium. Let dry. Coat sides completely with découpage medium to seal. This makes a lovely centerpiece.

Option 2

Smooth candle wax and roughly textured corrugated paper embellished with a creative patch of green sealing wax provide interesting contrast on this candle. Adjust paper size to fit the candle, cutting the paper a few inches shorter than the candle height. Cut paper width to overlap ⅛" (3mm). Wrap the candle, overlapping the ends. Tie the wrapped candle with raffia or ribbon. Drip hot sealing wax onto the overlap at the raffia knot, then press with a decorative or initial seal to finish.

Option 3

A collection of useful candles wrapped in lovely fabric and tied with a French wired ribbon makes a lovely and thoughtful gift. Use handmade candles to personalize this remembrance, or select ready-made tapers. Choose pure white or ivory, or a variety of hues to match a color scheme or seasonal theme. Select fabric and ribbon to coordinate. Add a few dried rosebuds under the ribbon knot to add a dash of interest.

Materials You'll Need

- Candles in a variety of shapes & sizes
- Twigs, greenery & bark
- Ribbon
- Raffia
- Craft glue
- Paintbrush
- Scissors
- Clippers

1 Measure a piece of wide ribbon to fit around a pillar candle, adding 6" (15cm) to allow for two 3" (7.5cm) tails. Wrap around candle, and tie into a knot. Trim tails.

2 Tuck a sprig of greenery behind the knotted ribbon, and trim sprig stem to fit. Select fresh greenery to suit a seasonal theme or use an artificial spray.

3 Use craft glue to coat the bottom one-third of the base of a tall square candle.

4 Place twigs in a natural pattern around candle, pressing twigs into damp glue. Finish one side at a time, allowing each to dry thoroughly. Wrap with raffia.

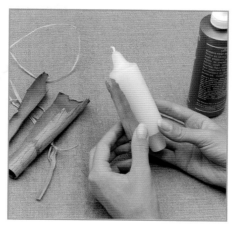

5 Trim pieces of curved bark to fit candle height, allowing for a complete wrap. Coat inside of bark with craft glue, then glue pieces around candle.

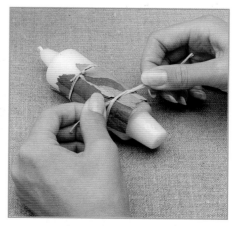

6 Hold damp, glue-coated bark pieces snugly against candle, then tie bark securely with raffia. Knot raffia and tie into a bow, or leave as a simple knot.

Index